D0457636

What's Come Over You?

What's Come Over You?

STORIES BY

Marian Thurm

DELPHINIUM BOOKS

harrison, new york   encino, california

Copyright © 2001 by Mariam Thurm

All rights reserved under
International and Pan-American Copyright Conventions.
Published in the United States by

DELPHINIUM BOOKS, INC.,

P.O.Box 703, Harrison, New York 10528

Some of these stories previously appeared in *Mademoiselle*, the *American Voice*,
Ontario Review, and *Michigan Quarterly Review*.

Library of Congress Cataloging-in-Publication Data

Thurm, Marian
What's come over you? : stories / by Marian Thurm.–1st ed.
p.cm
Contents: Moonlight – Earthbound – Passenger – Ancient history –
Jumping ship – Personal correspondence – Housecleaning – Mourners –
Pleasure palace – Cold –Marquise –Like something in this world –
Miss Grace at her best.
ISBN 1-883285-21-6
1. United States–Social life and customs–20th Century–Fiction. I. Title.

PS3570.H83 W48 2001
813'.54–dc21   00-065966
First Edition
10 9 8 7 6 5 4 3 2 1

Distributed by HarperCollins Publishers
Printed in the United States of America on acid-free paper

Book design by Krystyna Skalski

For L.A.T.
on his 80th birthday

*My thanks to Joe Olshan
for his help in the final shaping of these stories
and also for his friendship*

Contents

•

What's Come Over You?

Moonlight

I'll never admit it to anyone, but the truth is, I love the deep rich confident sound of my own voice, especially when magnified through the microphone on the lectern that's all mine every Friday night and Saturday morning and whenever else I'm needed. (If I hadn't, in fact, become a rabbi, I might very well have tried to break into radio or TV as an announcer, something my family had urged me to do a dozen years ago when I finished college.) Now, on this wintry Friday night in October, I listen for only an instant to the slight, annoying buzz coming from the microphone before giving it a sharp tap that awakens a woman in a wide-brimmed black hat sitting in the first row of the sanctuary, right under my nose. Winking at the woman, letting her know I've forgiven her for dozing off, I say, "And now Steve Sommers, president of the Men's Club and beloved by all, has a couple of announcements for us."

"Excuse me." Rising from her customary seat in the front row, Francee, my wife, marches up the six carpeted steps that extend the width of the dais, and heads for the lectern. Short and a little overweight, with a wide, pretty face and long glamorous blond hair, Francee is dressed in the same gray wool suit she wore to her law office today.

"What *is* it?" I murmur, and retreat from the lectern with a frown. Francee steps onto a small wooden box (kept handy for the shorter bar mitzvah boys whose heads don't quite reach above the top of the lectern) and swiftly gets down to business. "I have some news," she says in her own perfectly confident voice. "Regrettably, the Rabbi and I are splitting up, effective immediately." And, as an afterthought, "Thank you." For no particular reason, I happen to be staring straight ahead at the woman in the black hat, who turns to her husband and says in a stage whisper, "Holy shit!" Feeling unsteady on my feet, ignoring the whispering of a hundred voices that roars in my ears, I grab Francee's arm as she attempts to brush past me.

"Freeze," I order in a fierce whisper. "Move from this spot before I tell you to and you're dead meat." Much to my surprise, Francee obeys, and I return to the microphone to say, "And now for the final benediction." The whispering gives way to silence and heads are bowed dutifully, expectantly, as I ask for God's blessings in these uneasy times. There's a murmuring of "amen" and then all eyes are upon me as I walk down the sanctuary's center aisle in brand-new Italian loafers that hurt my feet, my black robes flowing dramatically, my wife of ten years just one step behind me, head held high, no doubt. When we reach the back of the sanctuary, I seize Francee's arm again, hurry her down a flight of stairs and into the caterer's office. I kick the door shut, kick off the miserably uncomfortable new shoes, and hoist myself on top of the big gleaming desk next to the window.

"God, Francee, what was *that* all about?" I ask, and light up a cigarette, ignoring the Plexiglas sign on the wall that reads

SMOKING ON THE SABBATH ON THESE PREMISES
IS STRICTLY PROHIBITED

"How could you do this to me?" I ask her. "Hasn't it been good all these years? Didn't we just come back from a Caribbean vacation to end all vacations?" I'm remembering all that strenuous sex in our hotel room in Barbados, every night for a week, except that first night when Francee was too sunburned for even the most delicate caress. "You love me!" I insist, and wonder if I am losing my mind.

"Ten years is a long time," Francee says vaguely, mysteriously, looking around the caterer's office, a room whose walls are decorated with photographs of jubilant brides thrusting forkfuls of wedding cake into their husbands' wide-open mouths. And, too, full-color close-ups of buffet tables crowded with chafing dishes and artfully arranged platters of salmon mousse and whole poached fishes, each with a single gold eye intact.

"A long time for what?"

"A long time to be with a person," Francee says. "As it turns out, I'm not the marrying kind after all."

"In that case, we better head straight for a marriage counselor."

"Oh, sweetie," my wife says, and smiles at me fondly. "It makes sense that you'd want to work things out, but it's just that I'm not interested. I just want to fly the coop, Danny."

My heart begins to race frantically; I'm sure my blood pressure is soaring as I arrive at my next question. "Are you in love with someone else?" I ask bravely.

"Unh-uh, but I wish I were, to tell you the truth. It would make things so much simpler for you, in a way, so much more easily understandable. And easier for me, too, of course, to be rushing off into the arms of someone else."

"Do you still love *me*?"

"I'm not sure," Francee admits.

"And how am I supposed to feel, hearing that? Am I supposed to feel hopeful?"

"Frankly, I haven't been giving all that much thought to how you might feel. Mostly, I've been concentrating on myself," says Francee, and gathers her hair on top of her head, letting it fall a moment later.

"You're having a mid-life crisis!" I say, pleased at how quickly I'm able to make a diagnosis. "That explains everything."

"I'm only thirty-five," Francee points out. "I'm in the prime of my life."

"You're having a mid-life crisis a few years ahead of schedule, then. And I'm absolutely convinced a marriage counselor could help us sort all this out."

Francee grips the edge of the desk with her long, professionally polished nails. "I had myself transferred to the firm's LA office," she tells me. "I'm going out there on Monday for a couple of days. To look for an apartment, I mean."

I am stunned by this additional piece of news, astonished that she has come to such a decision without letting me in on it until now, that partners in the firm knew what was up before I even had an inkling of the disaster that was in store for me.

"I'll come with you," I say. "I can take a couple of days off without any problem."

"Of *course* you can't come with me. What purpose would it serve?"

"We'd be together," I say in a small, hurt voice.

"Someday," Francee says, taking my hand and giving it a squeeze, "someday when you're happily remarried and I'm just a name on a New Year's card you open up and throw away with the junk mail, you'll—"

I drop her hand with a yelp of pain, as if I've just now discovered shards of broken glass in her palm. "Shut up," I say. "Just shut up, is that too much to ask?"

"I'll shut up in a second," she promises. "But I want you to know I went up to that microphone, got everything out there in the open like that, so you'd understand I really meant it, that there'd be no turning back. So *do* you understand?" Francee asks softly, a tone I'm not accustomed to hearing from her.

What I understand is that she is a woman of extravagant gestures, a woman who once shrieked at me so loudly in our kitchen that she set off the smoke alarm with her screams. (I no longer remember the reason for all that shouting, only that after I'd jumped onto the kitchen counter, reached toward the alarm on the ceiling and ripped out its batteries, the two of us burst into laughter, reeling about the room with our arms hugging our stomachs, wheezing hard.) And once, after we had been dating a short while and Francee had dropped by my apartment unexpectedly only to find me out, she'd left, as her calling card, a circle of vivid pink kissprints around my door knob. I kept the lipstick marks there for several days, careful not to smudge them when I turned the knob, wanting to preserve this unmistakable display of her affection. (That I had inspired such a gesture thrilled me; I'd never expected romance to come so easily into my life.)

"I'll never understand," I tell her now. "Not as long as I live."

• • •

The night that Francee flies to LA without me, promising to be back in three days, I drag myself to the synagogue for the weekly therapy group I conduct for a dozen or so members of the congregation. Usually I shine at these encounters, drawing people out almost effortlessly, offering comfort and insight week after week in a Hebrew school classroom decorated with a large map of Israel and posters urging contributions to Operation Exodus to help Jews emigrate from what used to be the Soviet Union. Tonight, though, I feel close to tears and very unsure of myself, in no shape to respond generously to the large and small sorrows of others.

"How's it going, Rabbi?" a teenager named Jamie asks as he slumps into his seat. He's dressed in a T-shirt that says "BLAH BLAH BLAH" across the front, and his dark hair is slicked back from his forehead with styling mousse that smells faintly of fruit or flowers, possibly both. "I was real sorry to hear your wife ditched you," he says. "Bummer, huh?"

"It's a bummer all right," I acknowledge. "And I don't want to talk about it, okay?"

"That's cool," says Jamie. "I guess it's like when my father died and I didn't want to talk about it for months. Of course, if my girlfriend dumped me, I'd probably want to shoot myself, you know, having to face running into her in school all the time, knowing she was alive and out there, but not for me. At least with my father, I knew he was dead, gone forever. You can forgive *that*, at least. Or I'm trying to, anyway."

"Get me a Diet Pepsi from the machine on the second floor, will you please, Jamie," I ask, and poke a cigarette into my mouth. I've been smoking too many cigarettes these past few days, drinking too much diet soda; even worse, a little gray has started showing up in my thick reddish mustache, I've noticed. (Once Francee's left me for good, I'll probably be a candidate for a horrendous mid-life crisis of my own, I suspect.) I watch now as the other members of the group begin to file in, mostly widows and divorcées in their fifties and early sixties, wearing sneakers and expensive sweatsuits and lots of jewelry. Two of them approach timidly, smiling at me shyly.

"Sheila and I just wanted you to know that our hearts are with you, Rabbi," Barbara says. It's been nearly six months since her husband took off with his gay lover, but Barbara's progress has been so slow and shaky that I've been thinking of referring her to another therapist who might do better with her.

"You're well rid of that wife of yours, Rabbi," says Sheila. "The woman was a viper."

"What?" I imagine Francee as a venomous two foot-long snake, threading herself over my shoulder, under my arm, around my waist, flicking her tongue, hissing at me disapprovingly.

"I was on the library committee with her twice, and she stabbed me in the back both times," Sheila reports. Her elderly and incontinent Yorkshire terrier was put to sleep several weeks ago, and she is still in mourning; her eyes are ringed with dark-green shadows of grief as she gives me a half-smile now. "I won't go into the sordid details, but believe me, I could tell you plenty."

"She's in mergers and acquisitions," I offer. "Everyone knows you have to be especially tough in that business."

Patting my elbow, Sheila says, "You're a good catch, Rabbi, a real cutie. The ladies will be beating down your door in no time. And if not, you could always run an ad in one of those magazines or newspapers, the respectable ones, of course, and choose someone nice for yourself. I have a friend who found herself a very lovely second husband that way. An accountant with a positive outlook on life and a house in the Hamptons with a hot tub *and* Jacuzzi."

"Thank you for your concern, ladies," I say, sighing. "Why don't you take your seats now so we can get started." Turning my back to them, I write Francee's name on the blackboard in tiny yellow letters, over and over again, then erase it all with a broad sweep of my sleeve. I slip into my sand-colored vinyl chair at the center of the U-shaped arrangement of seats and put my head down in my arms. I wonder if I can stay this way for the full two hours, leading the group with my eyes shut tight. Last night, not surprisingly, I'd been unable to sleep, and had left my bed several times between two and three-thirty, walking in and out of the rooms of my apartment, the tips of my cigarettes glowing, my bare feet colliding in the darkness with walls and furniture as I tried desperately to tire myself out. Francee slept peacefully through my wanderings, flat on her back in our king-sized bed, her beautiful hair spread abundantly across her pillow and mine. Whispering into her ear, I told her she was making a disastrous mistake, that she needed to take her time and reconsider. I remembered then that somewhere I'd read of people learning foreign languages while they slept, listening to tapes through headphones, awakening in the morning with *Comment vas-tu, Pierre?* on their lips. I contemplated making a tape of my own, in plain English, a tape that would list all the perfectly good reasons Francee and I had for staying together. Enumerating the list in my head, I fell asleep at last. In the morning, Francee left for work with her suitcase and carry-on bag, offering me nothing more than a quick embarrassed kiss to my forehead.

"Here's your Pepsi, Rabbi," says Jamie, and thumps the icy can on the table next to me.

I thank him without lifting my head, then peek out at the classroom, one eye open. "I'm appointing Jamie as my replacement for tonight," I announce, and close my eye.

"Cool," says Jamie eagerly. "Most excellent. So who wants to go first?"

"Rabbi," Sheila says, and I imagine her waving her hand in the air theatrically. "I'm sure I speak for all of us when I say that Jamie's the wrong person for the job. He's in high school, Rabbi. For all we know, his mind is on his geometry homework even as we speak. I really think a mature woman such as myself would be a much better choice."

"I'm a mature woman, as well," says Barbara. "I'd be happy to take over for you, Rabbi."

"Oh, man," says Jamie. "I'm sure the Rabbi has some real good reasons for picking *me*."

"Well, for starters, you've got a good head on your shoulders," I say. "And beyond that, I don't know, it was nice of you to go all the way down to the second floor to get me my soda." I can hear the shocked silence, lingering in the air like my cigarette smoke, and then the sound of a male voice, belonging to one of the two middle-aged men in the group.

"What is it, Hy?" I say. "What's on your mind?" I feel a special fondness for this man, who is always unfailingly generous and sympathetic in his reactions to everything he hears in this room, and who, at forty-three, is still on the lookout for the love of his life.

Hy clears his throat, then presses on bravely. "I think you need to talk about what happened Friday night, Rabbi. You're obviously in pain and I think you want to talk about it. To clear your head a little."

"Friday night?" I say. My voice sounds drunken, dazed. If only I had the strength to lift my head, raise myself to a standing position, and make my way toward the door. None of this seems possible, but at least I manage to open both eyes. "What happened Friday night was very unfortunate," I allow. "And I have to say that my ego is particularly fragile right now. We could talk about it forever. But that wouldn't be fair to you, Hy, or anyone else here, for that matter. I'm the one with the degree in counseling, I'm the one who's here to help *you*."

"You're the one whose wife pulled the rug out from under him in front of the whole congregation," Hy says quietly.

"I think it's awesome he had the guts to show up here tonight," says Jamie, and leads the round of applause that begins just before I surprise them all and exit from the room without apology.

• • •

As soon as the news gets out that Francee has moved into her furnished apartment in Beverly Hills, members of the congregation begin treating me as if I were bereaved and unable to care for myself—sending me wicker baskets of fruit and cheese and crackers, a couple of small, dressed turkeys, and, in one case, a black housekeeper in a white uniform who arrived to do my bathroom and kitchen floors and a few loads of laundry, she said. (Sending her on her way apologetically, with a twenty-dollar bill in hand, I had explained to the woman that I was perfectly capable of running my household of one on my own.) In fact, in Francee's absence, I've learned how to flip an omelet in a Teflon pan, to debone a chicken breast, and how to eliminate the mildew thriving in the corners of my stall shower. These small accomplishments strike me as something to be proud of, and I find myself silently boasting of them when, late one night, after a month or so of silence, Francee happens to call.

Not recognizing her voice at first, which sounds so small and sweet and distant, I say, "Who *is* this?" and nearly hang up, thinking it's a child on the line, someone much too young to be making phone calls on her own.

"You've got to be joking," Francee says, more boldly this time. "Didn't you think you'd never forget the sound of my voice?"

"Actually, I hadn't given it much thought one way or the other," I tell her. I keep one eye on the TV set, where an ancient rerun of *The Odd Couple* shows Oscar giving some poor frog a whirlpool bath in a blender.

"What's so funny?" says Francee.

"Believe it or not, I still find myself laughing from time to time. Life goes on, it seems, even in the face of terrible disappointment."

"Oh," says Francee.

It's unclear what she wants of me; I wonder if Francee herself even knows what has propelled her to the phone. "Did you want to talk to me?" I ask. I like the edge of impatience in my voice, the suggestion that I have better things to do than spend time on the telephone with someone who has so cruelly broken the bonds of affection and loyalty between us.

"Did I want to talk to you?" she repeats. "As it happens, I called to tell you about my toe. I was doing my exercise tape this morning and in the middle of a fancy kind of jumping jack, I smashed my baby toe into the coffee table. I had to wait nearly two hours for an X ray and then they tell me there's no treatment for a fractured toe. Nothing. Not even a Band-Aid."

"Poor baby toe," I say. I blush, imagining myself bending low to give it the lightest of kisses.

"It's purple and green!" says Francee, and bursts into tears. "And it hurts so much I've been on aspirin-with-codeine all day."

I listen patiently, long-distance, as her weeping mixes with a poignant hiccuping sound. "I love you," I murmur helplessly, and am relieved, an instant later, to realize that she's making too much noise to hear me.

"What?"

"Go to sleep," I advise. "You're bound to feel better in the morning."

"I have no friends on the West Coast," says Francee. "In the whole state of California there's not a single person who cares about my broken toe, not even the doctor in the emergency room. She was so bored, she yawned in my face while pointing out the fracture on the X ray."

"Well," I say, "I suppose you just have to be happy it wasn't anything worse."

Considering this for a moment, Francee is silent. "Thanks for those incredibly useful words of wisdom, Danny boy," she says finally, and hangs up on me.

I contemplate calling her back, and do not move from the phone. On the TV screen is a phone number and a blond woman in a leotard of sorts that reveals a spectacular bosom. "Confess your secrets," she urges me. "Or, if you like, hear the fabulous confessions of others. Dial 1-900-CONFESS!"

I have nothing to confess, I realize, except my own weakness for someone who wants my sympathy but not my love; someone who would fit in just fine with my therapy group, I realize.

•   •   •

In the back row of a crowded movie theater, I find myself feeding buttered popcorn to my date, the divorced mother of a thirteen-year-old whose bar mitzvah I'd recently presided over. My date, whose name is Deborah Mazzola-Weiss, delicately licks the salt and butter from my fingertips, then smiles at me in the dark.

"This is so sexy," she says, and sucks on one of my fingertips so enthusiastically that it makes an embarrassing noise when I pull it from her mouth.

"No more," I tell Deborah. She is hard and slender in all the places where Francee is soft and even a little flabby; the contrast depresses me, makes me nostalgic for Francee. This is my fourth Saturday night with Deborah in a month, and already she is leaping to mistaken conclusions. It's my fault and not hers, I know, and moan softly when she mentions her sister's upcoming wedding.

"It's a second marriage, of course, so it's not going to be a big deal, but I'm really hoping you'll go with me."

"Can I get back to you?" I ask. "It seems to me there's something big on my calendar for that weekend."

"Well, cancel it," Deborah says, sliding her small dry hand in my buttery one. "This wedding's going to be fun, you'll see. My sister's a panic."

"What's she in a panic about?" I pray for a way out of this; out of the sister's wedding, out of Deborah's life. It's all too much for me at this moment—I'm just not ready to let someone settle too comfortably into my life. If my prayers are answered, I'll quit smoking. Or at least cut back to half a pack a day. Sometimes my whole life seems only an attempt to avoid hurting people; offering small white lies along the way is second nature to me, something I've always done easily and well, and almost entirely without guilt. The guilt I save for bigger things, like the night last weekend when I allowed Deborah to seduce me on her living room couch while Barbra Streisand sang "People" on the CD player in a heart-stopping rendition that only intensified my guilt. *I need this*, I heard Deborah sigh as she went for my zipper. Or maybe, *I need you*; I'm not sure which. I needed it, too, urgently, and had undressed in record time, all the while doubting my modest affection for Deborah would ever deepen into love.

Afterward, I'd left in a hurry, refusing her invitation to spend the night, embarrassed and filled with regret at what I could only regard as a moment of weakness for me. When I got home there was a message from Deborah on the answering machine: "Just promise you won't forget me, Rabbi." Not a message I could ignore. And so I'd called her back immediately, sitting on my kitchen floor at midnight with my spine against the dishwasher, reassuring her that none of it had been a mistake.

As she laughs at me now in the movie theatre, Deborah says, "A panic, not *in* a panic. My sister's terrific—a funny, wonderful person. Her first husband was a fool to let her go."

"Sometimes," I say, "it's just not possible to hold on. You think you're willing to do anything, to handcuff yourself to that person and follow her anywhere, but of course you can't. You just can't."

"What your wife did to you," Deborah says sternly, "was outrageous. You can't even think about forgiving someone for that."

"You'd be surprised," I murmur.

Deborah shifts her gaze toward the screen, where a box of popcorn with a goofy, smiling face and spindly arms and legs dances its way into a garbage pail. "My husband, who was essentially pond scum, was having an affair with never-mind-who for almost five years. Five years that I knew of, anyway. Do you know how long five years is?"

I shake my head. I feel my arm moving toward her shoulders, her head tilting toward my neck, where it settles so sweetly, so lightly, I really can't complain.

• • •

The Hebrew school classroom has been converted, I see, into a living room of sorts; apparently someone had gone to a thrift shop and chosen this assortment of bean-bag chairs, this broken-backed corduroy couch and battered coffee table that my group is eyeing with such suspicion now. "Make yourselves comfortable," I urge as the last few members straggle in.

"Hey, I heard you got yourself a girlfriend," Jamie says buoyantly, and sinks into a bean bag next to me. "Way to go, Rabbi!"

My face blazes; lowering my head, I busy myself searching for my cigarettes and lighter.

"Not only that," says Sheila, "but she's Italian." The sweatshirt she's wearing has "HOT STUFF" spelled out in rhinestones; across the brim of her baseball cap is the same message.

"She's a convert," someone else calls out.

"I know someone who went to Sacred Heart with her all the way through high school," Sheila reports.

Releasing a white plume of cigarette smoke in the direction of a poster-sized map of Israel, I say, "Let's move on, okay?" (Actually, I have the impulse to grab Sheila's cap from her head and sail it across the room into a corner somewhere.)

"I guess you're telling us it's none of our business," she says.

"You're absolutely right. Now, who would like to begin to-night? Hy?"

"I'm afraid I can't accept that," Sheila persists. "Because of who you are to us, we really need to know more."

Hearing this, Jamie pushes himself up out of his bean bag. "No way," he says. "No one in this room should be forced to talk about things they don't feel like sharing with the group."

"Thank you," I say, enormously grateful. "I'm glad *someone* here knows which end is up."

"But I'm confused," says Hy, and taps his brow with the eraser end of a pencil. "I thought we were here to confront our fears, to speak openly about anything and everything that may have been causing us anxiety and confusion."

"True," I say. I can see where this is going and stir in my huge bean bag uneasily, accidentally getting Jamie in the shins. "Sorry," I mumble. And then, "But that's not what *I'm* here for."

"Your life isn't the same as when we first started this group," Hy says. "You're dealing with major trauma in your own life that could affect your judgment of the things you hear in this room. And that's why I think you owe it to us to be a little more generous in what you reveal."

"So what's the story on this chick you're dating?" Jamie says. "That's the kind of stuff we need to know about, right?"

I laugh nervously. "You want me to explain my life to you, is that it?"

"Just the important stuff," says Jamie. "The stuff that keeps you up in the middle of the night."

Now that I think of it, I've fallen into a deep satisfying sleep nearly every night these past few weeks, or at least every night I've seen Deborah. Sometimes, wary of her son asleep nearby in his bedroom, we limit ourselves to making out in front of the TV set, taking pleasure in the lengthy kisses we exchange, the simple act of entwining our ankles on the couch cushions, the quiet sound of our murmuring. I find it fascinating that she was raised a Catholic, that while we were growing up in neighboring suburbs on Long Island, we probably would not have given each other a second look. At her sister's wedding last month, fortified with several Scotch-and-sodas, I managed to charm her two little wizened old parents, managed to change the subject when her father asked what line of business I was in. It was what Deborah had wanted from me and so I had done it, promising myself that this was it for us, our very last date together. But later on at the wedding reception, watching Deborah arranging a bow in a niece's hair, escorting another little niece to the ladies' room, dancing with her sister's new husband, I found myself admiring how gracefully and easily she moved among people. This was something that Francee had no talent for, and it had always been a source of grief to me. She was impatient with people and did not know how to get past that; she seemed genuinely puzzled when I tried to explain to her that members of my congregation, especially the women, found her rude and difficult. ("So I can't keep up my end of a mindless conversation about how to roast a stupid chicken. So what? What does it matter?" she'd said tearfully on more than one occasion.) Seeing Deborah at the center of a group of her sister's friends at the wedding, her arms slung casually over the shoulders of a pair of women in identical dresses, I'd fantasized idly, briefly, about what it would be like to spend my life with her, a woman people found themselves drawn to, a woman who knew how to be of comfort. It occurred to me that I was the slightest bit drunk, that there was always the danger that everything she said and did that night might seem all the more appealing because of the three drinks I'd had, yet it didn't really seem to matter. Approaching Deborah, leading her away from her sister's friends and toward the dance floor, I held onto her tightly. "I'm putting myself in your hands," I said, and closed my eyes as she steered me around the room, guiding my leaden feet easily, whispering encouragement and unearned praise in my ear. When the slow music gave way to something fast and I tried to abandon her, she would not let me go. She flapped my arms to loosen me up, spun me around swiftly a few times, and somehow I kept going on my own, buoyed by the sound of the Ronettes singing "Be My Baby" and the joyous feeling that I was free of something I couldn't define but was absolutely sure I no longer needed.

"Come on, Rabbi," Hy is saying in his patient way. "There's nothing to be afraid of, isn't that your standard line?"

"And now I'm telling you," I say firmly, disappointing every one of them, "that in this room, at least, I have no choice but to keep my life to myself. Anything less than that would be very unprofessional." I take command confidently, for the first time in quite a while, it seems to me, and shift the attention to Sheila, asking if she's been feeling any less despondent over the death of her terrier.

Looking me straight in the eye, Sheila says, "You bet."

"That's wonderful," I say. "Time is always the greatest healer, isn't it?"

"Not necessarily," Sheila says. "Actually, I haven't been particularly truthful about any of this."

"You haven't?"

"A couple of months ago I dug up Cindy from her little grave in the backyard of my country house," Sheila says slowly. "I had her freeze-dried by a taxidermist, and now she's sitting at the foot of my bed, looking like her old self, except for the pair of glass eyes they had to give her, of course."

The room itself seems to draw in its breath, and then Jamie says, "No way!" My arms prickly with goosebumps, I'm once again humbled, reminded of just how little I know about any of them, really, and how presumptuous it is of me to ever think otherwise. I am speechless and can only nod at Sheila as if I understand.

"You can't imagine how much better I feel," Sheila says. "You just can't."

•　•　•

Deborah has dyed her short dark hair a shade of auburn that nearly matches my own, I realize when I see it tonight for the first time. I wonder if this was an act of love or merely a coincidence, and decide, as I thread my fingers through it gently, that I'd rather not know. Walking the short distance between her apartment and mine after dinner on this clear ice-cold winter night, Deborah drops my hand suddenly and says, "My T-shirt."

"What about it?"

"I left it in your freezer last week."

"What?"

"Oh," Deborah says, "there was gum on the pocket and since I heard the best way to get it off is to freeze it, I stuck the shirt up there in your sub-zero whatever and then I forgot all about it. So listen, weren't you wondering what a shirt was doing in your freezer?"

"Never even noticed it," I say, smiling as she rolls her eyes at me. Just ahead of us, working diligently, a homeless man dressed only in a bathrobe and backless slippers writes his name in the dust on the windshield of an old Corvette. "Archie is Archie is Archie," he prints with his index finger. When he sees that I'm watching him, the man says, "Give Archie money and he'll tell you a joke." He pockets my dollar in a flash. "What goes up but never comes down?" he asks hoarsely.

I shrug.

"Your age, right?" the man says, and laughs silently, with his mouth full of ruined teeth wide open. "No way you going to be young ever again."

"Thanks for the tip, Archie," I say, and hurry past him, as if what I have just heard were a foreboding of some new disaster. My breathing grows shallow, my palms clammy inside my leather gloves.

"Want to stop and get something for dessert?" Deborah asks.

I shake my head; I can't wait to get home and out of my clothes, to feel her now-familiar body under or over my own. I picture, admiringly, the sharp planes of her hips, the deep hollows beneath her arms when her hands are linked behind her neck, her small high breasts. It is still a surprise to me that I no longer feel nostalgia for Francee's softness. I have turned bad luck into good, I remind myself, and throw back my shoulders now as I enter the lobby of my building with Deborah on my arm.

Later, when the phone at my bedside rings a little after eleven, I assume it can only be a wrong number calling so late on a Saturday night.

"You'll never guess," I hear Francee say brightly, "but go ahead and give it a try anyway."

"Never guess what?"

"Give up?"

Absently stroking Deborah's bare arm in the darkness, I say, "Go ahead."

"I'm in a cast up to my elbow!" Francee shrieks, so loudly that I have to hold the receiver away from my ear.

"Calamity Jane," I say.

"The last time I talked to you it was my toe, and now this. Two bones in three months, isn't it amazing?" When I don't respond, Francee says, "Don't you want to know what happened?"

"What happened?"

"I was roller skating in Venice and I lost my—"

"You went to Italy?"

"Venice, California, genius. So I lost my balance and went down hard, right on my wrist. The guy I was with was a real sweetie and spent the afternoon with me in the emergency room, so at least I wasn't alone."

"What guy?"

"Just an attorney from the office."

"Are you in love with him?" I say, as Deborah gets up, pulls the top sheet from the bed and drapes it across her body like a floor-length shawl. Raising the blinds, she arranges herself on the window-sill, looks out at the flat rooftops of a dozen buildings in the near distance, at a silver plane casually crossing the darkened sky. From my bed, I have only a partial view of what is beyond the window; I concentrate on the mournful slope of Deborah's shoulders beneath the bedsheet. I gesture with my free hand for her to come back to bed, thump the mattress beside me with my palm. She ignores me, refusing even to turn her head in my direction.

"Don't be ridiculous," Francee says. "If I love anyone, I think it's safe to assume it's you."

"Me?" I say stupidly, and I'm filled with a curious mix of dread and exhilaration. "What do you mean?"

"I want to give it another shot, Danny."

"Another shot?"

"Why do you sound so dumb?" Francee says, clearly exasperated. But then she laughs. "I've been thinking about coming home. Bet you think that's pretty funny, all things considered."

"You can't," I say instantly. "I mean, you can't do this to me." I glance over at Deborah, who is entirely still, her knees drawn up under her chin. The phone in my lap now, I move toward the foot of the bed, trying without success to reach her with my fingertips.

"Do what to you?" says Francee.

"You've been away for months," I begin. "It's not as if life stands still, do you understand what I'm saying?"

After what seems like a lengthy silence, Francee says, "Oh God, *you* have a girlfriend, and *I* can't move my fingers. The cast cuts right across the middle of my hand but I'm supposed to be able to move my fingers, I'm supposed to be able to wiggle them. I'm trying, but I can't, Goddamnit."

"Don't panic," I say. "The numbness is going to go away. But if you panic, everything's going to get worse."

"Worse?" Francee shouts, and at last Deborah turns away from the window and toward me. "My fingers are paralyzed and my husband of ten years doesn't want me back. And you think things could get worse?"

"You're the one who set things in motion," I remind her. "You're the one who announced the break up of our marriage into a microphone."

"Nobody's perfect," says Francee mildly. "We all make mistakes."

This strikes me as so inadequate, so utterly beside the point, so hilarious, finally, that all at once I'm convulsed with laughter, doubled over, my head bent low to my knees, the telephone receiver gone from my hand and over the side of the bed, onto the floor. "Nobody's perfect," I repeat, and pound my fists into the mattress. Collapsing into a quiet, motionless heap, I hear a voice rising sharply from the floor. "I'm sorry," I say into the receiver as I hang over the side of the bed to retrieve it.

"You are one tough cookie," Francee tells me, but I know there is no truth to this, that I am simply someone who lets things happen—love, betrayal, and unexpectedly, miraculously, love, again. I think of the bright circle of her kisses surrounding my doorknob and the sound, years later, of her voice coolly broadcasting to a sanctuary full of people the news that our marriage had played itself out. Both of these seem startling to me even now, these markers that boldly frame my time with Francee. All the rest, all the months and years of my marriage, seems only a blur, indistinct and soundless, like something witnessed underwater.

"The numbness is going away—I'm getting some feeling back!" I hear Francee holler triumphantly.

"I told you," I say. "Didn't I tell you?"

"We're not done with each other, are we," Francee says. "Now that I can move my fingers again, I'm beginning to feel hopeful."

"Hope is always a good thing," I lie, and blush with shame.

"I can live with that," says Francee.

Hanging up the phone, I go in search of Deborah, who has slipped away unnoticed on bare, silent feet. I discover her in front of the open refrigerator, where she stands shivering in my bedsheet, her frozen T-shirt hanging stiffly from one hand.

"There's nothing here I really want." she says, slamming the refrigerator door shut. "And now that I've reclaimed my shirt, you can take me home," she says forlornly, but instead I lead her from the kitchen, past the moonlit dining room and to the window beyond it, where I offer her a splendid, perfectly round white moon and several handfuls of winking stars.

"This is what you want," I guess, and cast my arm across her trembly shoulders, drawing her into my heat.

Earthbound

Sometimes, Walter knew, people mistook him and his daughter, Sunny, for husband and wife. He never bothered to correct the impression, because, after all, it was nobody's business. It was the impatient way he and Sunny spoke to each other, the aggrieved looks they shot one another, as if, after years together, they'd both had just about enough. He was a young-looking forty, with pale skin and hair and a mustache so faint it was easy to overlook. Sunny had recently turned nineteen and was already the mother of two children—three-year-old Jenna, a fat little girl still in diapers, and James, the baby, who was about to celebrate his first birthday. The three of them were living with Walter in his apartment, where they all had their own bedrooms except Sunny, who slept on a pull-out couch in the living room and wasn't happy about it. (It was only because the baby was such a miserable sleeper, awakening two or three times a night and carrying on noisily, that he and Jenna had to have separate rooms.) Occasionally, Sunny spent the night at her boyfriend's: according to the arrangement she had with Walter, whenever she was going to stay over at Chick's, she was expected to call home and let her father know her plans. But often she forgot, leaving Walter a prisoner in his own home with two kids to babysit. Sunny's boyfriend was exactly her age; unlike Sunny, Chick looked as if he were still in high school. He had a rosy sprinkle of acne across his forehead, and skinny hairless arms and delicate wrists. He wasn't the father of

Sunny's two children, but he treated them as if he were, bringing them little gifts from the pet store where he worked, tickling their bellies, ruffling their hair affectionately. He hung around Walter's apartment almost every night after work, gazing admiringly at Sunny in her scoop-necked shirts and astoundingly tight blue jeans. Sometimes Walter felt as if he couldn't wait another minute for the two of them to decide to get married and find a place of their own. On the other hand, he regarded Chick as a loser, someone without much to offer his daughter and her children. It was, for Walter, what his wife would have jokingly called a "dilemna." She had died when their daughter was thirteen, before Sunny had got herself mixed up with Ben Ingerman, her high-school boyfriend who'd got her pregnant not once, but twice. (A hotshot soccer player, the kid was likable and bright enough, Walter had once thought: Ben had, to his credit, taken Lamaze classes with Sunny and seen her through both deliveries.) Shortly after James was born, Ben had gone off to the state university in Albany and never looked back. For a while, Walter remembered, there had been some talk about Sunny and the children following him up the Hudson, but nothing ever came of it. Walter was convinced that just to spite him, Ben would eventually turn out to be a big success—a wealthy businessman of some sort, with a limo and a driver and a glamorous blond on each arm. In his daydreams, envisioning this flashy grown-up version of Ben out on the street somewhere, Walter would simply march up to him and sock him one in the solar plexus, a blow so powerful it would knock Ben right off his feet. He thought of how satisfying it would feel to deliver a punch like that to the one person on this earth he truly despised. He wondered if Sunny ever thought of Ben at all, especially when she looked into James' ice-blue eyes, eyes that resembled a Siberian husky's and came straight from Ben.

Knowing Sunny, probably not.

•   •   •

They were five at dinner, including Chick, who'd stopped off after work to buy a family-sized order of fried chicken and a container of coleslaw. They ate on Styrofoam party plates, because the dishwasher was down again and Sunny had already predicted she was going to be too tired to clean up after all of them. From the dining-area window, they could look directly into the apartments of the high-rise next to them, where an elderly woman had recently been stabbed to death by her next-door neighbor.

"I'll tell you why it doesn't bother me much," Walter said, and tipped a small mountain of coleslaw onto his plate. "She knew her attacker and let him into the apartment. It wasn't as if he were some stranger who'd forced his way past security and into her home. Now *that* would be something to be upset about."

"What?" said Sunny. They'd had this discussion several times since the murder, and each time they ended up raising their voices, calling each other names they later regretted. "Are you out of your mind?" Sunny said shrilly. "An old lady was stabbed practically on your doorstep and you can sit and look out that window and not be upset?" She got up and lowered the blinds, yanking the cord so vigorously that they banged against the windowsill. "Now I can eat my dinner in peace."

"This is *my* home," said Walter, as he went to the window and pulled the blinds back up. "If you don't like the view you can get yourself a better one."

"Yeah yeah yeah," Sunny said. "Tell me something I haven't heard before." She wiped a vivid streak of ketchup from Jenna's cheek and picked fried-chicken crust from the baby's temples. "If we moved out, you'd miss us so much you wouldn't know what to do with yourself."

"Want to bet?" said Walter.

"Absolutely."

"You're dead wrong," Walter said, though he knew she was probably right. He tried to imagine what it would be like having the apartment to himself: just the silence would be enough to drive him crazy, he decided. He would have to keep the TV and the stereo going from the moment he returned home from work, and would fall asleep at night to the sound of a stranger's voice coming from his clock radio. Eating his meals alone would be bad news, too: without Sunny to cook for him, he'd end up eating two slices of pizza, one with mushrooms and one without, every night of the week. Unless his girlfriend, Charlene, decided to take pity on him, which seemed unlikely.

They'd been seeing each other on and off for nearly five years, but recently she'd talked about moving back home to the small town in Ohio where she'd grown up, a town with one supermarket, one movie theater and lots of Mennonites dressed in bleak colors. Although the affection he felt for Charlene didn't quite measure up to either his or her definition of love, for a long while she had been willing to make do with whatever he could offer her. This failure of his to feel something deeper for Charlene troubled him, but, in fact, he didn't expect to fall in love ever again. He'd explained to Charlene that in *his* life, at least, love came around only once; when he lost Meg, Sunny's mother, that was it for him. Charlene claimed that she understood, that love probably meant something different to everyone, anyway, and that there was little point in talking these things to death. But she knew what was what—why else would she even have considered leaving New York and going back to a place where her return would be noted in the local newspaper, probably with a big headline.

"You'll never believe what happened in Burger King today," Chick said excitedly. He had the baby in his lap now and was dangling his keychain in front of him, bringing it within James' reach and then snatching it away as soon as the baby, overcome with laughter, made a grab for it. "Silly silly silly," he told James approvingly, and turned to Walter. "This homeless dude asks me for money, and I'm just not in the mood to give him any, you know? So I offer him my soda and my onion rings instead. Fine. But then he goes to the table next to me and grabs a hamburger right out of the guy's hands. He starts to run away, and the guy chases after him out into the street, and he's yelling, 'Give me back my goddamn Whopper, you piece of garbage.' It was pretty sickening, actually—I couldn't even think about eating after that."

"So you let him have some of your lunch," said Walter. "That's something to feel good about."

Chick shrugged. He stood the baby at the edge of the table, and holding his hands, jerked his arms back and forth rhythmically so it looked as if he and James were grooving to music only the two of them could hear. "His mouth was black," said Chick. "Like he had some kind of disease. It was pathetic."

"I'll tell you something else that's pathetic," Walter said, but didn't finish. He watched as Chick swept the baby from the table and handed him over to Sunny.

Going through his pockets now, Chick came up with a pair of rubber squeak toys, one in the shape of an enormous pacifier, the other a cheeseburger on a sesame seed bun. "I wonder who these are for," he said.

"Me!" said Jenna, and jumped down from her chair to collect her gift. Certainly she didn't know they were dog toys, didn't know what Walter would have bet his life on, that Chick had swiped them from Pawsitively Pets, along with every other junky little rubber toy he routinely pulled from his pockets. Walter felt his fingers stiffening into fists. He shook his head as Jenna held the toys up to her ears and squeaked them, as Sunny smiled in her lover's direction.

"We have to talk, Chickie-boy," he said.

"Now what?" said Sunny. "You think he's spoiling the kids, is that it?"

Walter led him through the long-barren hallway and into his

bedroom. He was embarrassed at the sight of his unmade bed, at the pajamas that lay draped across the threshold of his walk-in closet, the stick of Arrid Extra Dry that, mysteriously, had been shoved halfway under his pillow. "Your girlfriend and I are a swell pair of house-keepers," he said mildly.

"She's busy with the kids all day," said Chick. "It isn't easy for her." He sat down on Walter's pillow and played with the stick of deodorant, taking the cap off and snapping it back on again half a dozen times until finally, with a sigh, Walter confiscated it.

"Sorry," said Chick. Up close, he smelled slightly fishy, like the inside of a pet store.

"Listen, kiddo, I'm far from perfect myself." This seemed to be a good lead-in, and Walter went with it, mentioning that he'd made a few mistakes in his life, just like everyone else.

"You're an okay dude," said Chick.

"That's right, I am. And you know why, because I wouldn't dream of stealing from my employer. Not a paper clip, not a box of number two pencils, nothing. If I took stuff out of my classroom I'd be cheating everyone: my students, the tax payers, you name it."

Chick rolled his eyes. "Whoa, a paper clip. That's like grand larceny, right?"

"It's the principle of the thing," said Walter. "You wouldn't hap-pen to know anything about principles, would you?" He fixed his eyes on Chick's, which were so narrow they gave him a perpetually drowsy look that did not inspire confidence.

Sliding off the bed and backing away, Chick said, "Get out of town! What do you think I am, a thief or something? You think I walk out of Pawsitively Pets every day with a five hundred dollar silver tabby Persian under my arm and nobody notices?"

"I didn't say that."

"So what's on your mind, then—a ten-pound bag of bird seed? A twenty-gallon fish tank? A couple of springer spaniel puppies?"

"Forget it," said Walter.

"How dumb do you think I am?"

"You made your point," said Walter. He shut the door after Chick and got into his unmade bed. Although it was late in June and uncomfortably warm inside the apartment, he pulled the covers all the way over his head. So his two innocent grandchildren had a shelf full of stolen toys meant for dogs and cats. It was too depressing to think about, really. He thought of Charlene and the pattern of freckles that spread across her chest and over her shoulders, of her soft behind that he loved to pat, of her bright, naturally red hair that was a little coarse to the touch. He tried to convince himself that he loved her, but that was depressing, too. If she moved back to Ohio, he would miss her, but he would not be devastated. After six years, it was still hard to forgive his wife for leaving him. He went to her grave once a year, every October, but standing there, his head hung gloomily, all he felt was a coldness, as if there were nothing there for him. Six years was an impossibly long time to be angry; he guessed that he wasn't ready to give it up yet, like a drunk who was perfectly willing to admit what he was but who just didn't want to stop drinking.

He could hear water running in the kitchen sink, the refrigerator door slamming, bright laughter that belonged to his daughter. Without warning, his door swung open and Jenna hurled herself on top of him. "Take me to the park, Poppy," she said.

"'Take me to the park, *Walter*,'" he said. "I'm not old enough to be anyone's Poppy."

"Silly!" Jenna shrieked. "You're so so so old."

"Says who?"

"Me me me."

"Great," said Walter. He got out of bed and put on his dark green suede sneakers and a souvenir T-shirt from his twentieth high-school reunion. The shirt listed every member of his graduation class, living or dead. Whoever had the shirts made up had spelled his name "Water Wilson." It hadn't bothered him before, but now, inexplicably, he found it unacceptable and went back to his dresser for another shirt.

He took Jenna by the hand and marched past Sunny and Chick, who were in the kitchen with their tongues in each other's mouths, a bucket of chicken bones on the stove behind them. James was on the floor, beating an overturned piece of Corning Ware with a wooden salad spoon.

"For those of you who are interested," Walter said, as he fastened James into his stroller, "some of us are going down to the park for a while."

Pulling away from Chick, Sunny wiped her mouth against her wrist. "Thanks, Daddy," she said, so warmly that he knew Chick had kept their conversation to himself.

"Go back to your make-out party," Walter said, feeling generous. "Enjoy yourselves."

They watched for the elevator at the end of the hall, an activity some of the tenants likened to waiting on a subway platform for a train that ran infrequently. Walter combed James' hair with his fingers as they waited, double-knotted Jenna's sneakers, listened to her sing endless verses of a song she had learned in her play group. Someone in an apartment nearby was smoking pot; the pungent odor had Jenna wrinkling her nose comically. It occurred to Walter that Sunny and Chick had probably lit up as soon as he left, triple-locking the door behind him, thrilled at the opportunity to exploit his absence. When, at last, the elevator arrived, he almost let it go without them. What would he have said to Sunny? He needed to get it just right, to come down hard on her but not too hard. *You're a mother, for crying out loud*, he wanted to say. He needed more than that, but nothing came to him. Reluctantly, he got onto the elevator with his grandchildren. He kissed the tops of their heads.

"You're too big to be wearing diapers," he said to Jenna.

"I don't care," she said pleasantly. "Not . . . at . . . all."

• • •

Several hours before James' birthday party, Charlene arrived with a Mylar balloon tied to her wrist and two trays of cupcakes she'd made from scratch. She and Sunny embraced extravagantly, as if they hadn't seen one another in years. Walter was always a little envious of how well the two of them got along, though he had to admit he took pleasure in it, too.

"Break it up, you guys," he said, and waited for his kiss from Charlene. She was wearing black leggings and a big knee-length shirt that went well with her carroty hair. She looked young and pretty, not at all like someone who'd be willing to waste five years of her life with the wrong man. He imagined her back in Ohio, living at home with her aging parents on ten acres that had once been farmland. He saw her in brilliant sunlight, slowly walking the expanse of her father's property and then beyond it, growing smaller and smaller until finally she disappeared into an endless cornfield, her eyes still straining for the man of her dreams.

Untying the balloon from her wrist, Charlene came toward him now. He kissed her urgently, guiltily, as the balloon drifted above them. The sun was sinking over the cornfield; he could see the weariness in Charlene's sloping shoulders, the disappointment in the downward turn of her sun-scorched mouth. "I'm sorry," he heard himself whisper.

"For what?" said Charlene. "Don't tell me you forgot to pick up your Big Bird costume. If you don't get over there by one o'clock, they're not going to hold it for you."

He had promised to be Big Bird for the afternoon, primarily because Sunny kept insisting the party would bomb without him. He must have been crazy to have made a promise like that, he realized now; who else but a madman would have agreed to spend a couple of hours imprisoned inside an elaborate costume on a hot summer afternoon? He liked to tell people he would do anything for his grandchildren, and he guessed it was probably true.

"You're very sexy for a grandfather," Charlene whispered in his ear.

"And also very young," he said.

"That, too."

As he left to pick up his costume, Charlene was twisting Jenna's hair into a French braid, and Sunny was adding silver sprinkles to the trays of cupcakes Charlene had labored over in her steamy windowless kitchen. Walter enjoyed the scene he was leaving behind, the thought of the many threads of affection that bound the three of them to each other, and to him. He recalled all the times Sunny had teased him about Charlene, saying, "What's up with the two of you, anyway? How come I've already voted myself in as maid of honor and you still haven't gotten your act together?" He hated to admit it, but maybe he was just too blind or too stubborn to recognize that this was as good as it was ever going to get, that something approximating love might be treasured as love itself.

On the street, he was almost trampled by an organized group of runners heading west toward Central Park, all of them dressed in silky blue shorts and T-shirts darkened with perspiration. He passed a man in an expensive-looking summer suit and red rubber thongs on his feet making a call from the phone booth on the corner. "The self is the only thing that exists?" the man yelled into the phone. "If you buy that crap, Joanne, you'll buy anything." Nearby, a mutt tied to a fire hydrant was eating from a ceramic plate of french fries, his owner nowhere in sight. By the time Walter arrived at the party store, just a few doors beyond Pawsitively Pets, it was already ten after one. He hoped they'd rented his costume to someone else, but no luck: the sales clerk handed it over to him with a smile.

"Hope your air-conditioning's working," he said to Walter

sympathetically. "You're going to melt in this thing."

"Do I get a discount for all the suffering I'm going to do?"

"Drink plenty of fluids," the clerk advised. "And take off your head if you start to feel faint."

He went past the pet store without stopping, then found himself turning around and heading back toward the store. He stood at the window and watched a pair of Siamese kittens dozing in their litter pans. He knocked lightly on the glass, trying to rouse them, but couldn't get their attention. At his post behind the counter, Chick was drinking what looked like Coke or iced tea out of a small fish bowl; Walter could see the price sticker on the bottom as Chick raised the bowl to his lips with both hands. He set it down on the counter and took a bite from a sandwich, then lifted up the fish bowl again. Walter stared, mesmerized, as if he were beholding something truly remarkable. And then, suddenly, he had to look away; the sheer dopiness of what he had seen, the casual, almost mechanical way Chick was drinking from the fish bowl infuriated him. "I'm nuts," he said out loud. But it wasn't unreasonable to want something better for his daughter—surely this had to be true.

A woman was beside him, holding a little girl up to the window to see the kittens. "Excuse me?" she said.

"May I ask you a question?" Walter heard himself say.

The woman turned, looked him over quickly. "Those kittens are Abyssinian, if that's what you're wondering about."

"Really?" Walter sighed. "This is just a hypothetical question, of course, but wouldn't you be horrified if your little girl grew up only to fall in love with a man who drank iced tea out of a fish bowl?"

"I have no idea," the woman said coldly. Then, "Is this a trick question?"

"No it's not," said Walter. "Thanks anyway."

● ● ●

Sunny tried to hurry him into his costume the moment he walked through the door. He had a beer first, then stood at the kitchen sink and ran cold water over his wrists to calm himself.

"Are you all right?" Sunny asked him. "Maybe we can get Chick into the costume instead. He should be here in an hour or so."

"No way," said Walter. It was Charlene who helped him dress, then took a couple of snapshots of him in his finery.

"The orange tights are . . . *you*," she said. "You've got just the legs for them." She kissed his bright yellow beak and ruffled what were meant to be his feathers but were actually something made of a woolly-looking acrylic. "Why do I get the feeling you've got stage fright?" she said.

"I don't *feel* like Big Bird," said Walter. "I'm just me, having a bad day."

Charlene stroked the huge yellow glove that covered his hand. "What is it?"

"We'll see," he said, and shrugged.

The party was to be held in the little concrete park adjacent to the entrance to Walter's building. Clumping in his enormous bird-feet out of the apartment and down the hallway, he got into the elevator with his family. Sunny had borrowed a supermarket cart and loaded it with paper goods, two vinyl tablecloths, and cartons of Hawaiian Punch. She and Charlene had already ornamented the trees downstairs with balloons and crêpe paper patterned with an army of Big Birds. On its way down to the lobby, the elevator made only one other stop; a bare-chested man in a bathing suit got on, reeking of suntan lotion. "And how are you, today?" he said, and reached behind him to pull on Walter's tail feathers.

"Cut it out!" Walter yelled irritably, though he couldn't feel a thing. "I don't like guys touching me, you know what I mean?"

The man laughed. "*Somebody* got up on the wrong side of the cage today."

"Fuck you," Walter mumbled behind his mask. He had spoken at normal volume but was sure no one had heard him; unaccountably, he was feeling very pleased with himself. He felt a kinship with all the excessively cheerful-looking costumed characters he'd seen once on a trip to Disney World. Inside their masks, he guessed, they were probably murmuring things that would have had Walt Disney rolling over in his grave.

Waiting for the guests to arrive, he sat on a wooden bench in the park with his orange legs crossed at the knee. Perspiration dripped from the tip of his nose into his mouth, and trailed down the slope behind each ear. He took off his head and set it down on the bench, and sipped at a can of Rolling Rock. A herd of babies came along in their strollers and Sunny shouted at him from across the way to put his head back on. Several of the babies burst into tears at the sight of him. "Hey, it's me, Big Bird," he said with false exuberance. "Isn't this super?"

A girl a couple of years older than Jenna, wearing a gold-lamé bikini and plastic slippers encrusted with jewels, circled him cautiously. "Can you fly?" she said.

Walter shook his head.

"Why not?"

"I'm too fat," he said, after a moment.

"Birds *fly*," she said and stamped her miniature foot in its gaudy plastic shoe.

"Well, this bird is earthbound," said Walter. He eyed his cold beer with great longing. "And also very thirsty." Just as he was about to remove his head, Sunny approached with a group of Jenna's pals.

"They want your autograph," Sunny said. "Do you think you can hold a pen?"

"I'm roasting in here," said Walter. "And what do three-year-olds know about autographs?"

"You think it's a dumb idea? I bought Big Bird stationery for party favors, and I thought you could autograph it for them."

"It's not in my contract," Walter said. "My contract states I just have to hang out and be, you know, available."

"Okay," said Sunny, which surprised him. "But you're not supposed to be sitting around. You've got to get out there and circulate. And be friendly. Ask the kids if any of them want to touch your feathers, shake your hand, that kind of thing."

He stood up and flapped his arms listlessly. "Anybody want to touch my feathers?" He moved his arms more vigorously. "Come on, guys," he said. "How do you think this makes me feel? I flew all the way here from Sesame Street and you're not paying any attention to me."

"You said you can't fly," the girl in the bikini reminded him. "You said."

"What I meant was, I can't fly on my own like other birds. I flew here in an airplane."

The girl gave him a contemptuous look. "You're a big fat liar," she said. "You can fly but you just don't want to."

"Big Bird doesn't lie," said Walter. He shook hands with a couple of kids and walked away, hanging his head so low his beak grazed his chest. He went over to the picnic tables Sunny had arranged side by side and draped in plastic, and lowered himself onto a bench. He watched the babies splashing in a green-vinyl wading pool, listened to the three-year-olds shrieking as they raced around aimlessly in the heat. Charlene was talking to the mother of one of the babies in the pool; bending down, she cupped her hands and tossed palmfuls of water over James' fleshy little shoulders. She was still young enough to have a child of her own, and Walter felt guilty about that, too. Whenever they were about to make love, he remembered to ask if she'd taken her birth control pill; always she murmured "yes" and always he responded "good girl," as if she were a child who never forgot to wash her hands before sitting down to dinner. Behind his mask, he smiled at her, and raised his enormous hand in greeting, but she was too busy with James to notice.

He closed his eyes for only a moment, then began to worry that he might doze off and suffocate somehow. He saw Chick bounding toward him, and groaned.

"Lookin' good, Walter," Chick said. "How does it feel in there?"

"Like I'm dying," said Walter.

"Want me to take over for you?"

"It wouldn't be right," Walter said. "When I start something, it's generally my policy to finish it."

"Want a beer, at least?"

Awkwardly, Walter folded his arms over his broad woolly chest. "I saw you enjoying your lunch at work today."

"You were in the store? How come I didn't see you?"

"I just happened to be walking by, but I didn't come in."

"Too bad. There's all kinds of neat stuff I could have showed you."

"You were drinking from a fish bowl," said Walter. He tried to sound casual, but began to tap his ludicrous three-toed orange foot impatiently against the concrete.

"Oh yeah?" Taking a stick of gum from his pocket, Chick unwrapped it delicately; he stared, as if in a trance, at the foil wrapper glittering in the sunlight. "Did you check out that amazing rabbit in the window? The tan one that was like as big as a fully grown cat? It's Angora—they go for a hundred dollars a pop."

"You're an idiot," said Walter. "I'm sorry, but you are."

With both hands, Chick grabbed him by his feathery throat. "Shut up, you asshole!" Heads swiveled in their direction; Walter heard a woman's voice shrill, "He's choking that poor Big Bird!"

Walter struggled to his feet, knocking over the bench behind him. Prying Chick's hands from his neck and kicking him in the stomach, he lost his balance. One of his tights tore, revealing a badly skinned knee. He whipped off his mask and tossed it aside as a small crowd of mothers and babies gathered over him. Chick was still standing, bent at the waist and holding his stomach. Sunny flew to him first.

"You're ruining the party," she hissed, but she had her arm around his shoulders and it was Walter she was glaring at.

"He tried to kill me," said Walter. "He had his hands against my windpipe and I was almost asphyxiated."

Moaning slightly, Chick straightened up. "I'd *like* to kill you," he said, sounding almost polite. "But of course there are plenty of things in this world I'd like to do." He blinked at Walter. "You can't always have it the way you want it, can you?"

Walter examined his scraped knee; the blood had pooled and was overflowing in a narrow stream down his orange tights. It was going to cost him something when he returned the costume. A guest at the party tried to kill me, he'd explain to the clerk, and hope for a little sympathy.

He felt a hand at the back of his neck, and smiled up at Charlene, who had James riding her hip. "It's just me," he said, "having one of those days."

Sunny cleared her throat. She looked wilted and miserable; somehow a smudge of royal blue eye shadow had settled across the bridge of her nose. "I want the two of you to shake hands," she said severely. "*Now.*"

"And I'd like a penthouse on Fifth Avenue," said Chick. "Forget it, man."

"Daddy?"

Waving his big yellow gloves through the air, Walter said, "I'm not even sure where my hands *are*, to tell you the truth."

"You two," said Sunny, disgusted. "Really." Shoulders thrown back defiantly, she went off with James to light the candles in Charlene's cupcakes and to lead the slightly off-key singing of

"Happy Birthday" in a big buoyant voice that carried all the way over to where Walter was still lying, and it broke his heart. Beside him, Charlene sat with the Big Bird head nestled in her arms. She stroked its beak absently, threaded her fingers through its bright fuzzy coat.

"Give it up," she said, and, leaving him, went to join the others.

"I can't," he murmured, as if she could hear him.

Passenger

"Basically, I guess you probably *could* say I have the worst nails in the whole entire world," Lacey admits, and this is no exaggeration—her fingernails are tiny chewed-up colorless slivers, painful to look at. Nina, her mother, has already paid out ten dollars in cash to Lacey on two separate occasions—one dollar per grown-out fingernail. But a week or two later the nails were back to their customary miserable state, and Nina was back on Lacey's case, nagging at her to get her fingers out of her mouth.

"So stop biting them," Nina says now.

"The day you stop smoking is the day I stop biting," says Lacey, who is twelve. They are stuck in rush-hour traffic in her mother's cab, and she is staring, fascinated, at the trio of life-sized bronze statues roped together in an open truck alongside them. The figures are nude males, their muscles finely delineated, their yellowish-brown skin gleaming. As the truck inches out in front of the cab, Lacey gets a good look at the statues' extraordinary muscled behinds, the sight of which makes her snort with laughter. "Nice butts!" she says. "How many real-live people do you know who look like that?"

Nina slams in the cigarette lighter with her palm and unrolls her window halfway. "Would you mind not using that word, please. Frankly, I find it very offensive."

"*Smoking* is offensive," says Lacey. "You're a drug addict, you know that? You're addicted to nicotine the way a crack addict is addicted to crack. And if you get lung cancer and die, there'll be no one to take care of me. I'll be an orphan," she wails, so loudly and theatrically that her mother reaches over and slaps at her thigh, but only halfheartedly.

Lacey's father, in fact, is alive and well and lives in Los Angeles with his new wife, whose name is Swan, though it had once been Cynthia; they have a six-month-old baby boy named Dakota. (A phony-baloney name if I ever heard one, Nina had said when he was born. Sometimes she refers to him as Montana, sometimes Idaho or Indiana.) Lacey had spent the summer with them and had arrived back in New York on Labor Day, only two weeks ago. She'd helped Swan take care of the baby, and brought her endless Diet Cokes whenever Swan asked for them, which was mostly as they sat around the pool in the backyard each afternoon, sunning themselves and trying to come up with something to say to each other. While in California, it became absolutely clear to Lacey that her mother was superior to her replacement in every way; at the very least, she was simply a much nicer person, someone who would pick herself up and get *you* a Coke, along with a glass, a handful of ice cubes, and a paper napkin meticulously folded into the shape of an arrow. And so all summer long Lacey was dying to ask her father why he'd moved away and married Swan. When, at last, she felt bold enough to actually pop the question, her father had looked at her in surprise, as if the answer should have been obvious to her.

"I was lonely," he said. "Even when your mother and I were in the same room together, I was lonely. And so was she. We weren't . . . connecting anymore. I don't know how else to explain it—it's just the way things were."

Lacey hadn't been sure what to make of this. "But when you and Swan are in the same room you're connecting?" Thinking of plugs and wires and electrical outlets, she almost laughed.

"Oh God, yes," her father said, so enthusiastically that Lacey had to look away. It didn't help that he'd cultivated an unnaturally dark tan and had started dressing in pink polo shirts, baggy white pants, and thin-soled black-suede shoes that looked like ladies' slippers with silly gold crests across the front. *Get out of those dorky clothes*, she wanted to say. *Lose that wife and that tan and come back to New York.*

Every day in California, Lacey had marveled at Swan's laziness. Her step-mother stayed in bed in the morning until after eleven, letting the housekeeper, Elena, take Dakota from his crib, change him, and feed him his first bottle of the day. She never made her bed, or cleaned up her bathroom after a shower. She wouldn't have lasted a day living with Nina, who had rules about putting things back where you found them and never leaving the apartment until the beds were made and the kitchen sink empty of dishes. She was very strict about these things but surprisingly easygoing in other ways. She let Lacey stay up forever, even on school nights, and for breakfast would fix her a bowl of vanilla ice cream sprinkled with a spoonful of instant coffee, which Lacey was crazy about.

"Your poor mother," Swan had said to Lacey one time toward the end of the summer. The two of them were drinking their Cokes poolside while the baby slept in his stroller in the shade of a grapefruit tree. Swan had her waist-length hair twisted into a braid and was wearing shorts and the top from one of her bathing suits, clothing that revealed a lot of flab Lacey would have preferred not to see. According to Lacey's father, Swan was a terrific athlete who could easily bike twenty-five miles a day, a world traveler who had once gone alone on a three-month trip to explore Thailand, Malaysia, and Singapore. This was years before Dakota's birth, Lacey knew, years before Swan had become lazy and boring and addicted to diet soda.

"We're not poor," said Lacey, who had no idea what Swan was talking about. "We have a piano and a million CDs and a microwave."

Swan laughed when she heard this. "I didn't mean *that* kind of poor," she said. "Though of course she's got money troubles, I guess. I meant that it can't be easy for her, living in a small apartment, raising a kid pretty much on her own, not having a man around, holding down two jobs, driving a cab all night. You know."

" 'All night'?" said Lacey, outraged. "What are you talking about? We're home by seven, usually. I wouldn't exactly call that 'all night,' would you? And her teaching job is part-time, too." Three mornings a week, Nina taught English as a Second Language at Hunter College, a job she enjoyed far more than chauffeuring strangers around town all day. She'd been hoping, Lacey knew, for the chance to teach full-time, but so far there'd been no offers.

Trailing her hand in the pool's luke-warm water, Swan said, "It's not a life I'd want to be living, let's put it that way."

Lacey gazed out beyond the chain-link fence surrounding the yard, out into the canyon, which was wilderness, really, just a lot of bushes and dirt and unseen coyotes that howled at night and sometimes tore apart cats and dogs who'd foolishly wandered from home. Above, the sky was enormous, something entirely blue and silent. Three thousand miles away, her mother was cruising the streets for fares, looking out at a sky so cluttered with immense buildings that sometimes there was nothing left of it but a narrow corridor of blue or white that was hardly worth an upward glance. In all the world there was no one Lacey loved more than her mother, who, as she'd imagined her then, was just a tiny figure behind the wheel heading into gridlock, her feet in their ankle-high black boots, tapping the brake and the accelerator impatiently, itching to get a move on.

"My mother," Lacey reported triumphantly, just before she left Swan's side and disappeared into the deep end of the pool, "thinks you're one lazy bitch." Surfacing a few moments later, she shook her hair from her eyes and flipped herself over onto her back. She drifted slowly toward the shallow end, hoping she looked thoroughly relaxed, grateful that Swan couldn't hear her labored breathing, the noisy thudding of her heart. After a while, her fingertips looked wrinkled and bleached, and a sudden breeze brought goosebumps to her arms. She stood in three feet of water, leaning back on her elbows against the ledge of the pool, a skinny little canal where stray leaves and dead mosquitoes floated aimlessly. What could she say to Swan, who had gotten to her feet and was lifting the baby from his stroller and coming toward her, offering a clean white towel like a truce.

"Are you planning on staying in there all day or what?" Swan said. "Don't be a jerk, kiddo."

"Are you going to tell my father what I said?"

Swan raised Dakota over her head, wiggling him from side to side until he laughed joyously. "You're twelve years old," she said, her voice impassive. "Do you think I take seriously anything a twelve-year-old says to me? And besides, what do I care what your mother thinks of me? She's nothing much in my life, just a name that shows up in my checkbook once a month."

Fearless, her throat choked with anger, Lacey's voice emerged husky and deep. "You're nothing in her life, either. What do you think, we sit around talking about you all day? Don't you think we have better things to do?"

"I'm sure you do," said Swan mildly. She lowered the baby to her chest, nudged his head gently against her shoulder. "Want to get dressed and come to the Farmer's Market with me? I've got a lot of stuff to buy for dinner."

Lacey had only nodded. She felt diminished, as tiny and power-less as Dakota. She ached for her mother, to be sitting at her mother's side in the cab, the two of them laughing it up at the moronic name her father and Swan had chosen for their baby. *Montana?* she could hear her mother saying. *Indiana?*

• • •

"Never hit me ever again," she tells her mother now, and rubs the leg that has been slapped so indifferently there's not a mark on it.

"Don't bug me about my smoking, okay?"

"Fine."

Her mother stops for a fare, a woman and a guy, both of them with long dyed-blond hair. The woman is all in black. On her feet are clunky-looking shining black oxfords, like policemen wear. Her companion has a safety pin fastened high up on the rim of his ear. They're going to lower Broadway, near Astor Place, the guy says, and slams the door.

"Why would I say I'm a witch if I wasn't?" the woman says plaintively. "If I tell you I can predict the future, you'd be really stupid not to believe me."

"So I'm stupid," says the guy. "Sue me."

Swiveling around in her seat for a better look, Lacey says, "I believe you." She has broken one of her mother's cardinal rules: no talking to passengers unless they talk to you first. (Let them have their privacy, she's told Lacey a dozen times. It's common courtesy, that's all.) But sometimes Lacey just can't help herself and has to open her big mouth.

"Thanks," says the witch. "I appreciate that."

"Don't you have any math homework to do?" Nina says. "What happened to all those fractions you were supposed to be converting to percents?"

"Homework!" says the guy. "Far out. I myself haven't had homework since the late eighties."

"Did it hurt when you put that safety pin through your ear?" Lacey asks.

"No way. My girlfriend sprayed Freon on it and yours truly didn't feel a thing."

"Ex-girlfriend," says the witch. "And Freon's what they put in your refrigerator, dummy."

Lacey is beginning to feel a little dizzy facing the back seat; reluctantly, she turns herself forward. "Can you see into my future?" she says.

"I need something that belongs to you, something like a finger-nail clipping would be good," the witch says.

"Ha!" says Nina, and thumps the steering wheel. "You see how a nasty habit like biting your nails can interfere with your life?"

"How about an earring?" the witch suggests.

Lacey hands over the silver teardrop that hangs from her ear. She knows she is going to hear something truly excellent, a prediction that will keep her going for weeks, maybe even months. She might even write a poem about it, which she has to hand in for an English assignment due at the end of the week.

An index finger finds its way into her mouth and she chews on it vigorously, waiting for the witch to come through for her. "Please please please," she whispers.

"You are," the witch announces with her eyes closed, "a woman of great passion. But the men in your life have always been a disap-pointment to you. Except one, a man you will meet sometime around your fortieth birthday. This is the man who will turn your life around, who will set you on fire, as it were."

Nina hits the brakes suddenly; the cab behind her taps her rear bumper, then blasts its horn. "That's me!" Nina says. "And that's my earring you've got in your hand."

"Awesome," says Lacey.

The witch's friend lets out a long leisurely whistle. "I'm blown away," he says. "But maybe it's strictly a co-inky-dink."

"No way! My mother and grandmother were witches, too. I told you, Howard, it's a gift that's passed down from generation to gener-ation." The witch asks Nina to let her off at the next corner. "I need to clear my head," she explains. "A nice long walk downtown is indi-cated, I think."

"What about me?" Lacey says. "I'm the one you were supposed to be working on."

"Sorry about that, sweetie," the witch says. "Maybe you should stay out of your mom's jewelry box in the future, you know?"

"Damn," Lacey says, and watches as the witch and her friend disappear down Broadway, their hands shoved into the back pockets of each other's jeans.

"There'll be other witches," her mother says. "Don't feel too badly."

They have come to a red light now; through the open window of the cab, Lacey hears the theme song from *The Brady Bunch* being played on the violin. The musician is someone in a Wolfman mask, tapping his sneaker to the music as he stands under the awning of a video store. "What a geek," Lacey says, and rolls up her window. She looks at her mother's hands resting on the steering wheel, at her small, nicely tapered fingers, her sleek, polished nails. Except for the nails, they could be Lacey's hands. Her mother's profile is hers too, dominated by a strong nose that loses its character whenever her mother turns so that she can be seen full face. Her mother is, in fact, strikingly pretty. She claims to have been born under a lucky star, a claim Lacey sometimes finds a little hard to swallow. If she had really been born under a lucky star, Lacey bets, the two of them would be living in California, lounging around their pool whenever they felt like it, waiting for her father to arrive home from work and open his arms to them, so welcoming and eager that they would fly instantly into his embrace. "What a loser," she says, thinking of Swan, a woman so unbelievably dumb that she is actually filled with pity for Nina and Lacey and their life together.

"Which loser is that?" Nina says.

"Swan feels sorry for you because you drive a cab," Lacey says.

"God, do I hate hearing that!" her mother says. "I hope you set her straight, at least."

"I told her she was a lazy bitch. Actually, I told her *you* said she was a lazy bitch."

Her mother laughs. "I can live with that," she says. "Hope she wasn't too upset."

"She wasn't."

"Well, that's good," says her mother, but she sounds disappointed. After a moment she says, "Not at all?"

"Not really," Lacey says. "That's the way people are in California, I guess."

Her mother is silent for a long while. It is dusk now, and a fine drizzly rain is falling; with a sigh, she hunches up over the steering wheel. "You know," she says at last, "I'm thirty-seven years old and it doesn't feel like I've got my act together yet. But of course in three years or so," she says, turning to look at Lacey, rolling her eyes extravagantly, "I'll be meeting the man of my dreams, so I guess it's just a matter of hanging in there, isn't it."

"You were born under a lucky star," Lacey reminds her.

"That's old news, Kewpie doll."

Lacey backs herself against the door, draws up her knees and rests her head on them desolately. Maybe it's the rain and the diminishing light that have gotten to her, maybe just the news that her mother has no faith in the witch's prophecy. "In LA," she says, "it never rained. Not once, the whole entire summer."

"Amazing," her mother says. "Kind of like paradise, huh?"

"We'd be happy there," says Lacey. She can see herself and her mother in her father's cool bright house, spreading their possessions throughout the endless closets, the two of them wandering from room to room just for fun, chasing each other up and down the winding staircase, collecting lemons and grapefruits from the trees in the backyard, falling asleep at night to the sound of howling coyotes. Swan and Dakota would be living in a house of their own, on some other planet. Her father, a tall guy with thinning blond hair, dressed in his New York clothes, tight black jeans and a faded denim shirt with pearly snaps, would be content in the company of his real family, connected to Lacey and her mother by a love so obvious that even strangers could see it in their faces. All of this comes to her now as clear as can be, vivid as a series of photographs snapped in just the right light, at just the right moment. She wants to show them to her mother, hear her murmur of approval, see the slow spread of her smile.

"What's so great about Swan, anyway?" she asks. "I just don't get it."

"You don't have to," her mother says. "And neither do I. We just have to get our checks in the mail every month."

Staring through the window, Lacey keeps a lookout for the witch, an ordinary figure in black striding along in policemen's shoes. She's dying to hear a forecast of her own life. Along with her mother's hands and profile, she's bound to inherit other things, as well—excellent driving skills and bad luck in the romance department, maybe. She remembers her mother's date a few months ago with one of her students, an Indian named Neville who spoke in a confusing sing-song and looked around their cluttered living room unsmilingly. He'd brought a half-dozen Milky Ways for Lacey in a paper bag, and white carnations for her mother. Returning home from her date with Neville, her mother had undressed immediately and then sat around in her underwear listening to old James Taylor albums, a sure sign that she was in her "depressed mode," as she called it. "Remind me never to go out with one of my students ever again," she told Lacey. After Neville came Timmy Wang, Odarkor Zinns, and Masato Kakuda. One day, Lacey realized, amazed, that she had memorized the lyrics to every song on the first two James Taylor albums. Her mother laughed when she heard this, but it wasn't funny.

Her father had found Swan right away, even before the divorce was final; Dakota was already six months old and her mother still hadn't met anyone she was willing to see more than once. It was hard to figure out why this was so or why her mother's happiness (or unhappiness) seemed to be linked to this. Lacey herself could be made happy by any number of things—an order of spare ribs from a Chinese restaurant, a social studies test that was postponed at the last minute, an invitation from her best friend to spend the weekend at her country house in Woodstock. These things, of course, could not do the trick for her mother, who, though generally cheerful and energetic in the daytime, went into her depressed mode at night — more and more, recently, this seemed to be true.

Probably, Lacey thinks now, if you'd always thought you'd been born under a lucky star and then began to suspect that maybe you hadn't been after all, you couldn't help but feel disappointed.

"Want something to eat?" her mother asks her, offering a bruised-looking banana from the glove compartment. "And take those fingers out of your mouth, please."

"I can't," Lacey says. "I'm all stressed out."

"What?" Her mother laughs, a little uneasily. "What are you talking about?"

"There are a ton of pressures in my life," Lacey announces. "I think we should move to California."

"I see," says Nina in a wobbly voice. "You want to live with your father, is that what you're telling me?"

Confused, Lacey begins to whimper. "We *deserve* to live there. In a big house with a heated pool and a housekeeper to pick our clothes up off the floor. Tell me why we don't deserve that." She thinks of all the hours she has spent riding around with her mother. Some days, after school, she goes home with friends, and once a week she has a piano lesson at the Y, but it seems to her that she spends half her life in this cab, observing the silent electronic accounting of the meter, listening to the exasperated sound of horns clamoring, her mother's exasperated voice telling her to quit biting her nails.

Her mother has double-parked and turned off the motor. She puts her arms around Lacey. Her hair smells of cigarette smoke as it brushes softly against Lacey's jaw. "Screw California," her mother murmurs. "Screw your father and what's-her-face." Lacey waits for the rest, but her mother has fallen silent, her eyes closed, tears leaking discreetly from their corners.

"Screw California," Lacey repeats dutifully, but that's as far as she's willing to go. If her mother wants to curse her father, that's *her* business.

Eventually, a man in a business suit and red snakeskin boots swings open the door and climbs into the back seat. "I need to get to the Upper East Side," he says. "Seventy-seventh and Third."

Nina looks at him as if he has asked the impossible, to be driven across the ocean, perhaps. "What?" she says. Then, "Can't you see I'm off duty?"

"I see that you've been crying," the man says without much interest. "But I don't see that you're off duty. The sign on top of the cab says you're on duty. And if you're on duty then you have to take me where I want to go. It's the law," he says reasonably. "You know that as well as I do."

"I'm off duty," Nina says, and flicks the switch that illuminates the sign outside the cab.

"You know what *I* think?" the man says. "I think you just don't feel like going to the Upper East Side right now. And that's against the law, as I've already pointed out to you."

"Take him," Lacey says. She draws away from her mother and turns to smile at the man. "Don't worry about it, she'll take you."

"It's raining," the man says. And then adds, as if looking for sympathy, "It's murder trying to get a cab in the rain." He rests his attaché case on his knees and snaps it open as the cab pulls out into traffic.

Lacey can tell that her mother is furious with her; she can see it in her rigid posture and the resolute way her hands have seized the steering wheel. In the back seat, the man is shuffling through some papers and whistling blithely.

"You're driving me crazy," Nina says, but it's unclear to Lacey whom she means.

"Me?" says Lacey, and listens for a response. Absently, she begins to sing along with the man's whistling: *Ohhh, it's enough to be on your way.* If the witch is right, and there's always the possibility that she might be, Lacey thinks, they've got a three-year wait for the guy who's going to set her mother's life on fire. Or is it that he's going to set her mother on fire, which is something else entirely. Either way, it sounds both dangerous and thrilling, and Lacey wants to be along for the ride, seated up in front, so close to the flames that they singe the fine, nearly invisible hairs on her delicate-boned, satiny arms, shaped precisely like her mother's.

Ancient History

Charles was slumped in an aluminum-and-suede director's chair in the basement of his father's house. Sitting in the dull light, sipping a watery Scotch on the rocks, he rested his left arm in his lap. There was a fiberglass cast on his arm that reached to his elbow; a tiny polo player that had been scissored off one of his Ralph Lauren shirts was glued to the cast at the approximate point where, two weeks ago, Charles's wrist had been fractured in a truly undignified fall from a bar stool. It was now ten in the morning. He was supposed to be at Melia's by eleven. They were going to the beach together for a couple of hours because Melia wanted some color in her face before the wedding. She was getting married tonight in a hotel on Central Park South, and Charles had promised he would sit in the front row and videotape the ceremony, but he just didn't know if he was going to be up to the task. He and Melia had been thick as thieves for nearly ten years—since they'd sat side by side in an honors geometry class, a lifetime ago, it seemed. The things she knew about him would have made his father's head spin. She knew all about the bars that were his second home, and the lovers who always seemed to give either less or more than he wanted from them. Melia was the one person he had been able to count on for almost everything and now he was going to have to get used to less from her, too. He'd suspected it was inevitable, that of course she would eventually marry somebody or other, but that didn't make it any easier on him. Once, he had fantasized out loud about the life they would have after college: they would share a house or an apartment somewhere, come and go as they pleased with their respective lovers, but still live together as best friends. Melia had laughed and shaken her head at him, and said he was off his rocker, but her face looked mournful, and that pleased him.

"What are you doing in here?" The room filled with artificial light and Charles saw his father at the top of the basement stairs. He was dressed in a short-sleeved sweatshirt and sweatpants, and he was holding a pair of gardening shears in his hand. Charles was still in his bathrobe.

"Hi," Charles said. He raised one hand in the air.

"Hi yourself," his father said. "Care to tell me what you're doing down here?"

"Not really."

His father sighed theatrically. "On an average day you don't say two words to me, you know that? You go to work, come home in the middle of the night, go to work the next morning, and then it starts all over again. Weekends, I don't see you at all. This isn't a hotel, for your information."

"I'm sorry," Charles said.

"About what?"

Charles took a sip of his drink and sighed.

Snapping off the light switch, his father said, "Sometimes it's hard not to lose patience with you, buddy." He turned around; his back was to Charles. "If you're so hot for this girl, why are you letting someone else marry her?"

Moments later the screen door to the kitchen slammed shut, and he was gone from the house.

• • •

Charles decided to take his father's Cadillac to the beach because it was air-conditioned and his Hyundai was not. He dropped the keys to the Hyundai on the kitchen table, then left without saying good-bye. When he got to Melia's parents' house five minutes later, he debated whether to go inside or just stay in the car and blow the horn. Her mother and father were probably home, and he didn't want to see them, so he decided to stay where he was. He smoked a cigarette and listened to the radio while he waited for Melia.

"Bonjour," she said when she got into the car. She was wearing cutoffs and a yellow V-necked T-shirt; large red-framed sunglasses hung from the V. Small and dark, her thick, wild hair tamed in a ponytail, she looked, Charles thought, far too young to be anyone's bride.

"What's so good about it?" he said. He kissed Melia on the cheek, then put the car into drive and tore up the street.

"Don't," Melia said. "I'm jittery enough as it is."

"What about me?" Charles said.

Melia leaned over and checked the speedometer. "Isn't one fractured wrist enough for you? Are you trying to do us both in, or what?"

Charles smiled. "Now, there's an idea."

"Get back to somewhere near the speed limit or I'm taking a hike at the first opportunity."

Obediently, Charles slowed down. "What do you want to get married for, anyway?" he said.

"Please," Melia said. "Just concentrate on the road."

"I'm not talking to you ever again," Charles said. "These are the last words you'll ever hear me say to you."

They stopped at a red light. Charles tapped his foot on the rubber floor mat. He whistled along with the radio, which was playing an ancient Barbra Streisand/Donna Summer song. The words and music were suitably melancholy, and he was enjoying the song immensely.

Melia touched his arm. "You worry too much," she said. "Things always turn out better than you expect them to."

"Oh, really," Charles said. "I hadn't noticed that." He was thinking about Jeffrey, her husband-to-be, a person who just didn't measure up, Charles felt. His wardrobe was the same year-round—jeans with finely shredded knees, jean shirts bleached nearly white, and orange-and-blue running shoes that were patched in spots with adhesive tape. He had published a novel soon after college, about a Jewish shrink and his disastrous relationship with his children; Charles hadn't read it and had no plans to do so in the near or distant future. (The only novel he'd read recently was *Gone with the Wind*, which he'd been in the habit of reading twice a year since he'd turned fifteen. As far as he could see, *Gone with the Wind* said all that needed to be said.) Jeffrey, he knew, was working on another book, and apparently was counting on Melia's job in the human resources department at MTV to see him through the writing of it. "It's a husband's responsibility to support his wife in the style to which she is accustomed," Charles said aloud.

"Is that what you've been worrying about?"

"No."

"I didn't think so," Melia said. "But it would have been sweet if you had."

"I'm not sweet," Charles said. "I'm a selfish beast."

Melia said nothing. She was staring into the rear window of the car stopped directly in front of them, where a little boy wearing a mustache was making faces at her. The mustache was bright turquoise and appeared to be made of Play-Doh. Melia pointed out the mustache to Charles.

"Kids," Charles said. "They send chills up my spine. Promise me you'll lock yours in a closet whenever I come to visit."

"Certainly," Melia said, and then she looked at him and laughed.

"I still don't understand what you have to get married for," Charles said. "It just doesn't fit into my plans at all."

•   •   •

As they struggled against the wind to get their blanket settled over a stretch of sand close to the water, Charles began complaining about the beach. "I always go home with sand in my teeth," he said. "And the ocean's always freezing; I hate it."

"What *do* you like?" Melia said, as if she didn't know the answer. She stripped down to her bathing suit and poured some oil into her palm. She rubbed it across her chest, and along her lightly freckled arms and legs. Charles stayed fully dressed in his pants and polo shirt.

"Drinking," Charles said. "That, and getting drunk. Although when I'm drunk, I tell the same stories over and over again. Or so I've been told. Still, it's the only attractive alternative to being sober."

"You drink a whole lot more than you should. It worries me."

"And, in addition, I've been known to smoke a minimum of forty-eight cigarettes in a single day."

"That, too," Melia said. "It all adds up."

"I'm living life to the fullest," Charles said. "At least that's how *I* choose to look at it."

Melia was lying on her back, her feet pressed together in the sand, her knees in the air. "Isn't this my wedding day?" she said. "Aren't I supposed to be at the hairdresser's or something?"

Charles poured sand on her feet until they disappeared. He smoked a cigarette and watched a hugely pregnant woman in a black bikini hurrying toward the ocean. She reached the lifeguard station and gestured with her arm over the water. The lifeguard was shaking his head; from where Charles was sitting, the guy looked cute enough in profile, but awfully young. "I'm starving," Charles said.

"I'll share some french fries with you," Melia said. "If you've got the heart to trudge all the way over to the snack bar and back again, that is."

When Charles returned, there was a small crowd gathered at the water's edge. Melia was propped up on her elbows squinting at him. "Missing child," was all she said. He offered her a paper cup filled with oily, nasty-looking fries, but she shook her head.

Charles polished off the cupful in no time. He licked the fingers of his right hand one by one. He watched the scene at the water. "Crowds," he said. "Don't they have better ways to spend their time?"

"The poor woman," Melia said. "Just imagine what she must be feeling."

A man with a small child riding his shoulders raced over the sand toward the crowd, which drew back as he approached. He lifted the child from his shoulders and handed him to the pregnant woman, who pressed the little boy's face against her and kissed his head. Then she set the child on the sand and smacked him for what seemed to be a long while.

"Can you believe this?" Melia said, astonished. "How upsetting is this?"

"What?"

"Obviously he's the love of her life, right? If she didn't feel so deeply about him, a kiss would have been enough. But if this is what parenthood does to you, makes you crazy like that, why would you want any part of it?"

"Now don't get all excited," Charles said. "Please."

"I can't take this," Melia said, shutting her eyes. "This is too much," she said, just as the woman lifted her weeping child into her arms and began to kiss him again.

"You want to go home?"

Melia nodded her head yes.

Charles said, "We'll go have a drink somewhere and then I'll take you back."

"Can't," Melia said. She stood up, and threaded her fingers together over the top of her head. Her diamond engagement ring glistened prettily; without any effort at all, Charles envisioned it buried deep in the sand, along with countless metal tabs from soda cans, rusted bottle caps, sharp bits of clam shells, worthless and lost forever.

"There must be a thousand things I have to do," he heard Melia say uncertainly. "Don't you think so?"

"Oh, well." They were shaking sand from the blanket now. "I guess I'll just go on home and polish my halo for a couple of hours," Charles said.

•   •   •

No matter how late Charles dragged himself in at night, there was always a light on in his father's house signaling the expectation of his return. That single light-filled window was something he was on the lookout for every night.

It hadn't always been just Charles and his father living in their two-story house on a quarter of an acre in the suburbs. Charles had a sister, Lori, who'd died at sixteen when the bicycle she was riding was hit by a laundry truck just three blocks from home. Predictably, his parents' marriage, which had never seemed a success, fell apart about a year later. His mother had withdrawn from both Charles and his father, as if, Charles thought, they, and not some stranger, had been the ones behind the wheel of the laundry truck. He was thirteen then, hurt and mystified by his mother's retreat from them; no matter what they did or said, it seemed, they weren't going to get her back. She had since remarried and was living in southern California. Every so often she sent Charles the briefest of post cards reporting the wonderful weather they were having. "Seventy-nine degrees and bright bright sunshine! What a life!" His mother was a space case, grinning like a fool in the California sun. Unforgiving, Charles never wrote back, but the post cards kept coming. He tore them up as soon as he finished reading them—standard procedure for all the junk mail he got.

Like his mother, his father concentrated on minding his own business. The tiny diamond stud that sat shining in Charles' earlobe drew no response from his father, nor did his hair, which was turning redder and redder every day from all the henna he'd been putting in it. Sometimes, when Charles looked particularly hung over and could barely keep his head up, his father would feel the need to say something. This was always at the breakfast table, the only meal they ever shared. *When do you sleep?* his father would say. *That's the part I can't figure out at all.*

But his father was all right—his heart was still in the right place, at least. Several months ago, when their fourteen-year-old Shih Tzu developed kidney problems and arthritis and had to be put to sleep, his father postponed telling Charles for as long as he could. He set out Frankie's plastic food and water bowls on the kitchen floor, filled them up every morning before Charles left for work, then dumped them out a few minutes later. This went on for nearly a week, until he was finally able to break the news. Charles was close to tears—not so much for Frankie as for his father, who had worked so hard to shield him from another loss.

• • •

In her childhood bedroom, Melia sits cross-legged on the carpet and stares at a tennis match on TV. There's an emery board in her hand; absently, she files her nails down to nothing, thinking of Charles. She remembers him in high school, taller and paler than everyone else, dressed in a fuzzy, royal-blue mohair sweater, carrying his books neatly in a pyramid—large history and science books on the bottom, a small grammar book at the very top. Except for a handful of girls he occasionally gossiped with in the lunchroom, he was friendless.

Once, soon after she and Charles became friends, Melia had been sitting in a first-floor classroom, next to a row of windows that looked out on the half-mile oval of track, and had seen him far behind the rest of his phys-ed class, his thick white legs barely moving, it seemed, until finally he stopped altogether and stood motionless, head bent, arms crossed over his stomach as if he were shielding himself from something. And then she had looked away, not wanting to know if the teacher was going to shoot across the track, blowing his whistle and gesturing furiously at Charles to get him moving again. This is the Charles she has conjured now, not the Charles she met downtown for lunch in early spring, the gaunt, bearded man in tight jeans and bomber jacket and cowboy boots, walking rapidly down Second Avenue, his back straight and his arms swinging, looking like someone who knew exactly who he was and exactly what he was after.

She is thrilled to be getting married—Jeffrey is just what she wants, she tells herself. Even so, he cannot be expected to understand Charles the way she does, to carry gracefully the burden of his friendship. The drunken phone calls at three and four A.M., the infinitely detailed stories of precisely how his heart had been bruised and broken, the depressing monologues about his life leading nowhere, and her own endless comforting—she has to find a place for all this within her marriage and she can't imagine how. And then there is the other side, Charles' frequent generous impulses; the gifts he is always presenting her with, the earrings and perfume and scarves and belts he can't seem to stop himself from buying for her. He has done his share of comforting too, holding ice packs to her jaws after she'd had four wisdom teeth yanked in one shot, doing a half-dozen loads of laundry for her in college when she was too depressed weeks after an abortion to even care whether or not she had clean clothes.

There is something like love between them and she does not think she will surrender it all so easily. Who else, she reflects, would have done her laundry, patiently pulling hot sheets and nightgowns and underwear from a row of dryers, folding everything just so, meticulously smoothing away creases with the flat of his hand, all the while singing their favorite Cole Porter songs to comic perfection? *I'm a worthless check, a total wreck, a flop*, she can hear him boasting cheerfully in the laundry room as he plunked imaginary piano keys across her arm. And, at last, drew a smile from her.

Who else, indeed?

• • •

It is the middle of the afternoon, but Charles has the shades in his bedroom drawn all the way to the window sill. Lounging among the stuffed animals crowded together on his bed, he makes a couple of phone calls. He arranges a dinner date with a bartender named Lonny who used to be a night proofreader at the *Times*. He is shorter than Charles and a little overweight—two strikes against him right there—but he has a weird sense of humor that Charles gets a real kick from, and is actually very good company. Charles makes a second date for around midnight with a college kid who seemed to admire him and kept calling him "sir" (much to Charles' amusement) when they'd met a few weeks ago.

After he finishes up on the phone, he goes to the window and lifts the shades up. He turns on the air conditioner and smokes a cigarette with his eyes closed. In a little while he gets up, pulls the shades down again, and phones the bartender.

"I'm calling to cancel," he announces.

"What's going on?" Lonny says.

"I have a wedding to go to tonight."

"Just get the invitation in the mail five minutes ago?"

"It's the truth," Charles says, "I swear."

"What the hell is wrong with you, Charles? I'm beginning to think you're a fucking mental case."

"I don't know why I called in the first place. I'm sorry," Charles offers, but he's already been disconnected. He stretches out on the floor next to his bed and rests a hand on his chest. He feels the rapid beating of his heart for a long time and then he falls asleep.

When his father awakens him nearly an hour later, Charles has to struggle to keep his eyes open. He is utterly exhausted, as if he'd spent the hour lifting weights instead of sleeping. With a plastic bag wrapped around his left arm, he heads into the shower and washes his hair, but, mysteriously, it doesn't feel clean at all. It takes him a minute before he realizes what he's done—he'd grabbed the bottle of conditioner instead of the shampoo, apparently. Exasperated, he pitches the plastic bottle over the top of the shower curtain and listens for its satisfying thud against the tile on the other side.

Afterward, he gets himself into the white linen suit he bought for the wedding and is pleased with the way he looks—very spiffy, he thinks. All that's missing is the boutonniere Melia has promised him.

"Ah, the ice cream man cometh," his father says as Charles makes his way into the kitchen for a glass and some ice. His father is emptying the dishwasher, but he stops as soon as he sees Charles.

Charles makes a face at him. "Keep it up," he says. "Just keep those compliments coming."

"There's no ice," his father reports. "So you can forget about that Scotch on the rocks you had your heart set on."

"What do you mean, there's no ice?"

His father shrugs. "It appears someone forgot to fill the ice trays."

"Someone?"

"You, me, whoever."

"I never forget to do anything I'm supposed to do. It must have been you," Charles says. "You used up the ice in all those diet Instant Breakfast shakes you're always making!" he hollers.

"I'd appreciate it if you didn't raise your voice in this house."

"Since when are you so sensitive?"

"Oh, I am," his father says. "I feel things very deeply."

"Tell me about it," Charles says.

His father leans back against the Formica counter and shuts his eyes briefly. "If only you had what you wanted," he murmurs. "If only I knew how to lead you there."

"Well, you're thinking about the wrong things," Charles says. "Don't waste your time."

"You're my one and only, buddy. Who else am I going to be worried about?"

Charles' head is lowered, as if to receive a blessing. He looks down at his father's feet, which are bare against the dark terra-cotta floor. His feet are delicate and very white, almost ladylike in appearance. Staring at them, Charles finds himself overwhelmed by a longing to shelter his father, as if, at this moment, it were the most important thing in the world that no harm come to him.

"I'm sorry," he says again, for the third time in one day.

• • •

He cruises into the city earlier than he needs to and parks his car in an indoor lot about ten blocks from the hotel. Walking aimlessly down Fifth Avenue, he stops and looks in the windows at Saks for a long while before deciding to go inside. On the main floor, he studies a rack of summer ties patterned with tiny pastel flowers, then kills some time spraying, on his good wrist, half a dozen different kinds of cologne, each of which turns out to be a disappointment. At the cologne counter, two deaf women in matching sweatshirts that say GUESS? on them stare at him, shockingly rude, then sign back and forth to each other, giving little grunts of laughter. It's clear they have been talking about him, and Charles is furious. He leaves the store, his heart ticking wildly, and lights a cigarette as soon as he gets outside. He stands in front of Saks and watches as an old woman with waist-length, tangled white hair walks by, pushing a beat-up baby carriage. In the carriage is a large bird cage filled with para-keets. "Seventy-five percent freaks in this town and that's only a conservative estimate," he hears a southern-accented voice say, but he continues smoking his cigarette and does not bother to look up to see who is talking.

By now it is nearly six; the wedding is set for seven. He thinks of Melia in her satiny gown, waiting for the hour to pass, gripping her mother's arm, needing to hold on to something. No, that was him, grabbing Melia by the elbow, saying, *Do you understand what I'm telling you? Do you?* It was the end of their first year in college and they were sprawled on the floor in his dorm room, near the window; the shade was pulled down to keep out the afternoon light. That was the year he'd been so in love with his economics professor that he'd lifted strands of pale hair from the man's pea coat, wrapped them around his finger and hurried back to his room to press them between the pages of a book, like flowers. The man was married, but he'd gone to a motel with Charles anyway. In six weeks it was all over; devastated, he'd spilled the story to Melia, who cried for him as she listened. After that, in the years that followed, it was easy to tell her things he had never expected to utter aloud—stories about the back rooms of bars where the unimaginable took place, where, in near darkness, people lost sight of who they were in daylight. Listening to him, Melia chewed the skin of her fingertips and kept silent. *Be careful*, she said at the end of every story. *Just promise me you'll be careful.* Like the lighted window in his father's house, she was a steady comfort—the sight of her, the sound of her voice, even her silence.

Sometimes, childishly, he imagines Jeffrey dead, lying like his own sister in a tangle of metal and rubber on concrete.

●　●　●

At the hotel, he takes the elevator upstairs and finds the bridal room, where Melia is seated on a rust-colored velvet throne, barefoot, her hands in her lap. There is no one else in the room, which is windowless and has floor-to-ceiling mirrors on two walls.

"I'm a wreck," Melia confesses. "Watch what you say to me."

"Where's your entourage?" Charles asks. "I figured you'd be surrounded by a cast of thousands."

"Nope, I'm all by myself," Melia says, "sitting here reviewing ancient history."

"Our history?" Charles sees a metal folding chair leaning against the wall; he drags it across the floor to the middle of the room, pulls it open, and sits down beside Melia.

Melia says, "Tell me what you're afraid of most."

He looks in the mirror at the two of them, all in white. He might have been mistaken for the groom, he realizes, and remembers a movie or two where a switch had been made at the last minute, hastily and with great excitement, where everything had fallen into place just when the audience had lost all hope.

He rises now and speaks to her, the words a surprise to him. "I have to go out," he tells her. "For a pack of Newports."

Melia stares at him, nods her head slightly. "You won't get lost, will you?" she says.

He goes out onto the street and heads toward Sixth Avenue, where he carefully counts, like missed opportunities, all the newsstands and delis that are shut down for the night. He walks along the avenue for endless blocks and then farther still, arriving at last at the perfect lie: he had lost track of time, place, everything. But then he turns, and, in what feels like slow motion, makes his way back to the hotel.

Jumping Ship

In three short days, my lovesick daughter has managed to run up a pretty impressive phone bill. If this were a hotel, I'd be hit with the tab at check-out time and fork over my credit card with a sigh. But we're staying with relatives—my mother and stepfather—in their Florida condo, and my guess is I'll never hear a word about the money I owe, unless I bring up the subject myself, which I fully intend to do.

"Noelle's too young to feel this way about a boy," my mother complains at the dinner table. "What grade are you in, darling?"

"Sixth," says Noelle. "But me and Kwame have been in love since fifth. He's so hot," she says emphatically, and drags a fingertip through the crimson puddle of ketchup on her plate.

"Kwame and I," I say. "And keep your hands out of that ketchup, please."

"Whatever."

"It's your fault," my mother tells me. "Why do you let her dress herself up like that?"

She's referring, I suppose, to the gleaming coat of black polish on Noelle's nails, the silver rings she wears on every finger, the four pairs of earrings that ornament her pretty little ears. The truth is, Noelle could pass for thirteen or even fourteen. She's eleven years old and already the hormones have started to kick in. Last month her period arrived, an event that caught me off guard and threw me into a depression that lasted almost as long as the period itself. Now I'm in a depression of another sort, the kind I sink into whenever I visit my mother and her husband in this impossibly cluttered apartment of theirs overlooking the Intracoastal Waterway. From my seat, I see magazines and newspapers in three-foot stacks at either end of the living room couch; a fortune's worth of yellowing sheet music piled high on the piano bench; and underneath it, a hideous oil painting of Noelle hung lopsided on the wall above the wicker couch; a half-dozen bath towels fresh from the dryer, dumped absently on top of the coffee table. I can see into the kitchen from here, but why would I want to look, knowing, as I do, that it's host to a family of roaches, vile creatures that scurry brazenly across the counter tops, appraising a milky shred of coleslaw, a pair of grapefruit rinds, tiny droplets of thickened gravy.

Instead, I study my mother, veteran of a thirty-year marriage and all the drama of its ups and downs. (My father, her first husband, died following a heart attack on the Long Island Rail Road, when I was four.) Her face is remarkably unlined, skin still porcelain and lovely; her hair is a gold helmet, brittle to the touch, thanks to her weekly visit to Hairsay, the beauty parlor where, she claims, she's greeted every Friday morning at ten like a beloved relative. The stress of caring for my stepfather, Murray, ravaged by Parkinson's, is evident in the perpetual hunch of her narrow shoulders, the way she keeps them drawn in at all times, as if to shield herself from his angrily mumbled, nearly incomprehensible demands. And, too, there are the numerous catnaps she takes throughout the day, the utter exhaustion that seems to overwhelm her after the preparation of every meal and the clean-up that follows.

"It's your fault," she repeats. "You're the one in charge."

"Since the day she was born," I say.

Murray makes a small choking sound.

"Honey," my mother says, "honey, what's in your mouth?"

Shaking his head, Murray points to me with a trembling index finger.

I know what he's thinking, that if I'd married Noelle's father, there'd be two of us in charge. As it happens, I never did figure out which of the three guys I'd been involved with was Noelle's father. Even then, over a decade ago, I'd had little interest in finding out whose DNA had mixed with my own in that now long-forgotten moment of passion. As soon as I realized I was pregnant, I cleared my life of all the men I'd been seeing, and settled on being a single mother. It had been hard, but not that hard, and I can't say that I made a disastrous mistake, much as Murray would like me to. He's still waiting for me to admit that I screwed up royally, but that's one confession he'll never hear from my lips. And if Noelle wishes she had a father, I'm sure I'd be the first to know it. So far, it hasn't come up, though God knows I've given Noelle ample opportunity to express herself on the subject. All in all, I would say my daughter's in terrific shape, except for this obsession with Kwame, which seems to have grown worse in the three days we've been down here.

I ask Murray to stop pointing his finger at me.

His head swings back and forth like a pendulum; his eyes widen. "You," he says, and the rest I just can't make out.

"He says you should marry Marshall, let him make an honest woman out of you," my mother explains.

"I *am* an honest woman. Honest enough to admit I don't need to be married to a man just because I happen to be in love with him."

Murray uses a handkerchief to pat, with a surprising daintiness, at the pool of saliva that has collected at one corner of his mouth. "Stubborn," he says. The disease has robbed his face of all expressiveness; what I see now is a smooth blankness suggesting there's not a thought in his head. This is a man who used to scare the shit out of me when, as a teenager, I displeased him in all the ways a sixteen-year-old could manage. Once, after I was arrested for drinking beer with my friends outside a 7-Eleven, he refused to bail me out and let me spend the night in the slammer. The only thing I learned from the experience was that I could count on Murray to add to my misery. When he and my mother forbid me to travel fifty miles to a Grateful Dead concert in New Jersey, I lifted the screen off my bedroom window in the middle of the night, climbed out, and ran away to a friend's house on the other side of town. "Your stupidity amazes me," Murray told me the next day, after I broke down and called home. At first I thought he was referring once again to the chemistry final I'd recently failed; then it hit me that it was my general, all-around stupidity he couldn't get over.

The chilly stares, offended, disappointed looks, occasional exasperating lectures delivered to my adult self in the booming voice of authority are gone from his repertoire, and I can't help but celebrate their passing. Declawed, Murray has become at last, it seems, a sympathetic figure.

He doesn't want my pity—that he gets in spades from every stranger on the street who sees him shuffling along with his walker, head lowered, hands clenched, as he makes his way laboriously to the corner and back.

"Oh, I'm stubborn, all right," I tell him, "but only in the best sense of the word."

"She wouldn't let me see *Pulp Fiction*," Noelle volunteers. "I had, like, a tantrum in the video store, but she was so mean and stubborn, she just kept saying no."

"What's that, a movie?" my mother says.

"*Hello?*" says Noelle. "A movie? It only won like the Academy Award."

"I'm not crazy about that tone in your voice," I say sharply, and help myself to a serving spoon full of baby carrots.

"I'm sorry," Noelle says, her voice offering a genuine sweetness now.

"We don't get out much," my mother says. "As you know."

Murray mumbles something in protest.

"Daddy reminds me that's not entirely true," says my mother. "We go to the speech therapist, the physical therapist, the regular therapist, the internist, the podiatrist, the neurologist . . ."

"You should go to the movies," Noelle recommends. She sets her elbow upright on the table, and sinks her chin into her palm in an attitude of longing. "Kwame goes to the movies like every other day. He's seen everything—he's seen *Fight Club* twice."

"His mother ought to have her head examined," I say.

"That's so mean!" Noelle cries. "You just don't like her because she's kind of an alcoholic."

"I don't like her because she's a bad mother."

"*You're* a bad mother."

"Shame on you," *my* mother says. "Your wonderful mother does everything for you and this is the way you talk to her?"

Noelle thinks this over. "I guess she's basically okay," she says a few moments later. "I wish she'd give me a bigger allowance, though."

"Break up with Kwame and I'll double your allowance," I say, and rise to clear the table. "I'll triple it."

"You are *so* annoying," Noelle says. She leaves the room in a huff, striding away from the table, arms swinging indignantly.

"She'll get over it," I announce, as the bathroom door slams shut.

"All's well that ends well," my mother says.

By the time I've carried all the dishes into the kitchen, she's dozing in her seat.

"Always tired," Murray says, and shrugs. He motions for me to hand him today's paper. The front page is decorated with a scattering of breakfast crumbs, which he shakes out onto the carpet industriously.

"Want some dessert?" I ask. "How about some ice cream?"

Formerly a big beefy guy—an imposing figure, really—Murray has shrunk dramatically during the years of his illness. He has trouble swallowing and only a passing interest in food. Put a meal in front of him and he endlessly rearranges everything on his plate, like a child at work on a jigsaw puzzle.

"Vanilla?" he says, or so I think.

"Vanilla?" I say, checking to make sure I've heard correctly.

He shakes his head and tries again, but I'm stumped; I go to the freezer and return with a half-gallon container and two pints. "The rocky road looks good," I say, and open the other two, as well. "You choose."

Pushing all three toward the center of the table, Murray turns his attention to the *Miami Herald*.

My mother worries that sometime soon he will simply stop eating altogether. I look now at his frail arms, at the gold stretchband of his watch drooping mournfully from his wrist bone. If I loved him, I tell myself, the sight would be nearly unbearable, wouldn't it.

• • •

In the kitchen, I wash a few pots, kill a few roaches. My bare feet stick to the linoleum floor. I load the dishwasher, discover a drowned roach lying belly-up in the silverware compartment. I look up the names of several exterminators in the Yellow Pages and write down their numbers on a paper towel. All of them have their answering machines on, and I decide to call back tomorrow. I wash the floor with a sponge mop; the sponge has gone from yellow to a deep gray by the time I've finished. Even in her prime, my mother was no housekeeper. The stationery store she and Murray owned, on King's Highway in Brooklyn, took up most of her time, and there was a woman named Ernestine who came to the house once a week to wash the floors and change the linens, gather together a few loads of laundry. But my mother has no one to help her now.

"You've got to get a housekeeper in here," I announce, as soon as my mother awakens from her nap.

She rubs the back of her neck with both hands and squints in my direction. "They steal from you," she informs me. "The last one took my best candlesticks. And the one before that walked off with a sterling silver candy dish. To tell you the truth, I don't need their help. My therapist says I can accomplish just about anything if I learn to organize my time properly. And one of these days, I may just prove her right. Or not," she says vaguely. She begins to doze off again, but awakens instantly when Murray thumps his hand hard against the table.

"Was that really necessary?" I ask him.

All of us are grateful when, a moment later, the phone happens to ring.

"If that's Kwame . . ." I say, heading for the phone in the kitchen.

I'm thrilled at the sound of Marshall's voice at the other end.

"How's it going, Diana," he says cautiously.

"Goddamnit!" I cry, and pitch a roll of paper towels at the microwave, where a solitary roach is strolling across the tinted glass door.

"I miss you, too," Marshall says. "I watched *NYPD Blue* without you last night, and it just wasn't the same."

Technically, Marshall is my boss, the director of the middle school where I teach social studies to seventh and eighth graders. The entire school is spread out along the top floor of a meticulously kept, century-old building overlooking the East River. There are twenty-six steps between floors and not an elevator in sight, even for the faculty. The morning Marshall hired me, I showed up barefoot for my interview on the fifth floor, my high heels in one hand, the other hand slapped against my chest. I opened my mouth to speak, but there was only the sound of a breathless woman panting furiously. Marshall had been fooling with the fax machine in his office when I arrived, and he stopped his tinkering and went to the little sink behind his desk to get me a paper cup filled with lukewarm water.

"The trick is to pace yourself as you're going up the stairs," he said. "And I guarantee you your heartbeat will be back to normal in no time."

It was August, and he was dressed in cutoffs, sneakers, and a T-shirt that said "It's Not That Life's Too Short, It's That Death's So Damn Long." His shoulder-length hair was tucked neatly behind his ears, and his large, handsome face was shining with sweat. "I love this school," he said, and offered me a seat at his desk while he settled himself on the window sill. "The kids are delicious and my teachers are absolutely devoted to them."

I never imagined the possibility of falling in love with a man who would use the word "delicious" to describe the two hundred and twenty preadolescents in his charge. It rubbed me the wrong way, hearing that word from him. It seemed lazy and imprecise and inappropriate; what I'd failed to consider, I later realized, was the exuberance with which he uttered it, the sheer generous enthusiasm with which he regarded his students.

But in a few hectic months he won me over. By then, of course, I knew all about the wife he'd lost to cancer two years earlier, his pain-in-the-neck widowed mother, the three long-haired cats who shed all over his clothes and in every room of his otherwise immaculate apartment on Riverside Drive. (Sometimes, after work, eating dinner at home with Noelle, I'd feel something impossibly distracting on my tongue and eventually withdraw a single cat hair from my mouth.)

"While you were watching *NYPD Blue*," I say now, "yours truly was filling out Medicare forms. A mountain of them."

"So how's the old guy doing?" Marshall asks.

Whispering into the phone, I say, "He's not exactly a happy camper."

"Why should he be?"

"No reason I can think of," I say without hesitation.

Marshall sighs. "Well, happy New Year," he says.

"That's tomorrow night," I remind him.

"True. And if I forget to call you, it's only because I'll be engaged in unspeakable acts of wanton debauchery and incapable of getting to a phone."

"Ditto."

Laughing, I hang up. I check on Noelle, who's positioned herself about six inches from the television set in the den, where she's watching a rerun of *Seinfeld*.

"You're too close to the TV," I warn. "Number one, it's bad for your eyes, and, number two, God knows what kind of radiation's leaking out from there."

"So what?"

"Listen, I'm sorry I tried to use bribery to break up your big romance with Kwame," I offer. "That was a mistake."

"Don't say you're sorry when you're not." Noelle shuts off the TV with her fist. Sitting at the edge of the fold-out couch, she pulls her knees up to her chin, lowers her head. "You'll never understand what a babe he is, will you? All the girls in my class understand—I don't have to explain anything to them. They think I'm lucky. Some of them are even jealous of me."

"He's cute," I admit, dropping down beside her. "That shining hair of his is really beautiful. But you're both too young to be so—"

"He's the best kisser," Noelle interrupts dreamily. "He—"

"He's *what*?" I grab her by the shoulders, turn her around so that she's facing me. "What are you telling me, Noelle?"

"Calm down, okay? We only did it like, maybe, twice."

"Did what?"

"Put our tongues in each other's mouths. You know . . ."

It occurs to me that this is one of those times when, if I knew for certain who Noelle's father was, I'd probably be on the phone with him in a heartbeat, angling for sympathy and advice. Instead, I console myself with the thought that kissing doesn't necessarily lead anywhere at all. I think of all the guys I've kissed, on doorsteps, in movie theaters, outside classroom doors; I see myself pressed against bookcases, kitchen sinks, wall-to-wall carpeting. Kisses that led nowhere, though they might have, if I'd allowed them to. Then, of course, there were the kisses that were simply a lovely prelude to deeper intimacy: There I am on the herringbone-patterned floor in Marshall's living room, my students' work scattered around me, a red ball-point pen between my teeth. Without warning, Marshall swoops down next to me, plucks the pen from my mouth, kisses me greedily. His hands are under my sweater, under my bra, gently kneading my flesh. He tugs the sweater over my head and flings it; it lands across a poorly written report on the Babylonians and the Code of Hammurabi. And then he's lifting my breast to his mouth.

"Don't be really really mad at me, Mom, okay?" Noelle is saying. "It's just skin touching skin, no big deal."

"No more kissing!" I say loudly. "Wait until you're fifteen, do you understand me?"

"Fifteen?" Noelle stares at me in disbelief, then begins to laugh. "That's like a joke, right? Like when you tell me I have to wear that stupid winter jacket I hate and we both know there's no way I'm going to put it on but you try to force me to anyway."

"That's a perfectly lovely jacket," I say. "Why won't you wear it?"

"I look like such a loser in that jacket!" Noelle shrieks. "It has fringes on it!" She's weeping now, her sweet little-girl face contorted in misery and confusion. She turns away.

My arms enfold her from behind; I rest my chin on top of her head. All she wants is a winter jacket that won't make her look like a loser, and a mother who will tell her she's free to enjoy her boyfriend's kisses, to go exploring anywhere she chooses.

"I want to go home," Noelle wails. "I just want to sleep in my own bed in my own room and wake up in the morning and see all the things that are mine, okay?"

"I know." I comb through her baby-fine hair with my fingertips, hold it in my hands. "We'll be back in New York at the end of the week, I promise."

"That's four more days. Kwame could have a new girlfriend by then. If he's cheating on me, I'll die!"

How does an eleven-year-old cheat on his girlfriend, I wonder. My mouth twitches, threatening a smile. "Let me tell you a little something about men," I begin, then decide to keep it to myself.

"What?"

"Never mind."

Drying her tears with a swipe of her shirtsleeve, Noelle says, "Can I call Kwame for, like, two minutes?"

I check my watch. "You've got until eight-sixteen. That's exactly five minutes."

"I love you," Noelle says excitedly, her hand already reaching for the phone. "And even when I don't, I still do."

Liking the sound of this, I say again, "I know."

In the living room sit my mother and her husband, who have made their move from the dining table to the couch. My mother has changed into a housecoat and pink-suede slippers, and there's a manila folder in her lap. Murray's hands are braced against his walker, as if he might be taking flight sometime soon.

"Graveside services only," my mother announces.

Dumping the pile of sheet music, I park myself on the piano bench. "Pardon me?"

"It's right here in this folder," my mother says, and holds up the file so I can see the words "FUNERAL ARRANGEMENTS" printed across the front in a familiar hand. "You need to take a look at this, darling."

"I don't *ever* want to take a look at that," I say, appalled. "Get rid of it."

"I'm trying to save you money," my mother explains. "Graveside services are a bargain compared to a whole funeral, trust me."

"Let's play Scrabble," I suggest. A mild wave of nausea passes over me; I can feel my dinner rising up at the back of my throat. "Where do you keep your set?"

"When the time comes, we want our bodies shipped back to New York, of course," my mother continues. "I'm afraid you'll have to come down here and then accompany the bodies on the plane. I hope it won't be too much of an inconvenience for you." She smiles pleasantly, as if she's just asked me if I'd mind doing a simple errand, like going to the post office for a book of stamps.

Murray lets out a muted growl; he falls back heavily against the couch cushions. As he struggles to make himself understood, the upper half of his body begins to sway drunkenly.

"We haven't been to the speech therapist in three weeks," my mother confides, ignoring the rhythmic lurch of Murray's shoulders. "I keep meaning to get over to her office, but somehow we never make it there." And then, to Murray, "Honey, I'm going to get a pad and pencil. You're just going to have to write it down for us."

I meet Murray's wide-eyed stare, but only for an instant. I remember the night I broke the news of my pregnancy, and Murray's chilly response into the phone. "Never a dull moment with you, is there?" he'd said, and handed the receiver back to my mother.

Murray and I have never been allies, have never been able to regard each other generously, and I've long given up trying to figure out why. In this apartment of his, I'm still the teenager who spent the night in jail, the twenty-five-year-old who slept around, got herself knocked up, and brought a fatherless child into the world.

So be it. At least my mother and I usually got it right.

I would, in fact, do anything for her; kill her roaches, mop her floors, accompany her coffin on its melancholy flight back to New York.

On the couch, Murray is still in motion, though he's slowing down now, like some wind-up toy running out of steam.

My palms are sweaty; I rub them together, and pray for Murray to come to a standstill. He has no use for my pity, but there it is, stirring inside me, thickening in my veins and arteries, traveling back and forth from my cold heart.

Arriving with a legal pad and a marking pen, my mother hands them over, along with a tiny Pyrex custard cup loaded with pills, and a tumbler of water.

Murray scribbles frantically, thrusts the legal pad at her. "YOU TALK TOO MUCH!" he's written, nodding his head vigorously as my mother reads his words out loud.

"Is that so," she says. She looks flustered at first, then incensed. "You," she says, "you sit there like a bump on a log thinking God knows what, telling me nothing, or at least nothing I want to hear. And you know what? I take pleasure in the sound of my own voice because it's the only pleasure I've got, thank you very much."

More swiftly than I could have imagined possible, Murray rises from the couch and shoves off, propelling his walker determinedly across the carpet. His pants slip slightly below his diminishing waistline, revealing the startling white flesh of his spine. When at last he reaches the threshold of the bedroom, he does a half-turn and slams the door shut.

"I'll kill him," my mother says. "I swear to you, one of these days I'm going to kill him."

"Please don't," I say, just as the tumbler of water left behind in a corner of the couch topples over.

"Why not? Why not put us both out of our misery?"

I start mopping up the couch with a handful of paper napkins. "Because I don't want to have to come down here and visit you on death row, that's why."

"I've got news for you, he's already on death row and I've got a seat right behind him."

The sodden napkins I'm holding are dripping water down the length of my arm; I pitch them onto the pile of towels on the coffee table, wipe my hands on my jeans. "You'll survive without him," I say in the merest whisper.

"The next step for him is a wheelchair," says my mother. "And then, after that, a nursing home." She shrugs. "The funny thing is, I don't even remember getting old. One day I looked in the bathroom mirror and there I was, someone you just couldn't call middle-aged anymore. What a shock. But you know, I can still remember as far back as Mrs. Hawkins, my first grade teacher. A witch if there ever was one. And there was a boy in my class, Ralph O'Connor, who came back from the lavatory one day with the buttons of his pants undone. They were tiny buttons, I suppose, or they'd been sewn on too tightly, whatever it was, he needed help with them. And you know what that witch did? She took a pair of scissors from her desk, snipped off the buttons, and told this poor little Ralph O'Connor, 'You tell your mother not to send you to school until you've learned how to button up your pants by yourself, mister.' And he cried right there in front of the whole class, poor thing," my mother says. Tears spring to her eyes. "My heart breaks for him, even now."

I nod; I want to take that pair of scissors and stab Mrs. Hawkins through the heart. Some of my own students, I know, are none too fond of me, either.

Unexpectedly, I yearn now to be back in my overheated classroom, begging my students to listen up. Sometimes they do, and there's that satisfying hum of excitement in the exchange of ideas; everyone in the room, even the sleepiest among them, finds something to nourish them. In any case, it's easier than being here, where, like Noelle in her fringed jacket, I'm a loser.

Murray is listening to an all-news radio station in his bedroom; through the wall, I can hear the details of a triple murder in downtown Miami. Someday, over the phone, perhaps, I will hear the inevitable news of his final battle with this disease that's already taken so much from him. Maybe then I will work hard to convince myself that there was, after all, something approximating love between us. Maybe then I will conjure up false memories of being steadied on my first pair of ice skates as my stepfather promises he will never let go; of being held aloft in his arms above the icy waves of the Atlantic; of being steered across the dance floor in his courtly embrace at a cousin's wedding, Murray impossibly, elegantly, straight-backed and tall. Stock images from someone else's family album that will bring tears to my eyes.

I enter the bedroom without knocking.

"Hello," Murray says. He's standing at the window, leaning against his walker. Across the pitch-black waterway are the lighted windows of one condominium after another, a cluttered landscape that was nearly barren when he and my mother first moved here. He was a golfer and swimmer in those days, perpetually tanned, perpetually on the move.

The truth: I will never confuse compassion with love.

"The next time you feel compelled to share your thoughts," I tell Murray, "do your wife a favor and make sure it's something she wants to hear."

At the window, a pale old man stands motionless, saying absolutely nothing.

• • •

My mother refuses to hand over the car keys. The four of us are going to the movies at the mall, but it's clear I won't be in the driver's seat.

"Why not?" I want to know. Riding down in the elevator that will take us to the condo's mirrored and marbled lobby, I say, "It's New Year's Eve—do you have any idea how many crazy drivers are going to be out there?"

"Let's just say I'll feel more comfortable if I'm behind the wheel," my mother confesses.

"But why?"

My mother bites her lip. "Daddy doesn't like the way you drive. He's afraid you'll get a speeding ticket."

"Well, if I do, it'll be a first for me," I say, marveling at the soft, dispassionate voice I've somehow managed to summon up. "I've never—"

"Never say never," my mother warns as we troop to the car, an ancient Buick with a tinted windshield to keep out the sun. I fold Murray's walker and stow it in the trunk. I help ease him into the front seat, and then I climb in back beside Noelle. My mother backs the car out of her parking space, maneuvering as carefully as if she were performing neurosurgery, though the spaces on either side of her are empty and there's no sign of life anywhere.

"Move it," I say under my breath. "Put your seatbelt on," I instruct Noelle.

On Beach Boulevard, my mother's cruising at a steady twenty-five, ignoring the parade of cars that passes her on the right and left, the bleating horns full of resentment. And in the back seat, I imagine myself jumping ship, knocking open the door with a single thrust of my shoulder, feeling adventuresome as I'm carried off in a swift warm current flowing in just the right direction, any direction at all.

"You're fifteen miles under the speed limit," I point out.

"Let them pass me, I don't care."

"You're kind of a hazard to other drivers," I say, as gently as I can.

"Tough toenails," my mother says. Beside her, Murray's head swings back and forth violently, uncontrollably.

We travel past a sprawling, brightly lighted liquor store called Big Daddy's, a block-long car showroom, a string of fast food restaurants. Cars continue to pass us, several at what seem like astonishing speeds.

"Where's the fire?" my mother complains. "So they'll get where they're going two minutes sooner, so what."

Suddenly a patrol car appears beside us. "You!" a voice calls rudely through a bullhorn. "Pull over!"

"Oh Lord!" says my mother, and drifts to a stop. "What's *this* all about?"

I sink down in my seat as the cop slams his door and approaches.

"Good evening, officer," my mother chirps, as if they were two pedestrians sauntering past each other on Main Street in some lazy little town. "Happy New Year," she adds.

"Oink-oink," says Noelle. "I believe I smell a pork product."

"Shush!" I say, clamping my hand over Noelle's mouth. "Are you crazy?"

The cop bends slightly, and places his palms flat against the side of the Buick. He stares through the open window at Murray, who's swaying frantically now, his head tilted to one side. "What's the problem?" the cop asks. He's a middle-aged man with a moon face and bad teeth. "Is there a medical problem here?"

"Actually, there is," says my mother, "but everything's under control. We're just on our way to the movies to see *Mission Impossible*. Part two, actually."

"Swell," the cop says. "License and registration, please."

Fumbling nervously with her wallet, and then reaching over into the glove compartment, my mother says, "I'm sure I wasn't doing anything wrong, your honor."

"You were driving twenty-three miles an hour in a forty-mile-an-hour zone. I'm going to have to write you a ticket."

"For what? For being extra careful?" says my mother, outraged.

"Look, don't give me a hard time, all right? Isn't it bad enough I have to work on New Year's Eve?"

Murray grunts, either in approval or disagreement. Or perhaps neither.

"Here you go," the cop says. He hands over the ticket impassively.

"What?" says my mother, shoving the ticket into the glove compartment as the cop takes off and Murray gives it another try. "Bastard?" she says. "Oh . . . bastard! You got *that* right, honey."

"Bastard!" Noelle says, jubilant. She leans forward and kisses the back of Murray's head.

"*Now* will you let me drive?" I ask.

"No way, José," my mother says, and floors it, as if she's decided to give us the ride of our lives.

Personal Correspondence

His friends, refusing to listen, had thrown him a fortieth birthday party even though he'd begged them not to, begged like mad to be left alone with his VCR, a couple of early Woody Allen movies and some chocolate hazelnut spread that he ate straight out of the jar with a spoon—his idea of heaven. Instead, in the end, Sam allowed himself to be dragged out of the city to an indoor tennis club in the suburbs where he and a dozen of his closest friends played for a couple of hours and shared a birthday cake sculpted in the shape of a Corvette. The word had gone out that he'd recently bought himself a Discman, and so most of his gifts were CDs, current music by groups whose names set his teeth on edge: the Dismemberment Plan, Phish, Smashmouth, Limp Bizkit. "We decided it was time for you to move on," one of his roommates from college explained. "I mean, how many years can you keep listening to the same old Dylan albums, over and over again?" No mention was made that night of Sam's wife, Carol, who had moved on, nearly six months ago, to a new life in Atlanta with her lover, an epidemiologist she'd met at a medical convention. Leaving behind Sam and their seven-year-old daughter, Sophie, Carol had hopped on a 727 with her beloved Dr. X (as Sam called him), promising to come back for Sophie when the time was right. Over my dead body, Sam told Sophie, causing his daughter to sob softly, even after he explained to her that "over my dead body" simply meant never. The shrink she'd seen for three sessions reported encouraging news: for a seven-year-old, Sophie was managing remarkably well. "She climbs into my bed every night at two-thirty," Sam complained ruefully over the phone. "Got any suggestions?" The shrink had just one: "Give her another week or so and then start locking your door. She'll get the message." The bill for this brutal bit of advice arrived in the mail only a day later, and was for one hundred and fifty dollars. Over my dead body, Sam thought, and filed it away in an overstuffed drawer where he'd never find it.

Now, several weeks after his tennis party, he waited uneasily behind his locked door for the rap of his daughter's small fist. It was only 2:12; he was expecting her in exactly eighteen minutes. Propped up on one elbow reading *Rolling Stone*, he saw, out of the corner of his eye, the shameful layer of dust that coated the laminated top of his dresser. He'd been meaning, for days now, to get out the can of Endust from under the kitchen sink and take care of it, but somehow, inexplicably, he just hadn't managed it. There were, he knew, stiff dots of toothpaste spattering the bathroom mirror, blackish mildew around the drain in the shower, piles of unopened mail on the counter in the kitchen. And twelve thank-you notes to be written for his birthday presents. There were some things, at least, that he was still able to handle: he showed up at work faithfully day after day, shopped for meals on the way home, cooked relatively nutritious dinners for Sophie every night (well, almost every night—once or twice a week, he scooted across Lexington Avenue for pizza or an order of pork fried rice and two egg rolls), ran the shower for her until the water was just the right temperature, played endless rounds of gin with her, read to her for fifteen minutes while she lingered over her bowl of triple caramel explosion ice cream, then slipped away just as she fell asleep. Sometimes he nodded off himself as he lay beside her, awakening in time for the eleven o'clock news and a movie he might have rented. Occasionally, while his daughter slept, he took the elevator to the basement of his apartment building and threw a load of laundry into the washing machine, hurrying back in case Sophie awoke crying for him. In the laundry room was a bulletin board cluttered with notices that had been tacked up by tenants and people in the neighborhood: index cards announcing a secondhand baby stroller or a laptop for sale, Xeroxed sheets from housekeepers and babysitters looking for work, business cards left by piano teachers, French teachers (Learn in your own home from a native Parisian!), and bridge instructors. And, from time to time, scraps of paper with threatening messages regarding laundry thieves: "TO THE FUCKER WHO STOLE MY RALPH LAUREN NIGHTGOWN FROM THE DRYER—BEWARE—GOD WILL GET PERVERTS LIKE YOU!!!" Remembering this, Sam laughed out loud, and then suddenly stiffened, watching as the stainless steel doorknob rotated quietly, tentatively, then more rapidly, rattling frantically now.

"Go back to bed, sweetie," he said in a monotone.

The rattling continued. "I can't sleep," said Sophie.

"How about some Tylenol P.M.?"

"What?"

"This is unacceptable," said Sam. "You're too old for this."

"My eyes won't stay closed. I tell them to, but they won't listen."

"Take your hand off the doorknob, Sophie."

"If you let me in, I'll only stay until I'm ready to fall asleep and then you can bring me back to my own bed, okay?"

"No dice, kiddo. Get back in your room."

A few moments passed in silence as Sophie considered this. "I love you," she said coyly. "I really really really love you."

"Me too," said Sam. "But in this household everyone sleeps in his or her own bed."

"Mommy doesn't."

"Mommy is no longer a member of this household," Sam said, and got up to open the door.

In the morning, he found Sophie lying diagonally across the bed, the tip of her index finger resting in her belly button. He stroked her fine, tangled hair, traced the outline of her small perfect ear. Opening one eye, she smiled at him.

"Get back where you belong," he said. "Scram."

"Buy me a kitten and I'll sleep in my own bed for the rest of my life."

"Promises, promises," Sam said.

• • •

At noon he lunched with a client who told him how terrible he looked.

"Define terrible," Sam said. He leaned forward and his tie grazed a little tin cup of cocktail sauce.

Christine, a best-selling author of a trio of self-help books, was thinking of writing her next book about either survivors of incest or preschoolers on Ritalin. She shook her head at Sam. "Your color's ghastly and there are these big pouches under your eyes," she said disapprovingly. "And you're certainly not your usual buoyant self." She was dressed in a flame-red suit without a blouse underneath and Sam allowed himself a good long look at her cleavage from time to time.

"I don't seem buoyant?" he said. "Well, maybe I need a nap."

"Two hundred units of vitamin E wouldn't hurt, either," said Christine. "Did you know it prolongs the life of your red blood cells? Four hundred units a day would really perk you up." Stretching toward him, she lifted his tie out of the cocktail sauce.

"You have, what, two kids?" Sam said.

"I've got three," said Christine. "Three very special boys, though the four-year-old's a big pain in the ass. He's sweet and adorable, but his energy level's way up there, which is why we've got him on Ritalin, if you know what I mean."

"Any of them ever try to come into your bed in the middle of the night?"

"Is the sky blue?" said Christine. "Do birds have wings? Did you read chapter four of my last book?"

"Yes, yes, and, I'm ashamed to say, I can't remember a thing about it."

"Well, every child in the world wants to sleep in his parents' bed.

And you've got to let them know that's a major no-no. You've got to nip it in the bud before things get out of hand."

"And I won't forget about those four-hundred units of vitamin C," Sam said.

"E," said Christine. "C's for warding off colds. You know, the Linus Pauling thing."

Sam nodded. He slid his credit card from his wallet and signaled to the waiter. He seemed to recall that Linus Pauling had been mistaken, or, even worse, that his studies had been fraudulent. He took another leisurely look at Christine's cleavage, and decided it was best to say nothing.

"So," Christine said, "Ritalin or incest, what do you think?"

•   •   •

On the laundry room bulletin board, someone had posted a notice that was unlike anything he'd seen there before. It was printed on mint-green paper and said:

> "Too busy to deal with your personal correspondence? Columbia grad student with excellent writing skills can make your life easier. I can send weekly letters to your widowed mother in Florida, birthday cards, anniversary cards, thank-you notes, etc. Reasonable rates. Leave message and I'll get back to you.
>
> HoneyRose 722-3636

"HoneyRose," Sam said aloud, and it sounded like the name of a stripper, or maybe even a hooker. Certainly not a Columbia grad student with excellent writing skills. He'd forgotten to bring down a laundry bag and his arms were loaded with toasty, neatly folded towels and sheets. It was time for the 11:00 news. Upstairs on the eighteenth floor, his daughter was sound asleep, her arms wrapped around the preternaturally gentle, very expensive Himalayan kitten he'd bought from a breeder in New Jersey. "HoneyRose," he said again, and memorized her number, at least for the short-term. In the elevator he wondered if it was too late to call this alleged graduate student. His birthday had come and gone almost two months ago and the thank-you notes were still nothing more than a hazy, guilt-provoking thought that plagued him once in a while. His widowed mother in Boca Raton had always been big on such niceties. (*Someone gives you a gift, you need to write a few lines to show your gratitude. If you don't, you're just being plum rude.* How many times during his childhood had he heard *that* from her?) She was currently in the habit of sending him sweet little notes, usually twice a week, which he couldn't be bothered answering. He felt bad about it, but not bad enough. He was a single parent, for Christ's sake; a phone call to Boca Raton every couple of weeks was the best he could manage.

Maybe this HoneyRose, with her promise to make his life easier, was onto something here.

Upstairs, he checked on his sleeping child, shoved the towels and sheets into the linen closet, and called HoneyRose. Her machine said she was unable to come to the phone, and he left a halting message that made him sound, if not exactly stupid, then ill at ease and inarticulate. Ill at ease about what? He had no idea, really.

Instead of the news, he watched *Charlie Rose* for a while. His guest was Carly Simon, who looked, Sam thought admiringly, pretty damn good for someone over fifty. He dozed off listening to her talk about her battle with breast cancer. When the phone rang, his mouth was dry and there was a damp spot on his shirt sleeve where he'd drooled. "Hello?" he said drowsily, and sank back into his seat on the living room couch.

"This is HoneyRose. So what can I do for you?"

She didn't sound like a stripper; she sounded businesslike and a little impatient. He didn't know what he was supposed to say to her.

Was this like a job interview? If so, he was the one doing the interviewing, wasn't he? "I've never done this sort of thing before," he said, as if she really *were* a stripper or even a hooker, as if there were something vaguely illegal going on here. At his feet, Jasmine the kitten meowed piteously; it was more like a whimper and so poignant that Sam reached down to pull her into his lap saying, "What do *you* want, darling?"

"What do *I* want?" said HoneyRose. "I want to know if you're serious about hiring me. Because if you're not, let's not waste anybody's time. And if we're going to do business together, you can't call me 'darling,' okay?"

"Actually, I was talking to the cat, but I do want to hire you. Or at least I think I do."

"Okay, look, what I can be is kind of like your social secretary, okay?"

"I have no social life to speak of," Sam confessed. "I'm a single parent and I don't get out much. But I do have a load of thank-you notes that I can't bring myself to write." He paused. "You probably think I'm incredibly lazy, don't you?" he said apologetically.

"I never pass judgment on my clients," said HoneyRose. "How many of these notes do you need?"

"A dozen."

"Well, let's see, how about . . . a hundred and twenty dollars for the whole deal? And I don't take checks or credit cards."

"No problem." That he was willing to blow more than a hundred bucks to dispense with some thank-you notes surely didn't speak well of him. You lazy bastard, he thought. "Did I mention my widowed mother down in Boca Raton?" he heard himself say.

"That's another one of my areas of specialization," said HoneyRose. "I know just how to deal with those old ladies. Too bad, I could have helped you pick out a Mother's Day present last month. I charge twenty-five dollars an hour to act as your shopping consultant."

"Sounds reasonable," said Sam. He could feel himself growing lazier and lazier as the conversation progressed, the will and energy to take care of anything at all draining swiftly from him. Even the thought of rising from the couch and going into the bathroom to wash his face and brush his teeth before bed seemed wearying. And showering and shaving tomorrow morning—forget it. Ever since Carol had flown the coop he'd been scrambling urgently to keep the gears of his daily life properly meshed, and sometimes—big surprise—the effort exhausted him. It *was* a big surprise. As it turned out, he'd underestimated what it would take to keep a seven-year-old happy. A couple of mornings ago, after he'd braided his daughter's hair to the best of his limited ability, Sophie looked in the mirror, frowned, and told him it was pigtails she wanted after all.

"With scrunchies at the top *and* the bottom," she said, like a diner in a restaurant decisively adding mushrooms and onions to her order.

"I don't *do* pigtails," he told her.

"You do," Sophie insisted. "It's easy. You make a part in the back, a *straight* part, and then you do the rest."

"I'm not good at those things." *Why can't you just do it yourself,* he almost said.

"But you have to be," Sophie told him. "You're the only one here, right?"

"Right," he said. He was close to tears, which frightened him. He contemplated calling Carol and ruining her day with a few carefully chosen words. How had he fallen in love with a woman willing to abandon her child in greedy, self-indulgent pursuit of her own fucking happiness? He'd underestimated a lot, it seemed, and recalled another one of his mother's incantations: *You wheel with people and you deal with people but you're a fool if you think you can ever really know them.*

Not even your own wife?

Apparently not.

He'd done a crummy job on his daughter's pigtails and could tell he wasn't going to get any better at it.

"So when do you want me to come over?" HoneyRose was saying.

The sooner the better.

•   •   •

He vacuumed and dusted in honor of her arrival, and printed out a list of names and addresses of everyone who'd been at his fortieth birthday, along with the gifts they'd given. He put Sophie and Jasmine to bed together, and shaved for the second time that day. He swept the coffee table clean of magazines and newspapers and videotapes, and brought out a bowl of low-fat vegetable chips. His khakis were pristine, the cuffs of his denim shirt neatly rolled past his wrists.

She was, he realized, the first woman to set foot in his apartment since his wife had vanished from the scene.

"Hey," said HoneyRose. "How are ya?" She dropped her briefcase to shake his hand.

"It's nice to meet you," he said.

Well, it was and it wasn't. She was slender but big-breasted, with a slightly sharp nose and pretty, hazel eyes. Her black jeans were very tight and her cropped T-shirt revealed an impressively flat stomach. The blazer that went over the T-shirt had a pin about the size of a half-dollar stabbed through the lapel; a Star of David was printed on it. Sam squinted at it, as if he were near-sighted, which he wasn't. "Oy vay, I'm gay!" the pin proclaimed in bright yellow, and it was like a kick in the teeth. He hadn't had sex in six months, a fact that was on his mind more than he'd liked to admit. Without sex, you had no life to speak of, not really. Or at least the life you had was a sadly incomplete one. There was no getting around it; he lusted after this girl with her exposed stomach ornamented with a gold ring that gleamed so compellingly in his living room. Never mind that he hadn't a prayer of getting his hands in her nearly pitch-black hair that was swept away from her face with two tortoiseshell combs, or that his mouth would never come anywhere near her breasts with their nipples that had hardened in the breeze of his air conditioner. Of course, if she'd been straight, he still might have lost out on everything, but surely there would have been a chance of winning her over one night while she worked composing clever, heartfelt expressions of his gratitude to his friends. Or so he imagined.

"Would you like some chips?" he asked indifferently as she sat herself down on his couch.

"They're pretty weird-looking," she said. "What are they?"

"Oh, yucca, taro, parsnip, all kinds of stuff that's probably good for you."

"I generally don't like stuff that's good for me."

"No?"

"I'm a drinker and a smoker," she confessed, "and I sleep about four and a half hours a night. But all that's going to come to an end soon enough." She took off her blazer and squashed it into her lap, then crossed her legs. He watched her every move with great interest; he just couldn't help himself.

"Really?" he said.

"Absolutely. My girlfriend and I are planning on having a baby as soon as we can, and since I'm the one who's better suited for this pregnancy, I'm obviously going to have to turn over a new leaf. But let's get to the thank-you notes." Unbuckling her briefcase, she took out a large manila envelope and opened the flap. "I brought along some samples of my work. Everything will have to be done on the computer, of course, since I can't possibly duplicate your handwriting, but don't worry, it's all going to be very personal."

"Why is it that you're the one who's better suited for the pregnancy?" Sam said recklessly. "If you don't mind my asking."

HoneyRose shrugged her slender shoulders. "Well, I'm twenty-nine and Lily's thirty-eight, does that answer your question?"

"What about graduate school?"

"One more semester and I'll have my masters."

"Raising a child is an enormous effort," he said. "It ain't easy."

"Thanks for the warning," HoneyRose said.

"And what about your parents?"

"Excuse me?"

"What do they think about all this?"

"I wouldn't know," HoneyRose said brusquely. "We don't speak. I mean we haven't spoken in a long, long while."

"I'm sorry," said Sam. "As a parent myself, I was just wondering, that's all."

HoneyRose smiled at him. "You're a very nosy person," she said. "But I don't mind, I'm nosy as well."

Was she? She hadn't, after all, asked him a single question about himself. "Well, my life's an open book," he said. "What do you want to know?"

"What style would you like to have the notes written in? Gracious? Affectionate? Funny?"

"All of the above," Sam said.

"Okay. I'll have them here for you in a week so you can sign them. Either I can mail them to you or I can come back and we can go over them together, just to make sure you're happy with them, but I get paid no matter what. Oh, and your mother in Boca Raton? What are your, uh, needs regarding her?"

To tell the truth, he'd forgotten all about her. "Could you write to her twice a week?" he said. "Something short—four or five sentences ought to do it."

"And what would be the subject of the text?" HoneyRose had a legal pad in her lap now and a pen in hand.

"Nothing," Sam said. "That's the beauty of it—you can write about absolutely nothing, just like she does. It's the idea of it, the idea of getting mail from me that's the important part here."

"Exactly what kind of nothing are we talking about?" HoneyRose asked. "The weather? What you had for dinner last night? The movie you went to last week?"

"Rented," said Sam. "The movie I *rented*. I never go out to the movies, it's just too much of a hassle to get a babysitter. And anyway, who would I go with? All my friends are married or remarried and I'm not the kind to be a third wheel, if you get the picture."

HoneyRose was writing furiously on her legal pad now. "You have a child, right? I need to know his or her name, of course, and age. What grade is he or she in school?"

Taking the legal pad from her, and the pen from between her fingers, he filled in the details. He tried to read the notes she had written, but, surprisingly, her handwriting was a god-awful mess and he could barely make out a single word. "What does this say?" he asked, pointing to what appeared to be two words separated by an ampersand.

"That?" HoneyRose said. "That's my own personal shorthand."

"So what does it say?"

"It doesn't matter," she said, retrieving the pad and pen and putting them back into her briefcase. There were silver rings on both of her thumbs, and her nails, which were child-sized, not much bigger than Sophie's, were polished a silvery pink. Her hands moved swiftly to zip and buckle the briefcase shut.

"What does it say?" Sam persisted. He guessed it wasn't anything of much consequence, but he needed to know anyway.

"Subject presents symptoms of lethargy and depression," murmured HoneyRose, keeping her head down.

"SUBJECT? What is this, a psychology experiment?" Sam said, outraged. "What kind of graduate student are you, anyway?"

"Don't get pissed off at me," HoneyRose said. She put her hand on his knee. "Please."

"Some social secretary," Sam said. "And your handwriting is abominable."

"Look," said HoneyRose. Her hand was still resting on his knee. "I *am* getting my degree in psychology, I'll cop to that. But I really am in the letter-writing business. And my interest in people makes me all the better suited for it, don't you think?"

"What I think," said Sam, "is that I'm capable of writing my own damn thank-you notes. Despite my lethargy and depression, that is." He stared coldly at the button on her lapel; he was on to her now. "You're not even gay, are you?" he said. "That's part of your experiment, isn't it? Just to see how people react."

"Oh, I'm gay all right," said HoneyRose. "And there's no experiment, believe me. I was just jotting down some clinical observations, that's all. Force of habit," she said. "Can't you forgive me?"

"Why would I want to do that?"

"Because fundamentally you're a nice guy, and because I need your business. And I'm a terrific letter writer. Your mother's going to be delighted with you, trust me."

"I ought to throw you out of here right now," Sam said halfheartedly. She was already at the door anyway; what was he going to do, scoop her up and toss her out into the hall?

"How about I do this all on spec?" she proposed. "I'll come back next week and if you're not happy with my work, you don't have to pay me."

"All right, all right," he said, and she smiled at him.

"By the way," she said casually as she opened the door herself, "Lily and I are in the market for a donor, so if you know of anyone, give me a buzz."

"Donor?"

HoneyRose looked him up and down, and smiled again.

"Sperm donor," she said, and shut the door behind her.

• • •

Now that Sophie was content in her own bed, it was the cat who insisted on resting her head against Sam's pillow night after night after she left Sophie. Jasmine had pale blue eyes, a wedge-shaped head, and chronic, though minor, respiratory problems. She kept Sam up with her wheezing and snorting, and no matter how many times he shoved her to the foot of the bed, she returned to his pillow, purring so blissfully that he didn't have the heart to lock her out. At the office he occasionally dozed over the manuscripts that cluttered his desk, and drank endless cans of Pepsi in an effort to stay alert. He tried, too, to avoid thinking about HoneyRose, to avoid fantasizing about proving himself to be the sperm donor of her dreams. It was a crazy idea, really, but in his moments of greatest optimism, he had to admit he had a lot to offer—he was smart and decent-looking and in excellent health, and there was no history of cancer or heart disease or diabetes in his family. And, of course, though this probably wasn't a point in his favor and might, in fact, instantly disqualify him, he was dying to sleep with HoneyRose. He would never let her know this, he decided, but would, instead, present himself as someone possessing a diploma from an Ivy League institution, excellent SAT scores, and twenty-twenty vision. Never mind that his wife had wearied of him and traded him in for an upscale model with an MD to his name; this, too, he would keep to himself.

When Christine called to say she'd decided to do a book on pregnancy after forty, he made no attempt to talk her out of it, even though he was sure there must have been dozens of books on the subject. A best-selling author was, after all, a best-selling author.

"This will be from my own personal perspective," she told him. "I myself was forty-one when my youngest was born and I came through with flying colors."

"Got any thoughts on sperm donors?" he said nonchalantly.

"Well, that's fine for people in desperate circumstances, I suppose, though not for a normal, healthy person with a normal, healthy husband for a partner."

"Of course not," Sam said. "I meant in extreme cases, of course."

"Maybe I ought to include a chapter on it," Christine mused, "for all those women out there in desperate circumstances. Thanks for the suggestion, cutie. And speaking of which, have you been taking your vitamin E?"

"Religiously," Sam lied. "Type up a proposal and an outline and fax it over to me, okay?" After he hung up, he rested his head on a 350-page epic poem and napped for a while.

• • •

On his way home from work, on a crowded shuttle between Times Square and Grand Central, he found himself seated across from a young guy wearing a soiled three-piece white suit and a dingy-looking stovepipe hat. "Sod-om and Go-mor-rah," the man sang tunelessly, again and again. And then, at last, he cut to the chase, and boomed, "GOD CREATED ADAM AND EVE, NOT ADAM AND STEVE! AND WOE TO THOSE WHO DO NOT HEED!"

"Shut up, you asshole, you're giving me a headache," a man in paint-spattered workboots and overalls growled.

"Me too," said Sam. A growl was what he'd had in mind, but the two little words came out in a whisper, and he hung his head, like HoneyRose when she'd diagnosed him with a psychoneurotic disorder or two.

Well, he had news for her: he was healthy as a horse. His depression had lifted, and he was, like the lunatic across the aisle, a man on a mission.

• • •

They went over the thank-you notes together at his dining room table. The perfume HoneyRose wore smelled delicious and expensive, like some extravagant dessert he couldn't wait for a taste of. Her mouth was glossed the same silvery pink as her nails and he imagined himself getting a taste of that, too. The thank-yous were printed on heavy, cream-colored paper that had been folded meticulously into note-sized cards. She'd done excellent work; each note was, as promised, humorous and affectionate, each slightly different from the one before it.

"And here's a note for your mother," HoneyRose said. "It touches all the bases—the weather, which I described as 'summerlike,' the Italian dinner you cooked for a couple of friends, the—"

"What friends?" Sam interrupted. "I never cook for friends."

"You do now," HoneyRose told him. "I used some of the names from the thank-you notes. Wayne and Adam, I think."

"Very clever."

"Yup. You fixed them homemade lobster ravioli, made fresh with your new pasta machine."

"And what pasta machine might that be?"

"I don't know, I'm trying to give you a slightly more interesting life here, all right? Don't you want to know what you had for dessert?"

"What?"

"Tiramisù, homemade, obviously."

"Have I taken a cooking course lately?"

"At the Y," HoneyRose said. "It'll do your mother's heart good to know you're keeping busy."

"I guess I'm impressed with the new me," Sam said hesitantly. This was rather like cheating, wasn't it, and probably he ought to put a stop to it. *Stick to the facts*, he should have told HoneyRose, *you know, the dry, unembellished truth*. So his mother thought he was out there making an effort; where was the harm in that, really? "Very impressed," he repeated, this time a little more enthusiastically.

"Thanks," said HoneyRose. "I told you I'd do a good job." She went through her purse and handed him several books of postage stamps. "So that's a hundred and twenty dollars, plus ten, plus twenty for the stamps."

"Fine," he said, but made no move to get his wallet. He stared at the clingy V-necked shirt HoneyRose was wearing. "Any luck finding a sperm donor?"

"Not yet," she said, "but we're working on it."

"I was thinking," he heard someone say, and then his mouth went dry. The hollows under his arms suddenly felt damp and his hands had turned clammy. Oh, for a beta blocker or two, he thought. He rubbed his gluey palms together in disgust.

"You were thinking what?" said HoneyRose.

"Actually, regarding the sperm donor search, I was thinking about me."

"You?" She looked at him with amusement and, perhaps, the slightest distaste. "You?"

"What's wrong with me?"

"No offense, but for one thing, you're not tall enough."

"I'm six feet even," he said defensively.

"No way!"

"Five-eleven and a half, I swear."

"In that case, I'd have to say your posture could be better."

She was right about that; he immediately sat up straighter in his seat, throwing back his shoulders hopefully.

"And for another thing," HoneyRose continued, "we were looking for someone with blue or green eyes."

Now he was truly incensed. "Oh, give me a break," he said. "How shallow is that? What kind of values do you people have?"

"Excuse me?"

"Look, here I am, a Phi Beta Kappa graduate of an Ivy League school, a guy in excellent health, willing to do you and your girlfriend a big favor, no strings attached, and you're ready to disqualify me because of the color of my irises? If that isn't the very definition of superficial, I don't know what is."

"Well . . . all right, what were your SATs like?" HoneyRose said, reconsidering, and he was back in the running again.

"Combined scores of 1530," he said proudly, though more than two decades had passed since anyone, including himself, had given a shit about them. "And that was without a prep course of any kind," he added.

"And what Ivy League school are we talking about here?"

"University of Pennsylvania."

"Penn?" HoneyRose said, and that not entirely benign look of amusement crossed her face again. "Well, it's an Ivy League school, but just barely. I mean, no offense, but what kind of cachet could it possibly have when people are always confusing it with Penn State?"

She was insufferable; he saw that now, and wanted to deck her, at the very least wanted her insufferable presence gone from his sight this instant. The V-necked shirt she'd chosen to wear for this business meeting of theirs showed, at the bottom of the V, a bit of black lace from her bra, and he couldn't help but envision his finger slipping gently under it, just to feel the warm, delicate flesh so close to her beating heart. "I was Phi Beta Kappa," he said meekly.

"Yeah, so you said. Can you prove it? Don't they give you a little gold key or something?"

He couldn't tell her the truth, which was that his mother wore it around her neck on a gold chain, along with a charm which said "#1 Grandma" and which had been given to her by Carol after Sophie was born. "Prove it?" he said, and then he was leaning toward her, his eyes half-closed now as his mouth met hers. It seemed an act both foolhardy and brash, even a little perverse, but what did he have to lose? Her lips tasted pepperminty and made his tingle, and he understood that she was returning his kiss, not tenderly but urgently, the lovely warmth of her tongue generously filling his mouth.

"Well, that proves something," she said, drawing back from him and wiping her mouth daintily with one finger. "Though I have no idea what."

"I can provide letters of recommendation as needed," he said.

"We're interviewing a couple of other candidates," HoneyRose told him. She touched his mouth with the fingertip that had just touched her own. "Or at least Lily thinks we are."

"Lily," he said darkly, and sighed.

"I'm so confused I feel as if my head is going to explode," said HoneyRose.

• • •

His mother called to thank him for his notes just as he and Sophie were sitting down to dinner. "Two in one week," she said jubilantly. "Imagine that." And then, sounding suspicious, "What's gotten into you all of a sudden?"

"Nothing," Sam said. He spooned some chicken casserole onto his daughter's plate and poured her a glass of Pepsi.

"I'm not hungry," Sophie announced.

"It's dinnertime. You have to be hungry," Sam said, and told his mother to hold on.

"Well, I'm not," Sophie insisted. "But if you let me watch TV maybe I will be."

"Nothing doing," said Sam. In the background, Yo-Yo Ma played a haunting, melancholy Bach sonata. "Dinnertime is classical music time, you know that," he said firmly.

"That chicken is so gross," said Sophie. "It's a yucky color and it looks like throw up, kind of."

She had a point there. "It's the cream of mushroom soup, I think," Sam said. "I followed the recipe exactly, and this is how it turned out."

"Talk to me, Sammy," his mother urged. "If you don't, I'm going to fall asleep with the phone in my hand."

Though they'd had pizza the night before, Sam slipped a frozen Pizza for One into the toaster oven. He let Sophie turn on the TV even though it violated one of the household's cardinal rules. Clearly he wasn't much of a father tonight; if anything, he was a cartoon of a father, a buffoonish figure easily manipulated by any child at all with half a brain in her head. Well, sometimes you just couldn't do any better than that.

"Sammy?" his mother said in her most plaintive voice.

"Sorry," he said. "I'm listening."

"Well, don't be angry at me, but I thought I saw your father again today. He was one of the EMS workers who came to get poor Mrs. David who lives on my floor. She's ninety-six and lives with her seventy-five-year-old daughter and has everything in the world wrong with her. But she's all right, it was nothing life threatening. But I took one look at that EMS worker and for a moment his face became Ira's and I'll tell you, I almost fainted. Sometimes, you know, I think I'm losing my mind. Do *you* think I'm losing my mind? If it's Alzheimer's I'd sooner shoot myself right now."

"You're not losing your mind," Sam reassured her, as he had twice before when she'd imagined she'd seen his father—once when a repairman came to fix her dishwasher, and once when her podiatrist walked into the treatment room where she'd been waiting for him and began to trim her toenails for her.

"Well, if I'm not losing my mind, then what is it?"

"You miss him," Sam said, "that's all." The canned laughter flowing from the TV set his nerves on edge and he yelled at Sophie to lower the volume.

"Missing someone that much can't be good for a person," said his mother. "Which is why I was so delighted to hear about this new girlfriend of yours."

"What?" He flew to the TV and put it on mute. "Get into your pajamas!" he hissed at Sophie, who looked at him as if he were deranged.

"I didn't have my dinner yet. And I'm watching *Friends* without the sound on," she complained.

"Go!"

"Not that three dates makes her your girlfriend exactly," his mother was saying, "but it's a step in the right direction, isn't it? I'm thrilled for you, pussy cat, even as my heart aches for yours truly."

"You've got to get out more, go places with your friends, join one of those reading groups where they discuss a different book every month or whatever," Sam said, desperate to end the conversation and call HoneyRose, who had already, in her second letter, gone too far. What chutzpah! Really! He'd have to establish some guidelines, set limits on this life she was so keen on inventing for him. Otherwise, next thing he knew, he'd have a new wife and a brood of stepchildren to contend with. And he wasn't even divorced yet.

"Well," his mother said, "at least one of us is headed in the right direction."

"A positive attitude, that's what *you* need," Sam advised. He was flipping through his address book frantically, searching for HoneyRose's number. He'd put his life in her hands and he didn't even know her last name, he realized.

He found her on the inside of the front cover, next to the numbers for Sophie's pediatrician and the Chinese restaurant where he got his fried rice once a week.

"I wish you the best," his mother said, "and please send my regards to this new lady friend of yours, this Stephanie."

"Stephanie," he said grimly. "I'll be sure and do that."

Dialing HoneyRose's number a moment later, all he got was her answering machine. His blood was boiling but he managed to keep his voice clipped and controlled as he left his message: "Please be advised that Stephanie and I are not now nor have we ever been, a couple." Was that enough? "And you and I need to talk," he added. "ASAP."

Sophie had returned and positioned herself an inch or two from the TV set; she was reading the actors' lips, Sam guessed. She was always such a patient, resourceful kid, reading to herself on the couch in the living room while he went over the manuscripts he often brought home with him at night, or working quietly at the dining room table with her paint box and a cup of water, determined, it seemed, not to disturb him. For a seven-year-old, she was pretty impressive, he suddenly realized. What planet was he living on that he'd failed to notice this?

Her nightgown was on back to front and she nibbled absently on the tip of her braid. Sam snuck up behind her and carted her back from the TV, but first he turned the sound on.

"I'm sorry I yelled at you," he said. "You're a terrific little girl and I shouldn't have yelled like that." Sophie sniffed a few times and he wondered if she'd been off crying in her room while he was on the phone. "Oh, sweetheart," he said guiltily.

She sniffed again. "The pizza's burning," she said. "Maybe it's on fire."

• • •

He was watching *Inspector Morse* on PBS when, a little after midnight, HoneyRose returned his call. Morse was a man after Sam's own heart—he was smart, cranky, and almost never wrong about anything. He probably wouldn't have made a particularly good husband or friend, but you had to admire the guy, Sam thought. He would, no doubt, have made an excellent sperm donor, with his clear blue eyes, splendid bearing, and his degree from Oxford. Knowing HoneyRose, she might have dismissed him simply because he fell several inches short of six feet, Sam thought irritably, and then had to remind himself that Morse was, after all, a fictional character, and that it didn't matter *what* HoneyRose's opinion of him was.

"What's up with that message you left me?" she said. "If you're going to criticize the work I'm doing, we might as well call it quits right now."

"You stepped over the line," said Sam. "I don't *want* an imaginary girlfriend, if that's all right with you."

"I'm adding texture to your life, okay? We don't want your mother thinking you're circling the drain, do we? Like she doesn't have enough to worry about."

Stung, Sam said, "Is that what you think of me, that my life is going down the tubes?"

"Relax," said HoneyRose. "Calm down and listen to me, will you. I actually have good news. It turns out Lily wants to meet you."

"Sweet!" he said. He'd forgotten all about Inspector Morse, who, detesting the sight of blood, had turned his head away as a corpse was being removed from the scene of the crime. "Hold it a sec," said Sam, and went to feed a tape into the VCR. It occurred to him that he'd been watching all too much TV since Carol had left him, but perhaps that was to be expected. What else was he going to do? Enroll in a cooking class at the Y with a bunch of desperate singles openly on the prowl? But HoneyRose was right; his life did need more texture.

"So let's make a date," she said.

"Stephanie's back in the game," he said. "I've reconsidered."

"Smart move," HoneyRose said. "Good for you!"

"So are we all going to go out for a drink or something?" he asked her. "Minus Stephanie, of course."

"Here's the thing." HoneyRose paused, just long enough for Sam's heart to sink in anticipation of what had to be bad news. "Lily wants to see you in your . . . natural habitat. And she'd like to meet Sophie as well."

"Sophie? No way. We're leaving her out of this, if you don't mind. And what's this about my natural habitat? What am I, an animal in the wild?"

"Look, I'm going to be straight with you," said HoneyRose. "Basically, I've decided you're my first choice, but there are still a couple of other candidates Lily's sort of hot on. And the competition's pretty impressive, that's all I'm saying."

Instantly, he envisioned a lineup of doctors, lawyers, and Harvard professors, all of them blue-eyed, well over six feet tall, and clever enough to charm the pants off HoneyRose *and* her girlfriend. How could he possibly compete with these people, these fucking *übermenschen* of his imagination? He let out a long, deep sigh of helplessness. He remembered the warmth of her tongue so unexpectedly filling his mouth; there might be more of that little piece of heaven but only if he won Lily's vote. Fat chance. He sighed again, this time with utter resignation. "She can meet Sophie, but only for five minutes," he conceded.

"She's not an ogre or anything," HoneyRose said. "She's the love of my life, for God's sake."

There it was: a sick headache that got him right between his unexceptional brown eyes. It descended with a cruel swiftness and intensity, and just before the room began its slow spin, he disconnected her without apology.

•   •   •

Leaving nothing to chance, he hired a housekeeper to turn the apartment upside down and shake out all the dust, straighten up his closets (in the unlikely event that Lily happened to peek inside), and wash the kitchen and bathroom floors, something he hardly ever remembered to do. He went for a haircut, not at the barber's, but at a trendy place on Third Avenue called Hair, Thair, and Everywhair, a salon where the stylists were dressed all in black and the guy who worked on him kept trying to convince him that a couple of artfully placed streaks of color were just what he needed. The haircut and shampoo set him back seventy-five bucks, and he cursed Lily silently but fiercely as he plunked down his Mastercard.

He told Sophie that a couple of new friends of his were stopping by and that, as a special treat, he would rent her a movie at Blockbuster.

"On a school night?" she said, astonished. "That's breaking the rules."

"Sometimes rules are meant to be broken," he said, but didn't elaborate.

"Can we break some other rules tonight?" Sophie asked, getting into the spirit of things.

"Nope, just that one."

"Well, I'd still like to sleep in your bed with you. Even though I have Jasmine, I'm still a little bit lonely."

Join the club, he wanted to say as she rested her head against his shoulder.

"I think I'm going to make a list of all the rules I hate the most," Sophie said.

"Do you need paper?" he offered. "Pencils?"

Sophie pursed her sweet, rosy lips disapprovingly. "You should be nicer to me," she recommended. "I'm the only child you have."

• • •

So this was the love of her life, this little blond shrimp with her short, gelled hair slicked back so severely, showcasing those ears busily lined with a dozen of the tiniest silver hoops. She couldn't have been more than five feet; beside her, half a foot taller, HoneyRose loomed like a giant in shorts and a T-shirt. The shrimp herself was wearing a black pants suit and a closed, unfriendly expression; clearly this was no social call. She was here on official business, like some caseworker who'd been assigned to evaluate his fitness as a father. (One false move and poor Sophie could wind up a ward of the state.) When she finally smiled at him, it was a smile that showed no teeth, no warmth, no sign that she knew damn well this was excruciating for at least one of them.

"Come on in," Sam said, resisting the impulse to yank HoneyRose inside and then slam the door shut as rudely as possible in Lily's cold white face. She was already looking him over appraisingly; what was he, after all, but a male of the species capable of providing stud service? He'd brought this on himself, of course, but what had he been *thinking*? Only of HoneyRose's hardened nipples grazing his bare chest, his hands cupping the sharp blades of her hips, their bodies so gracefully entwined it was obvious they were meant for this.

And now he was going to blow it all by saying exactly what was on his mind. "You know," he began, and ushered them into the living room, where the two women seated themselves on the love seat, nearly on top of one another, their thighs and elbows touching. "You know, I've never felt so uncomfortable in my own home before."

"That's terrible," said HoneyRose sympathetically. "This is not a big deal, I'm telling you."

"Not a big deal?" Lily said. "Are you kidding? What could be a bigger deal than this, honey."

"Is that Honey with a capital 'H,' short for HoneyRose?" Sam asked. "Or just an ordinary term of endearment?"

"I told you he was funny," said HoneyRose.

"Yeah, hilarious," said Lily. "Who plays the piano?" she asked Sam, gesturing toward the black walnut Yamaha fitted perfectly under the dining room window.

"That would be me," he admitted, feeling as if he'd just confessed to a crime.

"Well, could you play for us? I'd love to hear something."

What was this, an audition for Juilliard? He hadn't played in many months, not since his marriage had gone belly-up. And he'd forgotten to tell the housekeeper to dust the keys, he realized. He blew at them, scattering tiny gray puffs in the air, and played, resentfully at first, the opening of "Rhapsody in Blue." Though the score was in front of him and he flipped the pages at the right moments, he was playing by heart, doing a pretty good job of it, his fingers moving deftly along the keyboard, body and soul overtaken by the music as Lily and even HoneyRose became ghosts whose presence he could no longer feel. And then, in the middle of a page, he simply came to a stop, exhausted. He slumped at the keyboard, carelessly displaying his bad posture.

"Wow," said HoneyRose reverently.

"Thanks for the concert," said Lily. "I'd like to meet your little girl now, if that's okay."

"Second bedroom on the left," said Sam, pointing. "Just give me a minute."

"And I'd like a drink of water," HoneyRose said. She followed Sam into the kitchen as Lily went down the hallway toward Sophie's room. He poured her a glass of filtered water from a pitcher, but after one sip she set it aside on the counter. "I'm blown away," she said. "Totally."

He shrugged. "I took lessons for years and years," he said. "I used to play all the time, and then . . ." His voice trailed off. "Never mind."

"Tell me."

His hands were hidden in the back pockets of his khakis; she reached for one of them, drawing it out and turning it over gently, running her fingertip across his open palm, as if she might discover something there. It seemed an intimate gesture, full of promise.

"Come with me," he said.

"What?"

"It won't take long."

He closed the door quietly behind them; in the elevator they stood next to one another shyly.

"Why do I feel like we're on some kind of weird date and you won't tell me where you're taking me?" HoneyRose said. "Not that I'm complaining."

"There's something I want you to see," said Sam.

When they got to the basement he led her by the hand into the laundry room, which was sweltering and deserted. A washing machine on spin cycle trembled convulsively, as if it might self-destruct at any moment, and a couple of dryers, their portholes steamed over, revolved endlessly. At the back of the long, linoleum-lined room hung the cork board where HoneyRose's mint-green notice was still pinned. "ARE YOU FOR REAL?" someone had scrawled across it in black marker.

"*Are* you?" Sam said. He had her by the shoulders now, but lightly, tentatively; she was free to bolt at any moment. It was always a mistake to ask too much of someone; even a simple question could be a burden, he knew. Unaccountably, he'd stumbled and fallen for her, but he wasn't saying a word. Let her watch for it in his eyes, let her feel it in his skin that sizzled now under her surprisingly cool, wandering hands.

The washer stopped its wild shuddering, the dryers at last fell silent. "*Are* you?" Sam said again, lightheaded in all that heat, listening hard for whatever she might offer him—a murmur of assent, of longing, or, perhaps, something else entirely.

Housecleaning

The young husband-and-wife team the cleaning service has sent over arrives ten minutes early, which pleases me no end.

"There's nothing like starting off on the right foot," I tell them buoyantly, and hold the door open as they drag in an industrial-strength vacuum and a shopping cart full of cleaning supplies. The man, who introduces himself as Dell, is startlingly tall—halfway between six and seven feet, I'd guess—and has a cigarette tucked behind each ear. His wife, Starlet, a tiny figure in a zippered teal-blue jumpsuit, has her hair just like Mary Martin's in *Peter Pan*. I eye her worriedly, already convinced that Starlet is too small and delicate for the heavy work load in store for them.

"And who's this?" I ask. Hanging back behind the threshold of the doorway is a little girl; as the child stands there gazing downward at the rubber welcome mat, I admire her dress, which has a large black-and-white likeness of a winking cat across the front, one eye ornamented with a rhinestone. The child is wearing black leggings that end a little past her knees and beat-up-looking sneakers with Velcro closures.

"That's Princess," Dell says. "Just stick her in front of the TV and you won't hear a word out of her."

"I'm hungry and I have to go to the bathroom," says Princess, but remains in the doorway. She flicks away the thin dark bangs that are hanging in her eyes and takes a single step forward.

At my temples and in the space between my eyebrows, I feel a headache brewing. "You know," I say to Dell, "I've got mattresses that need to be turned, heavy couches that have to be pulled away from the wall . . . there's actually quite a lot for you to do. Do you really think your wife's strong enough for that kind of work?"

"Not to worry," says Starlet, and places her hand briefly on my shoulder. "We're the best in the business. We're a great team."

At fifty dollars an hour you ought to be, I almost say but do not. (Having lived through the Depression, I can still remember when you stopped in the street to pick up a penny because it was worth the effort.)

"Fine," I say now. "My husband's being discharged from the hospital tomorrow and what I'd really like is to have everything spotless. If you can manage it."

"Heart attack?" Starlet says.

"What? No, he's asthmatic. He had a very severe attack. It scared the hell out of me," I say. "He—"

"The master bedroom's that way?" Dell asks. "We'll set up in there first."

I nod, waving him past. My husband, Simon, had stopped breathing halfway through the eleven o'clock news last week, and if not for a neighbor in our condominium who knew CPR, I would have lost Simon right there in our den, just as the weather forecaster in his smart-looking blue blazer was poised in front of his map predicting three straight days of rain for the Miami-Fort Lauderdale area. Roger Parrish, the neighbor who resuscitated Simon and summoned the paramedics, happens to be a courtly, handsome man with not a hair on his head. Twice-divorced and a champion tennis player (at least on the local senior citizen circuit), he's much admired by the numerous widows in the building. He drove me to the hospital in Fort Lauderdale the night Simon was carried off in the ambulance;

later, the two of us went for coffee in the hospital cafeteria. Holding my shaky hands between his own steady ones, he listened patiently as I talked a nervous blue streak, outlining my worries one by one, thanking him extravagantly, then returning to my long list of fears before setting out to thank him again. (What a frazzled wreck I'd been that night, all wilted and dry-mouthed and unable to keep silent for even a moment.) I remind myself now to pick up some small gift for Roger, an expression of gratitude for bringing Simon back to life.

"You do have a TV set, don't you?" Starlet is saying. "Princess is just a lost soul without her TV shows."

"Shouldn't she be in school?" I say.

"Not if I don't want to," says Princess. "And today I definitely don't want to."

I don't know what to make of this. "In my day," I tell them, "they used to send the truant officer after you. But of course my day has come and gone."

"Princess is a school-phobic," Starlet explains. "It's like a disease, sort of. Sometimes she wakes up in the morning and throws up, just because she's afraid of going to second grade. The school district has a special counselor for her. It's part of her treatment—two hours a week with a very sweet lady-psychologist."

"School-phobic," I say, marveling that they already have a name for it. "What will they think of next?"

"Oh, it's real common these days," says Starlet blithely. She puts on a pair of elbow-length turquoise rubber gloves and rummages through the shopping wagon. "There's lots of kids like Princess all over the district," she says, and trails down the hallway, arms loaded with sponges and an assortment of bathroom cleansers.

"Swell." I look at Princess, whose fingernails are rimmed with an accumulation of moss-green dirt. "Would you like to wash your hands?" I say. "And then Mrs. Sugarman will slice up an apple for you. Would you like that?"

"Who's Mrs. Sugarman?" Princess says suspiciously.

"Me."

"Why do you call yourself 'Mrs. Sugarman'?"

I smile at this. "Because a long, long time ago, when I was very young, I married Dr. Simon Sugarman. And that's how I became Mrs. Sugarman."

"I'm hungry for a baloney and cheese sandwich on an onion bagel."

"It's nine o'clock in the morning," I say, as shocked as if Princess had asked for a martini.

"I'm hungry."

"Didn't your mother give you breakfast?"

"Maybe, but I threw it right up," says Princess. "How about if you make me a hamburger? I like it red on the inside and burnt on the outside, okay?"

"I can't give you a hamburger so early in the morning. It wouldn't be right. What about a bowl of cereal instead?"

Princess looks me straight in the eye. "You're not so nice," she says. "I thought you were, but you're really not."

"Excuse me," I say stiffly. "Right now you're a guest in my home. And in this house we don't insult people, we speak nicely to them, do you understand what I'm saying?"

"This isn't a house," says Princess. "It's an apartment. Why do you call it a house?" She saunters from the foyer into the kitchen, where she heads straight to a half-open cabinet and selects a bag of salt-free pretzels for herself. "We live in an apartment, too. It's Dell's apartment, actually."

"Actually," I say. I follow Princess into the kitchen and shake my head now as the little girl tears open the bag of pretzels with her teeth.

Lowering her voice, hunching down over the cellophane bag, Princess says, "Dell's not real nice, either. Well, sometimes he is, but mostly he isn't. Once, on purpose, he made my mother fall, and she broke two ankles. Wait, that's not right, I mean she broke one and sprained the other one. I had to do a lot of things for her, like make her sandwiches and change the channels on the TV for her because the clicker was broken. And she was such a grouch."

I shiver in my air-conditioned kitchen. I imagine Dell thrusting out one of his extraordinarily long legs to trip Starlet, imagine Starlet's shriek of astonishment as she goes flying. "Poor thing," I murmur. "And is Dell your father?" I ask Princess.

"No way. He's like the biggest dork," Princess says.

"Then let's not talk about him." The truth is, I don't want to contemplate whatever dark things might or might not have transpired in somebody else's household; I just want my apartment shining by noon. There's plenty to do today, but I can't remember what's first on my list. It's Princess and her chatter that's thrown me off course. I try to recall my plans, but my mind is a dull stubborn blank. Simon's homecoming, which I'd been looking forward to all week, suddenly seems like something I'd rather postpone. What if having been brought back from the dead has permanently altered him? In the hospital these past few days, he seemed pretty much his old prickly self, though he'd been a little passive, I'd noticed, a little too eager to have me take charge of things, asking me to brush his teeth and his hair for him and even to strap his watch around his wrist. Yesterday I'd glimpsed, through the fly-front of his cotton pajamas, something droopy and sad between his legs; for only an instant, I'd been appalled at the sight, but then, recovering, remembering all my affection for him, I'd pulled the thin blue hospital blanket up under his arms and launched into an entirely irrelevant story about one of our neighbors. The humiliation he would surely have felt if he'd seen, in that instant, what I had seen, was my humiliation, too — wasn't that always the way it was when you loved someone? Observing Simon in his bed, it came to me that I couldn't imagine Roger Parrish lying in a hospital, vulnerable and exposed like that.

The half-hour or so we spent together in the deserted cafeteria that night seems to have taken on, for me, a dreamlike quality, and also a bright sheen of romance and possibility. In my mind, I keep returning to it, remembering the feel of his cool hands over mine, his soft, subdued voice gently reassuring me, his head gleaming brilliantly under the cafeteria's fluorescent lights.

At the kitchen table now, I let out a lingering sigh that ends in a little moan of pleasure and longing. I listen to the distant heavy rumble of the vacuum cleaner. "See how hard your mother's working?" I say.

"This is pretty boring," says Princess. "Don't you have any coloring books for me?"

"If you were in school, where you're supposed to be," I say, "you'd be too busy to be bored. You'd be reading and writing, and borrowing and carrying numbers, and probably your teacher would be reading you *Charlotte's Web.*"

Princess hisses noisily, puffing out her cheeks. "My teacher," she says, "is an A-hole."

"What?"

"Don't you know what an A-hole is?"

"As a matter of fact, I do," I tell her. "But we don't allow people to talk like that here. If they want to talk like that, they have to step outside into the hallway."

"Do they get to come back in again?"

"I suppose so," I say. "It varies from case to case, I suppose."

"I want to see my mother," Princess says in a wobbly voice, and runs from the room. I brush some crumbs from the table into my hand and put the bag of pretzels back in the cabinet. I've frightened off Princess, which isn't surprising: the truth is, I've never had a way with young children, not even my own. And my two daughters would be the first to tell anyone who'd listen that I just didn't have the endless patience that would have made all the difference, that, years ago, would have sweetened the tone of our household. Instead, I lost it, and dug my fingers into their slender wrists, shrieking, *Why can't you listen to me? I'm not asking you to climb Mount Everest, I'm just asking you to take those filthy feet off the couch. Am I asking the impossible?* I would cry, never breaking their delicate skin but marring it with tiny violet marks shaped like crescents on the underside of their pure white wrists. *No I am not — all I'm asking for is a little consideration!* And now Simon and I are in Florida and the girls are nowhere in sight, Renée comfortably settled in the suburbs of Boston, Joanna in San Francisco. Unaccountably, both always seem to have their answering machines switched on, no matter when I happen to phone. ("This is your mother calling from Florida," I say self-consciously at the cool, electronic sound of their respective beeps. "Don't you think your father would love to hear from you more than once while he's in the hospital? Don't you think the familiar sound of your voice would do him a world of good?") It's been ages since we all lived together under one roof; sometimes the thought of our separate, distant lives still makes me a little weepy. The therapist I dragged myself to nearly twenty years ago — when both girls married and moved away within months of each other — had been sympathetic but firm. "You had each of them for what, eighteen years?" Dr. Hirschorn asked me. "Well, you have to remember they were really only visitors, just passing through. And take it from me, it can't be any other way, not really."

A fundamental truth, maybe, but one that sometimes strikes me as absolutely heartbreaking.

Silently I make my way into the bedroom now, where I discover Starlet and Princess standing over my dresser, fingering the bottles of perfume I keep lined up in two precise rows on an ornate mirrored tray. "I happen to know this one over here is like forty-two dollars an ounce," Starlet is saying to her daughter. "So you can figure out what a bottle this big must have cost. Want to try some on your wrist?"

"Excuse me," I interrupt. My heart is thumping away in my

chest, and I feel a wave of dizziness sweep over me. "My husband gave that to me for an anniversary present," I inform them.

Starlet swings around to face me, the bottle upright in her palm. "That's real sweet," she says, shaking her head, as if in astonishment. "What would it be like to have a husband like that, I wonder."

"Put that down, please," I tell her warily. "I'm sure I speak for all of us when I say we'd be very upset if it broke."

Unscrewing the cap, Starlet tips the bottle against her fingertip. She guides her finger slowly down the side of her neck, then under Princess's nose.

"Yummy," says Princess.

"You had some mildew inside the shower," Dell announces, suddenly emerging from the bathroom. "Nothing too serious, but I took care of it. Better to nip that kind of thing in the bud, that's my policy." He slides a cigarette from behind one ear and pokes it into the corner of his mouth. "Just taking a three-minute break before I start on the other bedroom."

"My husband's an asthmatic," I say. "The smoke is very bad for him."

"Your husband's not here," Starlet points out. Picking up a comb from the perfume tray, she runs it languorously through her hair, then frowns at herself in the mahogany-framed mirror above the dresser. "This is just the worst haircut, don't you think? They call it a pixie cut but I'd say it makes me look like a little mouse. Maybe if I had it streaked with a touch of blond, I'd look more, you know, glamorous."

"You're not the glamorous type," says Dell matter-of-factly. "Never were and never will be." He taps the ash from his cigarette into his cupped palm, making me wince.

"I'm sure I can find an ashtray somewhere," I say. "Maybe in the kitchen." I picture myself dialing 911 from the phone on the kitchen wall, whispering urgently for a patrol car. *She used my perfume without my permission. And also my comb. And he smoked a cigarette in my bedroom when he knew I didn't want him to.* I can hear the snort of laughter from the operator at the other end: *Don't you know better than to be tying up the line with that kind of silly stuff? Call back when one of them puts a gun to your head, lady.*

"What do you mean, I'm not the glamorous type?" says Starlet, as Dell steps into the bathroom to ditch his cigarette. "I could be if I wanted to. Why do you think my mother named me Starlet? She had high hopes for me, probably still does."

Dell stands framed in the bathroom doorway, a Marlboro lingering behind his left ear. Caressing the cigarette, as if it were something beloved, he says, "Your mother's a big fat fool. The day she moved to Tennessee with that pathetic excuse of a boyfriend was one of the best days of your life, whether you know it or not." He nods in my direction, saying, "This mother of hers is a deluded tub of lard and a nosybody besides, calling every hour of the day and night to give out advice nobody in their right mind would listen to."

"A deluded tub of *what?*" Starlet's pale blue eyes widen; she seizes a spray bottle of Windex With Vinegar and aims the nozzle at Dell's belt buckle.

"Don't you pull that trigger, miss," Dell says. His hands are on his hips and he is staring down at Starlet grimly. I can see the ten-gallon hat tipped back against his head, the dusty boots with spurs at his ankles, the spurs glittering silver in the Wyoming sunlight.

"Oh Lord," I murmur.

Hearing this, Princess lets out a squeal and dives under the bed, the soles of her little white sneakers peeking out from under the bedspread. Starlet squeezes the plastic trigger; a delicate spray of something sour-smelling darkens Dell's faded dungarees just under his belt. "You slimeball!" she says in a screechy voice, and then aims the trigger at his heart, soaking his shirt. Swiftly, Dell cracks her on the wrist and the bottle of Windex pitches to the floor.

"That's it! I'm out of here!" he announces. "And I'm taking the vacuum with me!"

"Like I give a flying you-know-what," says Starlet, rubbing her wrist against the side of her face. "Like I need you, right?"

"Like a hole in the head," says Dell, in a falsetto that somehow sounds menacing.

Starlet looks at him, surprised. "That's right," she says. "How did you know?"

Looping the vacuum cleaner cord fiercely around its handle, Dell sighs. "Because you're so fucking predictable, that's why."

"Will you please," says Starlet. "Not in front of Mrs. Sugarbaker."

"Sugarman," I correct her. On my knees now, I flip up the bedspread and speak to Princess. "Are you all right, cutie?" I ask. "Would you like to go see what's on TV?"

"No."

"You can put some of that delicious perfume behind your ears if you'd like."

"Can I take the bottle home with me?"

"Come out and we'll talk about it." I wait a few minutes, listening to the sound of the front door banging shut, and then Starlet's rapid footfalls approaching down the hallway.

"Get yourself out here right now, Princess," Starlet says. "We've got to go and call ourselves a cab." Her eyelashes are wet and gleaming, and she's sniffling into a handful of tissues patterned with pink and blue flowers. "I'm going to count to three. Here goes: uno . . . dos . . . tres."

"I peed in my pants, I think," Princess confesses in a tiny voice. "I tried to hold it in but I couldn't."

"I know," Starlet says. "I know you tried." She blots her eyes with the clump of tissues. "Listen, we'll rinse out your undies and use the hair dryer on them, how's that?" And then, to me, "Got a blow dryer for us?"

"What a terrific idea," I call out from my place on the floor. "Don't you think so, Princess?"

"Oh yeah," says Starlet. "I'm just full of terrific ideas."

"Don't be so hard on yourself," I say as Starlet stands up. "I don't know that spraying your boyfriend with Windex was the smartest thing you could have done, but we all have our ways. One time when Dr. Sugarman said something very cruel to me, I poured a cup of coffee into his lap. Lucky for both of us it was lukewarm, or he might have ended up in the burn unit at Jackson Memorial." Stricken with shame at having shared this with a stranger, I hear myself gasp. "That was a lie," I tell Starlet. "I would never lose control like that. I was just trying to make you feel better, that's all."

Starlet grabs Princess by her skinny little ankles and pulls her out across the carpet. "Let's have a look," she says, and shoves a hand down her daughter's back. "Damp," she reports. "Not too bad at all, actually. But what I'm real interested in knowing is, what was it your husband said to you that got you so ticked off?"

"I don't even remember," I say, "but even if I did, it wouldn't be right for me to tell you, would it."

"Why not?" says Starlet. She and Princess are back at my dresser, stroking perfume on their wrists. "This is my absolute favorite," she says. "Escape, by Calvin Klein."

"Why not? Because some things should remain private between husband and wife, that's why."

"You mean like sex?" Starlet says. "That's not as private as it used to be, you know. You ever watch any of the talk shows? Some people, and I'm not saying I'm one of them, are perfectly willing to let forty million people in on their little secrets. And sometimes it turns out that I can, like, relate to what they're saying. Like these three ladies whose boyfriends were into tying them to the bedposts with silk scarves and stuff. Not that Dell can afford silk—polyester is more his speed—but the idea is the same."

All at once, the air seems saturated with a mix of sickeningly sweet fragrances; breathing in, I feel confused and light-headed. For a moment I can't place the two small figures in my bedroom. The one all in teal looks elfin, like Peter Pan. I don't want to imagine her tethered to her bed with silk scarves as her lover eagerly lowers himself onto her, overcome with passion. After a long slow cooling off, there is no longer any passion in *my* life; sometimes it seems that it's inexplicably dried up like a parched, neglected flower, turned brittle and then to dust. I find myself wondering what Roger Parrish's smooth handsome head would feel like against my flesh, in my hands. He'd saved my husband, breathed life into Simon's open mouth while I'd looked on fearfully, utterly helpless. The connection between us, between me and this man whose lips had touched my husband's, is something I can feel simmering under my skin; whatever it is, it is miraculous, something to be savored.

"You've got to get rid of this Dell," I hear myself say. "I just know you can do better."

"If he bought me perfume like this, I'd be in heaven," Starlet says. "Fat chance."

"I can see you're not going to listen to me. Neither of my daughters listens to me, either," I say. "Well, I'm used to it."

Starlet nods. "I *am* going to clean your house, though. But first thing, you got a full-length mirror?"

"Behind the closet door." I watch as, motionless and unsmiling, Starlet inspects herself in the mirror, then slams the closet door shut.

"I need six-inch heels and a miniskirt," she says glumly. "And a job behind a desk—you know, answering phones, opening the boss' mail for him, ordering his lunch. You can't be glamorous and be in the housecleaning business, they just don't mix."

"Mom?" says Princess. She's been silent so long that I'd forgotten all about her. "When are we going home?"

"Never!" Starlet says exuberantly, rushing toward her and swooping her up in the air. "We're going to move into this nice apartment and have Mrs. Sugarbaker cook for us and do our laundry and take such good care of us we'll never want to leave. How would you like that?" she says, and parks Princess at the edge of the dresser. "Wouldn't that be cool?"

I smile faintly. My heart is racing, alert to danger and also, I have to admit, an inexplicable excitement. I imagine myself flipping the most delicate of omelets for Starlet's breakfasts, roasting chickens for her dinners, folding her laundry, leaving foil-wrapped mints on her pillow at night. And I could never explain to Simon how it happened, how it was that I'd been unable to resist a stranger's neediness.

"I'm teasing you, baby!" Starlet says, but Princess has already burst into tears. "Tell her I was teasing, Mrs. Sugarbaker."

"Of course she was teasing," I say, and wait for my heart to slow. "Don't be a silly goose."

"Why do you keep calling her 'Mrs. Sugarbaker'?" says Princess. She licks at the tears that have made their way slowly to the corners of her mouth. "A hundred years ago she married Dr. Simon Sugarman and that's how she became Mrs. Sugarman."

"A hundred years ago. No way," says Starlet.

"It's true," I say, and sigh. "Grover Cleveland was in the White House and life was sweet."

"Who's this Grover Cleveland character?" says Starlet. "Anyone I should know?"

"Never mind," I say, but I'm surprised at how disheartened I feel. It could be that I expect too much of people, wanting my daughters to fly to their father's bedside, my husband to be moved at the sight of my flesh, my cool, elegantly bald neighbor to appear wordlessly at my doorstep simply because he can't stay away. I slide my hand now along the surface of the night table next to Simon's side of the bed; dust darkens my fingertips, dangerous stuff for a man with asthma. There's probably dust everywhere in the apartment—in the week since Simon's been in the hospital, I've done very little with my time except try to keep him entertained with a steady stream of talk that exhausts us both. Sweeping the sleeve of my sweatsuit across the table, I send dust into the air, above the three bright rectangles of sunlight that pattern the avocado-colored carpeting and rise halfway up the bedroom wall.

"I've got to call a cab," Starlet is saying, her hand on the telephone. "It's like I can let Dell stew in his own juices for only so long and then it's real bad news."

"Have some coffee before you go," I offer. "Your boyfriend will wait."

"Well, maybe one cup. A little milk, two Sweet 'n Lows. And I swear to God," Starlet says, "I'd finish up the work you hired me for if I could. But I know I couldn't do a super job right now—my heart just wouldn't be in it." She seems to be puzzling over something, running a hand through her Peter Pan hairdo, then resting it awkwardly on top of her head. "I think maybe I just quit the business," she says uncertainly. "As of this minute."

"Good for you," I say. "I like to see a young person taking charge of her life." In the kitchen, I boil water for instant coffee and set out two blue-rimmed ceramic mugs on a Lucite tray monogrammed with my initials. I arrange some Oreos on a plate, and napkins and spoons. It's been a while since I've had company, I realize, since any of the neighbors have stopped in to ask how Simon's doing. Everyone has his own troubles here—cancer, heart disease, Parkinson's. *What a crew*, Simon had said one afternoon down at the pool, looking around him at all our waxen neighbors sunning themselves on chaise lounges. Fresh from a couple of sets of tennis, Roger Parrish had been the sole swimmer in the water, making his way vigorously from one end of the pool to the other. Silently, I'd applauded him, watching carefully as he pulled himself from the pool and draped a white towel across his tanned shoulders. Even then, before he figured in my daydreams, he had been someone to take notice of.

At the edge of the glass coffee table in the living room, Starlet and Princess sit mesmerized by the sight of a newly selected contestant on

The Price is Right. The woman, tall and scrawny-looking, wearing sunglasses and a racing cap and hoop earrings large enough to put your wrist through, is embraced by well-wishers in the audience as she approaches the stage. Asked to bid on a brass crib filled with stuffed animals, she looks back over her shoulder for advice from the audience.

"One thousand dollars!" Starlet urges, ignoring me but taking a cookie from the tray. "Fifteen hundred!" The audience clamors suggestions of its own; the woman crosses herself, then opens her mouth. "Two thousand dollars?" says Starlet. "No way, lady."

"Drink your coffee before it gets cold," I say. Beside me, Princess splits open an Oreo and scrapes her front teeth across the bright white cream, leaving behind what looks like trail marks in fresh snow.

The woman in the racing cap raises her arms in triumph; it's her bid that's come closest to the actual retail value of the merchandise. The emcee thrusts the microphone at her, looking on in amusement as she speaks into it breathlessly. "This is the happiest day of my life," she pronounces. "This is it."

"She doesn't mean it," I say. "It must be that they coach them before the show and tell them to say things like that, but you just know she doesn't really mean it."

"Of course she does," says Starlet. "And anyway, what do you know about her? What do you know about her life?"

I pretend not to hear. I think uneasily of Dell, cooling his heels, listening for the sound of Starlet's apology, of Simon waiting in his hospital bed for the start of visiting hours. Not long ago, the morning before the asthma attack that nearly killed him, I emptied a cup of coffee into his lap. We were in the kitchen, lingering over breakfast, sections of the *Miami Herald* spread across the table between us, neither of us speaking. Dreamily I opened my robe to him, shyly guided his hand to my breast. He pulled away so swiftly, so instinctively, it was as if his fingertips had been scorched. *You're embarrassing us both*, he said in a whispery voice, as if I'd disgraced myself in a roomful of people. Seizing the coffee cup, just for something to hold onto, I suddenly let go, casting my arm in Simon's direction without looking at him. Afterward, I made no offer to help him into dry clothes or to mop up the kitchen tiles where the coffee had spilled in a thin muddy pool. *What's eating you?* Simon asked me. *Could you give me a hint, at least?* Fleeing, I went downstairs for a swim and then out to a string of malls, searching half-heartedly for something that might appeal to me. At home, my husband waited all day for my apology, is still waiting for it, for all I know.

Starlet is smiling at the TV screen now, at a freeze-frame of the woman who won the brass crib caught in a jubilant pose, arms stretched high over her head, mouth opened wide, utterly enraptured. "Will you look at that!" says Starlet. "Will you?"

"I'm looking," I say, and see myself somewhere beyond reason and self-control, my ankles and wrists bound in bright silk, as my lover's knowing hands drift lightly along the smooth path of my flesh.

*M*ourners

The night Kay's husband leaves her, colliding with a pair of trick-or-treaters at their door dressed as a devil and a hippie, he acciden-tally knocks a pitchfork from the devil's hand and keeps right on going—into the BMW in the driveway and out of the neighborhood, past countless glittery angels and princesses, and tiny monsters in grotesque rubber masks who stream slowly down the walks on both sides of the street. Retrieving the pitchfork, Kay throws extravagant handfuls of miniature Milky Ways and Snickers into the devil's shop-ping bag until at last the little boy (or girl—who can tell?) says, "No more, okay?" and backs away from her as if she is someone to be afraid of. Kay is wearing pointy-toed shoe-boots peeking out from under a long black skirt, and a splendid witch's hat; the angry tears that trail down her face have wrecked the elaborate witch-makeup she'd so diligently applied an hour earlier. For a few minutes, she continues to greet the trick-or-treaters, a weeping witch with a muddy-looking face and blackened front teeth who silently tosses too many candy bars into their waiting, wide-open bags.

Her daughter, Daphne, who is ten, is spending the night with a friend; without changing out of her costume, Kay flees to the garden apartment complex where her lover lives, a fifteen-minute drive that she has made at least once a week since last winter. Lance isn't at home when she arrives and so she sits on the curb next to his assigned parking space, her head in her hands, and watches the trick-or-treaters parade past. She remembers the first time she was here, just after Christmas last year. Lance had led her into the living room, sliding her jacket from her shoulders as she looked around a little hesitantly, trying not to appear too nosy, too impatient, too eager. There hadn't been much to see; the room was rather stark and impressively neat, with a few books, and a great many CDs in orderly rows on little painted-white shelves. Seating herself at the edge of a scratched leather couch, she waited as Lance searched through his CD collection, his back turned to her. Broad-shouldered and skinny, he had a headful of shining, prematurely silver hair that he usually wore pulled back in a pony tail. Paradoxically, he was intensely mellow, his manner so casual, his voice so uninflected, that it was, at first, hard for Kay to understand just what he was after. (He had been Daphne's fourth-grade teacher last year, and they'd met at Back-to-School Night. As he stood in front of a classroom packed with parents, pacing as he talked, Kay found herself feeling light-headed in his presence. Her cheeks were burning and her eyes hurt. In the dozen years of her marriage to David, she had never felt this way in another man's company. Approaching Lance at the end of his talk, armed with a question about the science curriculum, she allowed her hand, as he gently shook it, to linger a bit too long in his. When he called several days later, wanting to meet for coffee, the sound of his voice over the phone made her trembly, and she'd wondered if he could hear the receiver knocking lightly against her chin as she fought to steady herself.) That first afternoon in his living room, he'd drawn her up and into his arms for a long slow dance as the Beatles sang *It's you, you, you, you-oo-oo-oo*. Suddenly she was thirteen years old and empty of experience, dancing on a glossy gymnasium floor, nearly in a swoon at the lovely unfamiliar feel of a boy's arms around her, her head tipped shyly against his hard shoulder. Lance switched the Beatles CD to Handel's "Water Music" just before he and Kay made love, but Kay was only dimly aware of the music, of the harsh sound of the blinds being lowered and shut, of Lance vanishing and reappearing in an instant with pillows and a blanket. Afterward, she had him play the whole disk over again. The leather couch, icy at first, had been warmed by the heat of their bodies, Lance's long and bony, like David's, but quite a bit hairier, a novelty to her. Idly, she threaded the hairs at his collarbone through her fingers as the two of them sat back against the couch, their toes touching, a satin-edged blanket around their shoulders.

"I feel guilty for not feeling guilty," she heard herself murmur.

"You came here because you wanted to."

She had to acknowledge that this was so, that no one had pointed a gun to her head. "But I'm happily married," she said, and was surprised at the sound of his gently mocking laughter.

"Shh," he said. "You're not saying any of the right things." She liked the way his mouth came down sweetly over hers, and the surprisingly tentative way he kissed her. Exhilarated, she felt herself rising above her own life and everything in it that was ordinary and tiresome.

When she was dressed and almost ready to leave, she followed him into the kitchen, wanting something to drink but feeling too timid to ask for it. On the refrigerator door was a black-and-white snapshot of his sons and ex-wife, who lived in Boston, two hundred miles away. "It must be hard," she said, smiling at the little boys in ice skates posed to the left and right of their mother, a small woman in a bulky sweater whose arms were stretched wide to accommodate them both.

Lance shrugged, and opened the refrigerator, gulping orange juice directly from the carton. She drank from it, too, something she would never have done at home, and a bright trickle of juice ran down the front of her pale gray turtleneck. It seemed she was no longer the person she knew herself to be, and after a moment of fear came and went, she felt electrified, as if she had just received a startling and possibly wonderful piece of news.

"Sometimes," said Lance, "I actually ache for my kids—it's something physical, something I can actually feel in my chest. But I get to see them once a month, and it's okay, really. My wife remarried last year and that's okay, too. As divorces go, it was a pretty good one."

"I didn't know there was such a thing as a 'good' divorce."

"I just meant it was quiet, very genteel; there's wasn't a lot of shrieking and accusations, just a feeling of resignation and disappointment, I guess."

"Still," said Kay. She wiped at her sweater with a wet paper towel but could see that it was hopeless.

"Still," he murmured, agreeing with her, nearly inaudibly.

They managed to see each other every week, whenever Daphne had after-school activities and the carpooling responsibilities fell to one of the other mothers. In between, Kay tried not to think too much about him, about what they were doing together. She understood that she had a crush on him, that the affection she felt for him was rather shallow and schoolgirlish, that it was only his long silver hair and his gentle, almost passive manner that aroused her sexual passion. They had never fully revealed themselves to each other, never dug too deeply; for Kay, this was what kept the relationship safe, something she could live with quite comfortably. She knew that she could give him up at any time, just as she had given up cigarettes cold turkey years ago. She could walk away unharmed, taking with her memories of the pleasures he'd offered.

As Lance pulls up now in his ancient Volkswagen Beetle, she runs around to the passenger side, flings open the door and arranges herself next to him in the front seat.

"Cool costume!" he says admiringly. "I wouldn't want to run into you in a dark alley somewhere, that's for sure."

In the moonlight inside the car, she can see how his perfectly straight silver hair shines against his shoulders. "Someone from school," she says, "I don't know who, called David at work and spilled the beans."

"Your front teeth are black," says Lance, staring at her in amazement.

"He left me," Kay says. *Don't,* she hears David say. *Don't talk to me, don't touch me, don't even look at me.* And then, pitching one of his shoes against the bedroom wall, *You blew it.*

"He split? Bummer," Lance says, and shrugs.

Watching his shoulders lift so slightly, she sees, with profound disappointment, that he has no gift for compassion, that her sorrows are her own. He had once laughed at her when she announced she was happily married; why then, should she be surprised that a shrug is all he can manage now?

"I wonder who gave us away," says Lance, drumming his fingers against her thigh. "My guess is it's one of the teachers I'd been seeing before you came along. In fact, I bet I know just who it was."

"Before I came along . . ."

Before Lance, she had never stared hungrily at other women's husbands, at any man at all, never wondered about their lives, what they were thinking, whether they found her appealing. Her life was with David, whom she'd loved unfailingly. She complained that they didn't see each other enough, that David spent too much time working and worrying about the small but flourishing printing business he owned, that eleven o'clock was too late for him to be returning home night after night, but these complaints had nothing to do with love. It was true, though, that in the months before she met Lance, she'd been aware of a lingering, melancholy boredom, both inside and outside her marriage, that seemed impossible to overcome. She was barreling toward forty, an utterly terrifying milestone, she sometimes thought. It simply didn't seem possible (or just) that she had already used up half her life. There was nothing she could point to in her own life that she had done exceptionally well, nothing in particular that marked her, defined her, and she had begun to ache for that definition. A month or so before Back-to-School Night, she had lost her social services job through budget cutbacks and no fault of her own; unable to find anything at all suitable in the job market, she found that she had fallen into an affair instead.

Crossing the parking lot now, a tiny skeleton with fluorescent bones holds the hand of a tall figure wearing a cat mask; a substantial-looking fluffy tail trails behind the six-foot tall cat. Kay touches her forehead to the dashboard and closes her eyes. She thinks of how desperate she had been, these past few weeks, even months, perhaps, for David to notice that something had changed. She began to see his thickheaded blindness as an insult to her, and to their marriage. (That her affair was an affront to their marriage was another matter entirely, one she tried to ignore.) It seemed intolerable that he could not see that she had been altered by the attentions of someone else, by the touch of someone else's hand upon her. In bed with David, she approached him eagerly, even boldly (propelled mostly by guilt, she knew), and though he seemed grateful, he was clearly too exhausted to spend less than a moment contemplating where this was coming from; plunging swiftly into a deep, hard-earned sleep was always his way. *What's come over you?* she'd longed to hear him ask. She had no idea how she would respond, except with relief and perhaps, too, a welcome little jolt of fear.

"I blew it," she says out loud.

Lance fools with the radio, running the tuning selector from alternative rock to hard rock to classical; unable to settle on anything, he switches it off. "Well, don't beat yourself up about it," he advises Kay. "The guy had no time for you in his life and now he's pissed off at *you*? Give me a break." Raising her hair from her shoulders, he searches for the back of her neck. She feels, for the last time, his mouth against her feverish skin, and trembles slightly.

•   •   •

Sitting at her grandfather's funeral two weeks after Halloween, with Daphne beside her, Kay tries hard to concentrate on thoughts of the man who had played endless card games of war and casino with her during her childhood; who held her hand tightly while the two of them watched *Gunsmoke* and *The Twilight Zone* and *Perry Mason*; who let her listen to her own heartbeat with his stethoscope and look into his ears with his otoscope. She sniffles quietly through the funeral service and more vigorously at the cemetery. Daphne, high-strung and given to melodrama, weeps openly, though her most recent and vivid memories of her great-grandfather are limited to her visits to the nursing home where he'd sat entirely motionless, dazed and senile.

Immediately following the burial, the family and a few close friends retreat to their cars and drive from the cemetery to the house where Kay grew up. There's a light lunch waiting for them there, an assortment of bagels and hard and soft cheeses that Pearline, Kay's mother, had ordered the night before in a wobbly voice not her own.

"So be it," Pearline says now, and adds a slice from a beautiful deep-red tomato to an onion bagel which she hands over to Kay. "Life was good to my father. Except, of course, that he outlived his wife. Men," she says, shaking her head at Kay, "should never outlive their wives. It's not the natural order of things."

"It's not?" Kay says.

"They can't do for themselves like we can, and that's why they should be the ones to go first. Your father, for example, doesn't even know how to turn on the dishwasher in his own house. Apparently, finding the right button to press is too much for him."

"Untrue!" Nathan says, appearing in the dining room from out of nowhere and draping his arm around Pearline. He's a small dapper man who looks a lot like the virtuoso Vladimir Horowitz — coincidentally one of his long-time heroes. (Once, about ten years ago, he happened to see Horowitz himself in the city, sauntering up Madison Avenue with a pretty girl on his arm, but he hadn't found the courage to ask for the great man's autograph, or even to simply nod and say hello. This failure was one of the most deeply felt disappointments of Nathan's life, or so he claimed.) "These hands of mine can do anything and everything," he announces now.

"It's not your hands I'm complaining about, it's your attitude," Pearline says.

"Here we go," Nathan says, and rolls his eyes.

"We're not going anywhere," says Pearline. "I'm officially in mourning for the next seven days and the only plans I have are to sit right here in my house and contemplate the ebb and flow of life. And, of course, receive condolences from anyone who happens to come and offer them."

"Speaking of which," Kay's father says to her, "are we going to be seeing your phantom husband anytime soon?"

"I hope so," says Kay in a weak little murmur. "I mean, absolutely," she tells her parents, who know little of any consequence about her life. "As soon as he finishes with that emergency at work."

"Frankly, I think it was terribly shabby of him to have missed Grandpa's funeral. Owning your own business is tough, of course, but a funeral isn't something you can just skip, like a meal."

"Sell the business, that's my advice," says Pearline. "Why knock yourself out day after day, coming home at ungodly hours, never seeing your family, missing out on practically everything, for what . . . money? What's so wonderful about making all that money if you don't ever have the time to enjoy it? I love David dearly, as you know, but I can't help thinking he's on the wrong track."

Hearing this, Daphne bursts into noisy tears. Kay hadn't even noticed her daughter in the room and now here she is the center of everyone's attention in a tiny black-leather skirt and black tights, her irresistible dark blue eyes spilling tears, her shoulders trembling pathetically. In an instant, Kay is leading her from the table, with Pearline following at their heels, loyal as a dog with a nose for trouble.

"Sorry," Kay says when they arrive at the little guest bathroom down the hall. She snaps the door shut rudely in her mother's face. "Look, sweetie," she tells Daphne, "you promised me you weren't going to do this. Not in front of other people, anyway. And especially not in front of your grandparents. This is just the wrong time for them to know about Daddy and me. You understand that, right?"

"*You* promised me he was coming home, but you lied. I'm not some stupid baby, you know, I'm the smartest one in my class. Of course, it's a very stupid class, but I'm still smart."

"I know you are," says Kay as the doorknob rattles from the outside.

"What's going on in there?" Pearline says, and goes for the door-knob again. "I'm not stupid, you know."

Kay laughs. "This family is overflowing with geniuses," she says.

"Are you making fun of me? I'm in no mood for this, believe me."

Kay imagines her mother's thin-lipped mouth puckered in annoyance, hands slapped against her hips, foot tapping impatiently. Pearline is a big sturdy woman, her bearing confident and even a trifle self-important, and Kay often feels herself shrinking in her presence, losing height and substance and years of experience. Accordingly, she feels like an undersized teenager at this moment, and in need of a good, long reassuring look at herself in the mirror. The one over the bathroom sink is draped with a bedsheet, as is every other mirror in the house; they will remain this way until the period of mourning is over.

Breaking into a sweat, she contemplates taking a peek under the flowery sheet, then decides against it. "Tell me something, cookie, do you think of me as a grown-up?" she asks Daphne.

"Are you crazy? Of course you're a grown-up. My feet are as big as yours, but you're still a grown-up."

"Just checking," Kay says.

"Good-bye and good luck," Pearline calls out, and then there is the welcome sound of retreating footsteps.

Kay combs through her daughter's thick blondish hair with her fingers, pushing the bangs delicately from her face, revealing Daphne's high, freckled forehead. "You're so beautiful," she says, and sighs.

Daphne scoots across the toilet seat cover, and yanks Kay down next to her. "When are you going to tell everyone that Daddy's living in a hotel?"

"Motel," says Kay. "And it's a secret I'll take with me to my grave."

"*What?*"

"I'm just mumbling to myself," Kay says. "Don't pay any attention to me."

"If he's never coming back," Daphne says, "he must be really mad at you. Why can't he just chill out and come home?"

"Sometimes," says Kay, "grown-ups are dumber than you can imagine."

Looking at Kay sharply, Daphne says, "So who's the dumb one — you or Daddy?"

"It's complicated," says Kay. "Too complicated to discuss with you right now."

"I'm ten," Daphne points out. "That's double digits. You can tell me anything, even things that are secret. You can trust me, okay, really." Earnest, and utterly, heartbreakingly innocent, she goes on begging until Kay reaches over, and, without hesitation, catches her daughter's face in her hands and holds onto it, ardently, greedily, staking her claim. "I just can't," she says.

"Oh my God, I really hate you!" Daphne cries, pulling away. "Of all the mothers in the whole world, you're the meanest and the worst!"

"No," Kay says. "That's wrong. No matter what, I've always taken good care of you. That's the way it's always been, and it's the one thing you can always count on." It's a relief to acknowledge this, to feel certain that she has done *something* right.

"So what," says Daphne, unimpressed.

"I see," Kay says. "Would you like to trade me in and try out someone else's mother for a week or two?"

"No way."

"How about an apology?"

"Only if you let me put on some of your makeup," Daphne says.

"One has nothing to do with the other."

"Okay okay okay, I'm sorry I said you were the meanest and the worst. Can I borrow some of your lipstick and stuff?"

Emerging from the bathroom a few minutes later, her lips Electric Lilac, eyelids Coco-Loco, cheeks Rosemist Blush, Daphne seizes Kay's hand and kisses it. "You're excellent," she says. "Totally."

In the dining room and beyond it, in the den, small clusters of people dressed in somber colors are sipping their coffee and talking in hushed tones. It is noon, but all the drapes are drawn against a weak wintry sun, and only a few lamps have been switched on. To Kay it feels like dusk, like the beginning of the end of an exceptionally long day. "There's such a thing as living too long, you know," she hears one of her mother's cousins tell his wife. "I'd blow my brains out before I'd put myself in those adult-sized diapers you see in the supermarkets these days."

"Oh great," says Pearline as Daphne approaches the buffet table. "Does your mother know what you look like?"

"She's feeling better now," Kay says. "End of discussion."

"I'm not even going to *tell* you what she looks like," says Pearline.

"That's good." Kay adds four teaspoons of sugar to her coffee, ignoring her mother's sigh.

"You know how I feel about sugar," Pearline says, and disappears into the kitchen.

The doorbell rings and heads shoot up in surprise; the custom is to simply walk in unannounced, rather than disturb the mourners. The bell signals the arrival of a stranger, someone who surely doesn't know any better.

Kay offers to answer it, and goes to the door, where she nods at a tall stooped man in a flimsy-looking navy blue windbreaker and brand new leather sneakers, unnaturally white.

"Kay Rosen, please," he says politely. As he speaks, his breath makes little smoky clouds in the icy air; he cups his hands and whistles into them, shifting his weight from side to side. Tucked under one arm is a large brown envelope with a perfect circle of a grease stain on it.

"Speaking," Kay says. "And who are you?"

"No one," the man says, and looks down at his new sneakers. "I mean, I'd rather not say."

"Did you know my grandfather?"

"What?"

Sidling up to the door with a cake fork pierced through a chunk of peach pie, Nathan says, "I don't believe I know you, sir. May I ask your name, please?"

"Here," the man says abruptly, and thrusts the envelope at Kay. "Just take this, okay?"

"Hold on a minute," Nathan orders, but the man is already fleeing down the driveway to his car, a two-tone turquoise Plymouth with rusty fins that he's double-parked in front of the house. He stops to light a cigarette, then leaps into the car and races down the street, barely acknowledging the stop sign at the corner.

"Somebody lit a fire under *him*, all right," says Nathan. Swallowing down a mouthful of pie, he clears his fork of crumbs, then taps the envelope with its tines. "Got any idea what's in there?"

Kay says nothing, but her heartbeat accelerates as she undoes the clasp. Beside her, positioning himself so that their shoulders touch, her father breathes heavily and leans over to see what's inside.

"Maybe you won the lottery." Nathan glances at the papers in

Kay's hand, then lifts his eyes to her. "That guy was a process-server," he says in astonishment. "What is this, you're being sued for divorce? Shame on him for serving papers in a home where people are in mourning!" He runs out the door and across the lawn, brandishing his cake fork at no one. Kay goes after him an instant later; when she catches up with her father, he is stabbing a hardy clump of azaleas with his fork.

"That lousy bastard," Nathan says. "I'm talking about your husband, of course. I guess now we know why he didn't show up at the funeral."

"He's not a bastard," Kay says. "Not exactly." Across the street, two little boys in fluorescent-lime down vests are poking each other with branches broken off from a crab apple tree. They throw themselves down, one on top of the other, laughing, and begin rolling along in the grass in a tight embrace.

"*Their* mother's divorced," Nathan says darkly. He digs the toe of his wing-tips into the partially frozen grass. "Well, at least Grandpa didn't live to see this."

"He was senile," Kay points out. "He wouldn't have seen anything." Coatless, trembling in her ill-chosen summery silk dress, she tilts her head upward as her nose begins to run. *I feel guilty for not feeling guilty*, she remembers telling Lance, and the kiss that soon followed, silencing her.

"Only a bastard," Nathan says, offering her his handkerchief, "would decide to serve divorce papers on the day of a funeral. Where the hell is he, anyway, the shameless little creep?"

"He's moved into a motel next to that Chinese restaurant on Route 25 we always go to when you come to visit us," Kay reports. "And I'd appreciate it if you didn't refer to him like that."

"I'm sick," says Nathan as she steers him back into the house. "Heartsick," he tells Pearline, who is watching for him at the doorway, a homemade angel food cake on a platter in her hands.

"My father lived a full life. He had a wonderful career, a loving family . . . there's no need to be heartsick, believe me," says Pearline.

Nathan shoots her a pitying look. "Wake up," he says. "Your daughter's marriage is over. Finished." He gestures with his index finger across his neck as if to slit his throat.

"What?" says Pearline, and whitens. Easing the cake platter into one hand so that she can grab Kay's arm with the other, she says, as if Kay isn't there, "That's impossible. They just finished remodeling the kitchen at the end of the summer. You don't undertake a major project like that when you're thinking of splitting up."

"Maybe they weren't thinking of it last summer. Maybe it's something that just happened," Nathan says softly. "Who knows what they—"

"You're thinking of remodeling the kitchen?" a woman named Lorraine interrupts. She is Pearline's childhood friend, someone who shows up cheerfully and faithfully at every funeral but rarely accepts invitations to anything else. "A new floor wouldn't be a bad idea for you, I'll tell you that. I have this wonderful white ceramic tiling in my kitchen that looks like a dream."

Thrusting the cake at Lorraine, Pearline says, "Be an angel and take this over to the table, okay?"

"I really recommend that ceramic tiling," Lorraine persists, as she ambles away. "Linoleum is so . . . ordinary. And incidentally," she calls over her shoulder, "you look so pale it scares the hell out of me."

"Oh God," says Pearline, hammering herself on the chest a few times. "She's got to go. And so does everyone else. You'll have to ask them to leave, Nathan. This minute."

"That's crazy," Kay says. "I'm the one who needs to go home. In fact, I *am* going home." She imagines herself climbing into bed with Daphne, imagines the two of them clinging together under a comforter, embracing each other til their arms grow heavy and tingly, her daughter's breath warming the side of her face as they drift toward sleep.

Pearline ignores her. "Make an announcement, Nathan. Tell

everyone I'm feeling a little under the weather. It's the understatement of the year, anyway. And if I don't sit down right away, I'm going to faint." Staggering over to a velvet chair next to the piano, Pearline sinks into it with a sigh. "Just get rid of all the cousins and anyone else who's still here."

"It's kind of rude," Nathan begins. "Here these people drove all the way out to the cemetery and back and now you're asking me to throw them out?"

"I'm going home," Kay repeats, and sits down on the piano bench. "Just give me a minute or two and I'm on my way."

Pearline shuts her eyes as Nathan disappears. "Is there someone else?" she says.

"What?"

"Is David having an affair?" Pearline says in a stage whisper. Opening her eyes, she gives Kay a plaintive look.

Kay's arm slips from the music rack where she has been resting it and comes thumping down on the last, deepest octave of keys. The sound is spooky, funereal.

"No music!" Pearline says. "For God's sake, we're in mourning, honey."

"Sorry."

"What about the affair?" Pearline whispers again.

"I don't think so."

"Are you sure?"

Kay nods.

"Well, then, what's this all about?"

One day, Kay fantasizes, when her daughter is old enough, she may share with Daphne what she cannot share with her mother and father; in ten years' time, Daphne will perhaps be forgiving of something that Kay's parents will never be able to make sense of, a truth, for them, as impossible to swallow as a mouthful of sharp-edged stones. She *knows* her parents, knows just how far she can take them.

The place where she has allowed herself to wander, to drift so smoothly and effortlessly, is simply too distant for either of her parents to travel. She will not beg them for a leap of understanding that is beyond them, beyond even their love for her.

"I'm waiting," Pearline reminds her. "You're not going to tell me it's none of my business, are you, because if it's *your* life it's *my* business."

"I see."

"Don't raise your eyebrows at me like that," says Pearline. "You're my baby, that's all I meant."

"Some baby."

Pearline waves her arm dismissively. "I didn't say you were a baby, I said you're *my* baby."

In the background, they can hear Nathan making his apologetic announcement, telling everyone that Pearline is having a little problem with her blood pressure, nothing serious, but that she needs to rest. Soon the cousins and friends are filing past, murmuring sympathetically, taking Pearline's hands in their own, delivering kisses, then finding their coats on the steel rack that's been set up for them in the foyer, before slipping out the door into fresh, winter-cold air. Kay watches them enviously, imagines herself sneaking out unnoticed with the rest of them, her shoulders hunched, head ducked low in shame as she makes her escape, Daphne slouching behind her.

"Well," Nathan says, and closes the front door. "So you got what you wanted—a nice empty house."

"Wonderful," says Pearline, her voice utterly expressionless.

Nathan stares at her. "It's what you wanted, isn't it? Now let's hear what this is all about. Anything you ladies would like to share with me?"

"Your daughter's not sharing anything," Pearline says. "A big mistake, in my opinion."

"Maybe when the time is right," Nathan says, sounding hopeful.

"And then again, maybe never," says Pearline.

Looking down safely into her lap, Kay is silent. "Mom?" she hears Daphne say, and there is her daughter approaching shyly now.

"Can I turn on the TV, Mom?"

"We're in mourning!" Pearline says. "In mourning, for crying out loud!"

Daphne considers this for a moment, then stares at Kay. Her cheekbones are remarkably, ludicrously crimson, her mouth gleaming a purplish-pink, her eyelids dusted heavily with the deepest brown shadow. "Oh," she says. "Oh."

Pleasure Palace

It took me a while to realize it, but the quality of the construction job in my fabulous new bathroom began to deteriorate as soon as the contractor broke up with his lover, who happened to be my hairdresser. Stuart had been doing my hair forever, and he was the one who set me up with Ronnie when he heard that I was in the market for a contractor. I'd been putting off the construction for months, though originally Jordan and I had planned on a starting date of July first. On April 12, Jordan died of a cerebral hemorrhage that had left him brain-dead, lingering in a coma for six days. The hemorrhage was caused by the cancer that had tormented him for a year and a half, but it came as a complete surprise to everyone, including the squad of doctors on the case. The truth was that from the start, none of them had been particularly optimistic, but I never did tell Jordan that, thinking the knowledge wouldn't have been the least bit helpful to him.

He was thirty-four years old when he died; we'd been married for thirteen years and had been in love for even longer than that, since high school.

The last time I saw him conscious, only hours before he disappeared into the coma, he was sitting up in his hospital bed enjoying smoked turkey and Dijon mustard on a croissant. Crumbs littered the bedclothes, and if we'd been home, I would have gone after them with the Dustbuster. But since he was in the hospital (recuperating from a low white count that resulted from his chemotherapy treatments), I just let them stay where they'd fallen.

Jordan was looking pretty good: his bald head was wrapped in a dark blue-and-white bandanna, and the little gold earring in his left ear (I'd pierced it myself with a cork and a sewing needle) gleamed beautifully. He looked like a person who led an exciting life—a rock star or a pirate, maybe. (In fact, he was a lecturer in the art history department of a local college and would have been an assistant professor if only he'd finished his dissertation.) After the first cycle of chemo, he lost every bit of his thick, unruly dirty-blond hair. It fell out in handfuls in the shower over a period of about two months, and one day there was simply nothing left. Jordan was depressed, but not too depressed, because he'd been told it would all grow back—maybe even thicker and more beautiful than before, maybe even a different color, but in any event, it *would* grow back. At least that's what they told him. What they didn't know, of course, was that he wouldn't live long enough for any of it.

That last night, as he sat up in bed with his smoked turkey sandwich, his fingers occasionally went to his temples, which he rubbed in an absent way.

"Headache?" I said after the third or fourth time I saw him do this.

"Umm."

"Want to ask the nurse for some Tylenol?"

"Nope. I can live with it."

We gossiped a while about some friends of ours and the problems they were having with their severely dyslexic son, and then the talk turned to the new bathroom. It was going to be a pleasure palace—large as a generous-sized master bedroom, with a skylight, a Jacuzzi, an elegant sink and new toilet that flushed silently, track lighting, a small bookcase loaded with favorite paperbacks. All the fixtures were going to be black and the floor an imported black-and-white tile that cost a small fortune. The new bathroom would transform our house from a three-bedroom to a two-bedroom, and everyone said that just wasn't good business sense. What if we decided to sell in a couple of years? Who'd want to buy a two-bedroom house?

What if, what if, what if? I said.

We're not going anywhere, Jordan said. Not in two years or twenty. We're just going to hang around forever enjoying our pleasure palace.

"I want heat lamps in the dressing area outside the shower," he told me that last night. "I hate standing there shivering in a towel."

"Me too," I said.

His fingers flew to his temples again and I went out and got one of the nurses. Jordan swallowed down the two Tylenol caplets and lay back against the pillows. I sat by the bed in a salmon-colored plastic chair, holding his warm hand. As soon as he fell asleep I left, though often, during his countless hospital stays, I'd remain a while longer, sometimes breaking down and weeping with frustration, self-pity, hopelessness, studying the beloved planes of his face. That night, though, I walked away from him without having done any of that, dropping a kiss on his cheekbone and hurrying out, as if I had something better to do than watch over him. I did, in fact, have a headache of my own, which was probably why I wasn't particularly troubled by his.

In the elevator, a husky little kid about five or six, and his mother—the only other passengers on board—gave me the once-over. The kid was holding a black plastic box about the size of a small camera, ornamented with a row of neon green plastic buttons. He pressed one of them and there was the electronic sound of a phone ringing.

"Answer the phone," he said to me. When I didn't respond, he said, "*Answer* it."

"Hello," I said. "Wrong number."

The kid smiled and pressed another button. The sound of bombs dropping filled the elevator, and my headache worsened. Then the phone rang again and the kid said, "It's for you."

"She has a headache and can't come to the phone right now," I said. I stared at his mother, a weary-looking, overweight woman in a lavender sweatsuit and matching basketball sneakers. I wondered if it were her husband she'd been visiting and if, like me, she routinely wept every night before going to sleep.

"Really," I said. "I really do have a headache."

"Turn it off, Michael Isaac Markowitz," the boy's mother said. "*Now*."

"I hate you," he said amiably enough, and I understood it might have been me he was talking to.

•   •   •

When Jordan had been in a coma for three days, the sweetest of the handful of doctors assigned to the case took me aside in an empty waiting room and told me that my husband could be taken off the respirator and allowed to die peacefully just as soon as he passed a couple of tests.

"The EEG shows a bit of residual brain activity," he said in a whispery voice. "But that's normal after a massive hemorrhage like this one. As far as I'm concerned, he's brain-dead, but we've got to have a completely flat EEG on two consecutive readings before we can let him go. *If* you want to let him go, of course."

"I do," I said, because I knew that was what Jordan wanted. He was already gone anyway—every time I went into his room to hold his swollen, waxy-looking fingers, to watch the slow rise and fall of his chest, to murmur into his deaf ears, I could see that he'd left me for good.

"But of course I have to talk with his mother first," I said. "Simply out of courtesy. You know."

"Absolutely," said the doctor. We both looked down at our shoes, as if they were objects of great fascination, and then I began to weep, but very quietly. The doctor, who was about my age, opened his arms to me, and I leaned into them without hesitation. He had a good thick head of dark-brown hair, and more than anything I wanted to thread my fingers through it, to savor the feel of a man who wasn't dying. Slowly my hands rose up from his shoulders, but I caught myself in time.

"God, I'm going to hate being single," I heard myself say as I drew back from him. It seemed astonishing that I was capable of saying such a thing and yet there was the doctor nodding his head in agreement and sympathy.

"Your husband was an extremely cool guy," he said. "Very intelligent and funny and . . ." His voice lost energy and trailed off. He looked away from me at a stack of outdated news magazines arranged haphazardly on an end table, at squashed soda cans, and Styrofoam coffee cups marked with lipstick stains left behind by somebody's distracted family.

"And what?"

"And life is shitty."

"Thank you," I said, because it was, at that moment, utterly gratifying to hear the simple mean truth.

•   •   •

The bathroom now has two entrances: one leading from my bedroom, the other out in the hallway. I walk in unannounced from the bedroom and find Ronnie staring up at the skylight, at the snow that is drifting down so lightly upon it. The room reeks of a recently smoked joint and a portable tape player is blasting the lyrics "I smell sex and can-dy." Stepping over a ladder resting on its side, I turn down the music and frown in Ronnie's direction.

"What's up, Ronnie?" I say.

"Oh, stuff and junk," he tells me. He's tall and pale and a little too skinny; he's wearing cream-colored overalls and a black cap with "Beastie Boys" emblazoned across the visor. "It's snowing," he says in amazement.

"I wish you wouldn't smoke pot on the job. It just strikes me as kind of irresponsible."

"Well, we all need to mellow out now and then, you know?" Ronnie says lamely.

I take his hand and lead him to the drop cloth spread out in the center of the room. "Let's sit down and talk."

"We *are* talking."

"Sit," I say, and give him a little push. "I had my hair permed a couple of weeks ago and while I was there I—"

"Oh yeah? It looks good. Makes you look kind of relaxed and freaky."

"And while I was there," I continue, "I heard from Stuart that the two of you'd decided to go your separate ways."

Ronnie's head droops, and with his fingertips he draws swirling shapes on the drop cloth, one after the other. "You heard wrong—*he* decided, not me. He met some lawyer at a Smashing Pumpkins concert in the city, and now it turns out he wants to marry her."

"He *what*?"

"I know," Ronnie says. "It's fucking incredible, isn't it. And who could believe in these dangerous times that a woman would even take a chance with someone like him. But he was married once before, years ago, right out of high school. He even has a kid who's a teenager now and living with his mother somewhere on the West Coast."

I can feel Stuart's capable fingers neatly rolling my hair onto thin plastic rods, can hear the confident, satisfying click of the scissors as he thins my bangs into something feathery. He came to Jordan's funeral in a beautiful dark suit, his hair moussed back proudly.

When he kissed me, I inhaled the scents of his cologne and mousse and face moisturizer, and nearly swooned.

It's beyond belief that there could be a wife in his past and one in his future.

"I'm so sorry," I tell Ronnie. But really I'm not; frankly, I don't give a shit one way or the other. Because my grief is purer, sharper, more deeply felt. After all, *I'm* the widow here; the love of *my* life's been transformed into ash and chips of bone while Ronnie's heartthrob is alive and kicking and heading back to the altar for another shot at it. Call me crazy, but the sympathy vote goes straight to me. And furthermore, I win by a landslide. *So cry me a river, Ron, baby*, I tell him silently.

Sighing, he lights a cigarette with trembly hands. "I'm the enemy," he says. "He's the guilty one, dumping me without even an apology, but I'm the enemy for making him feel guilty. He told me he won't forgive me for that, and that now he isn't sure he ever loved me at all."

"No way."

Ronnie lets out a thin trail of white smoke and begins to cough; tears leak from his eyes. "We were so happy together. You can't imagine how happy we were."

Wanna bet? The loss of my nearly perfect jewel of a marriage pierces me cruelly now. I've lost too much—love, friendship, romance, passion, sex. The sight of Jordan's long narrow almost-pretty feet hanging over the edge of the bed in early morning. The feel of his mouth against the side of my neck. The sound of his voice over the telephone. The sloppy heap of his pajamas and bath towel waiting outside the shower door. It seems no credit to me, but merely a fluke that I've survived these losses. Just a few days ago, going through the top drawer of Jordan's dresser, determined to throw out everything that was still left, I found myself holding his contact lenses in my palm. Weightless, nearly invisible, entirely worthless.

Tenderly I replaced them in their plastic case, as if they were heirlooms.

Raising my head now, I look around in my pleasure palace, at the graceful black sink and matching toilet, at the deep-set Jacuzzi, its chrome hardware dazzling, at the well-placed window that overlooks my snow-covered lawn. Cartons of tile stand in disorder against one wall, Ronnie's tools litter the floor. I get up to examine the shelving he made for towels and supplies of soap and shampoo. The boards are unevenly cut and haven't been planed to a smooth finish. The track lighting has been installed carelessly, at a peculiar angle. And the door that leads out into the hallway, I notice, falls about three inches too short of the floor.

"What's going on, Ronnie?" I say, as if it's all a mystery to me.

"What?"

"Your work was so professional at the beginning," I tell him. "But it's clear your heart's not in it anymore."

"Look, I'm doing the best I can," he says irritably.

"You're coasting," I say. "Just getting by."

"Just getting by," he agrees, surprising me. "I wake up in the morning and I think, 'I can't *do* this.' I can barely brush my teeth. I stand there in front of the mirror with the toothbrush in my hand and I can hear Stuart telling me in a stranger's voice that it's possible that in the three years we were together he never loved me at all. And just like that he's gone from my life and I'm nowhere. I'm not even in this room with you," Ronnie informs me. "I don't know *where* the hell I am."

I'm so angry now, I want to shake Ronnie until he goes limp. *Do you realize who you're talking to, you miserable little self-pitying sad sack?* I want to tell him. *Go cry on someone else's shoulder, buddy.* But then it hits me that maybe by a wild stretch of the imagination I'm the lucky one here, that although there's an excruciating absence of love in my life, a deep hollow I'm almost always aware of, at least I know for sure that Jordan was mine until that very last moment before he slipped away in his hospital bed littered with sandwich crumbs.

• • •

Keeping watch at Jordan's bedside an hour or so before they took him off the respirator, his mother and I could only make small talk. When we ran out of that, we fell into a miserable silence.

I fixed my gaze on Natalie as she touched her brightly powdered cheek against Jordan's ashy one. Sixtyish, her hair dyed an alarming orangey-gold, she was overdressed for the occasion in a pink silk suit and pearls, which she fingered incessantly. Her lashes were mascaraed, and her mouth was polished with lipstick that matched her hair. For whose benefit, I wondered. Hers? Mine? Her comatose son's?

Natalie let go of her pearls and went after a thread on her skirt.

"I bet that suit spends half its life in the dry cleaners," I said. I jammed my hands into the back pockets of my jeans and came up with two sticks of gum. "Would you like a piece?" I offered.

"What's that, wintergreen?" said Natalie suspiciously. "I hate wintergreen."

"It's Winter*fresh*," I said. "It has nothing to do with wintergreen."

"That's what *you* think."

"Well, at least it's not spearmint."

"Actually, I like spearmint," said Natalie. "But every time I chew gum I get a headache, so what's the point?"

I slipped the gum back in my pocket.

Sighing, Natalie put out a manicured hand. "You might as well give me a piece anyway. I'll get rid of it as soon as I feel a headache coming on."

"Well, you can never be too careful," I said.

We chewed our Winterfresh discreetly. "Jordan's in Mexico," my mother-in-law announced after a while, already loony with grief, her voice oddly animated, enthusiastic, even.

"Pardon me?"

"Oh, he's not here. He's in Acapulco, lying on the beach with the sun in his eyes."

"Acapulco," I said. "Of course." Leading her away from the bed, I laced my arms around her soft fleshy back and felt her face tip clumsily against my shoulder. "Acapulco," I murmured. We'd been there several times over the years, enjoying the sharp blue water beautifully surrounded by mountains, the ferocious sun that appeared without fail every morning, the wild, bumpy rides in speed-boats, the leisurely trips in glass-bottomed ones, the wet, pebbly sand under our feet at the water's edge. It was true that we'd taken pleasure in those things. That our life together had been filled with many pleasures.

"Don't you just feel a hundred percent better knowing he's in Acapulco?" Natalie persisted. "Don't you?"

I couldn't bring myself to tell her what she wanted to hear. Jordan was Natalie's only son, her only child, in fact; her husband was long gone. The loss she was about to endure might very well prove too much for her, I thought, sending her over the edge and into some hellish place that I didn't even want to contemplate. She and I had recently become pretty good buddies in the way that soldiers in a foxhole together might, but I was unnerved at the prospect of the two of us clinging fast to each other in the weeks and months to come; I could see us fixed in a weepy embrace forever, our lives motionless as swamp water. What I felt there in the hospital room just before Jordan's death was an extraordinary, overpowering selfishness. And so when the nurse squeaked into the room in her Nikes to tell us that she was ready to start the procedure, I backed away from Natalie and headed for the door.

"Where are you going?" she said, sounding terrified.

"I can't stay here," I told her. "It's like I'd be witnessing an execution."

I could hear Natalie sucking in her breath at the word "execution"; perhaps she understood exactly what I meant. But a moment later she said, "That's crazy. How can you even think of leaving him alone?"

Marla, our favorite of all the nurses, years younger than I was and very pregnant with her first child, squeezed my shoulder. "Some family members prefer it that way," she told Natalie. "But I'm sorry, you can't stay in the room while I'm . . .working in here."

Impulsively, I reached out a hand and placed it on Marla's hard, taut stomach. I felt a couple of good swift kicks and Marla's smile upon me. For years Jordan and I had been ambivalent about having children; when at last we decided to go ahead and give it a try, we learned that I had all sorts of problems that required surgery and more surgery, and so we'd agreed to forget it. Now, of course, I wished I'd been braver, wiser, more resolute. If we'd had children, there would have been something left for Natalie to hold onto, as well.

Examining her stricken face, I apologized out loud for having failed in the grandchildren department.

"Oh Lynnie," she said, and I caught her in my arms as she fell hard against me.

"Take a ride with me," I told her. "We'll drive down to the water and . . ." And what? I was going to make my escape but the truth was I had no plans at all.

"I couldn't," Natalie said. "I have to stay here till it's over. But you go. I'll see you back at the house, I guess."

"Would you like me to call and let you know the time of death?" Marla asked me. "It may take a few hours. Or less. Everyone's different."

I've got a better idea. Would you like to trade lives with me? You give me your husband and your baby and I'll give you nada. Zip. Zippo. Zilch. Deal?

Marla looks horrified.

Can't say that I blame her.

I kissed Jordan on the mouth, my lips unintentionally brushing against the plastic tubing of the respirator that snaked from his mouth and behind his shoulder. "Who knows if I can live without you," I murmured. "Or even if I want to give it a try." My hands lingered along the bones of his skull that lay under the blue-and-white bandanna; lifting my fingertips from him for the very last time seemed the most terrible thing I had ever had to bear. There was a crushing pain in my chest and it occurred to me that I was having a heart attack and would die right there on the floor beside his bed. This seemed a good thing, maybe even something I had willed. But then there I was walking from the room, down a long, waxed, linoleum aisle, past nurses at their stations monitoring the vital signs of the living and the dying and sipping from cans of Diet Coke and joking around with their lovers and husbands on the phone.

Driving home in a trance, I stopped instinctively at red lights, accelerating when they turned green, but seeing and hearing nothing. The pain in my chest subsided and I realized the obvious, that it was only that my heart had turned to glass and shattered soundlessly against the solid brick of my grief.

I walked up two flights of steps to the attic, which we'd redone as a den of sorts before Jordan got sick. The hardwood floor was pickled white and there was a pair of chrome and leather Breuer chairs positioned across the room from a top-of-the-line CD player and a large-screen TV. A triangular window overlooked the Sound below, and I stood by it and watched the sun set, watched as spectacular bands of crimson and deep blue marked the sky. A cluster of anchored boats remained visible as a full glittery moon and a luminous spray of stars appeared. The phone rang on a little table behind me, instantly raising goosebumps all along the path from my wrists to my shoulders. I should have been prepared, but of course I wasn't. Something bitter rose in my throat and I began to choke on it, coughing uncontrollably as the phone went on ringing. After a while the answering machine in my bedroom picked up and I imagined the sound of Marla's voice carefully announcing the precise moment at which Jordan had taken leave of this earth.

There were friends I could call, and my sister in California, my father in Florida. And of course there was Natalie, who would be putting in an appearance at any moment, a woman deprived of absolutely everything, including hope. But I preferred to be here alone in the darkness of my attic.

• • •

"Will you get a grip," I advise Ronnie now. My voice rises unpleasantly. "Tell your sob story somewhere else. How about a chat room on the Internet?"

Ronnie looks at me in astonishment. "You of all people," he scolds. "You—"

"That's right," I say, and then I clam up, saving my breath. But he already knows the worst of it, that I'm running on empty; there's nothing left for anyone but me.

"Listen, I swear to God, I don't know which end is up anymore," Ronnie confesses.

"Go home," I tell him. "Come back to work when you're feeling up to it and not a minute sooner."

• • •

In the evening, after a hot, leisurely bath, I gaze out through my skylight. Loony as my mother-in-law, I watch the sky for signs that Jordan has, at last, arrived at some distant place, perhaps settling himself comfortably on a star as small as the earth, or one infinitely larger, as great as the earth's orbit.

Cold

Freezing, my hands and feet ice-cold as I sleep, I dream that I'm lounging, late on a steamy summer night, on the terrace of a motel somewhere close to home. In the dream, I'm smoking a cigarette, watching the pale smoke drift toward the full, shockingly brilliant moon cast high above me. I watch the swimmers horsing around in the glassed-in pool across a narrow strip of parking lot. A trio of teenaged girls joins hands before leaping all at once into the water, and it is as if I'm viewing a silent film, for I cannot hear the sound of their splash, their good-natured shrieking. Enormous black clouds float along the face of the moon; for some reason the sight terrifies me, and I awaken in a panic. Jesus Christ Almighty, I say out loud to no one. It is so cold I can actually see my breath in the bedroom of the tiny cottage my wife and I had always referred to as our beach house. Until recently, it would never have occurred to me to even consider the impossible expense of winterizing it. But a few weeks ago, shortly after New Year's, my wife, Amy, let me know she'd had enough—enough of me and our ridiculous, wilting, half-dead marriage, she said—and coolly told me to get my things together and scram. When I asked where exactly it was I was supposed to go, she said, in a chilly voice I'd never heard from her before, "I don't know, and truthfully, I don't care. Anywhere out of my sight would be fine."

And so, after offering a clumsy and unsuccessful defense against

Amy's angry list of charges, I'd been evicted from our three-bedroom home just outside of Boston and exiled to the cramped little beach house that sat across from a lovely wide lake where Amy and I had waterskied each weekend in a succession of summers.

This was my punishment for an assortment of offenses, the most serious of which was a momentary affair with a patient who'd come to me with a pair of badly chipped front teeth needing crowns, and who had seduced me two visits later while both the hygienist and receptionist were out on their lunch hour. The patient, a woman named Sasha Resnick, had—just my luck—an irresistible urge to confess to her husband, and it was the husband who called Amy with the news, weeping and cursing and repeating "Why *me*?" until Amy finally lost patience and hung up on him. Other sins, according to Amy, were my failure to spend what she unhesitatingly (and without any irony at all) called "quality time" nurturing our five-year-old son, my laziness when it came to helping out with the housekeeping, my insistence on going to sleep early (and alone) when I'd known from the beginning of our marriage that Amy was a night owl and could not possibly settle into bed before midnight. Listening to her grievances, I'd nodded politely; to appease Amy, to diminish my guilt about Sasha Resnick, I forced myself to admit out loud that maybe I'd made a few mistakes along the way, that somehow, during the seven years of our marriage, I'd gotten offtrack, perhaps turned the slightest bit selfish and self-absorbed.

"I'll clear the dinner table and load the dishwasher every night," I promised Amy. "I'll read Matt's favorite books to him and get him ready for bed instead of collapsing on the couch with the newspaper and leaving everything to you. Those are the kinds of things you've been talking about, right?" I said hopefully.

"Don't try to bargain with me," said Amy. "Screwing that root-canal patient was the last straw."

"It was a couple of chipped teeth," I said, as if that might pacify her. "She was in a car crash and her mouth hit the windshield."

"You're a spoiled little boy," Amy said wearily. "You're pathetic." She had always seemed terrifically energetic, someone I could rely on to keep my life running in good order. Girlishly, she wore black-velvet headbands in her dark, glossy hair, and child-sized clothing that accentuated her flatness, her small delicate bones; even then, when she'd stared at me so bitterly, I understood that I absolutely could not bear losing her.

But I had lost her and any sympathy and patience she had once had for me. Eating dinner every night these past few frigid weeks in the beach house, in my down parka with the hood thrown up over my head, I tried to imagine what might inspire her compassion or her pity. I thought of having a friend photograph me as I sat bundled up, picking at my TV dinner from a wicker snack tray, the maroon plaid scarf around my neck getting in the way of the forkfuls of limp, overcooked beef teryaki. ("This is the man you once loved," I would have written on the back of the picture, "trying his best to keep warm at the dinner table.") Knowing her cold fury and her disappointment in me, I doubted she would have been moved by the image and could see her pinning the snapshot to the refrigerator with a magnet, next to a reminder to herself to call her lawyer.

Now, awakened at five in the morning by a dream of a sultry summer evening, I decide that, like Amy, I have had enough. I will find my friend Josh before work and hint around for an invitation from him for a few nights' room and board, just until I settle things with Amy. Just until the rock-hard ice of her contempt begins to thaw and she is ready to welcome me back. If not into her arms or into her bed, then at least into the spare bedroom with the varnished parquet floor and the antique oak dresser and the twin bed covered with a heavy wool afghan crocheted by my grandmother. I envision myself wrapped in it now, envision my fingertips warm and rosy-looking. (There is a bluish-gray cast to them now, or so I imagine.)

Driving the hour-long trip to my office just after sunrise, I keep the heater in the car roaring full blast, enjoy the film of sweat that coats the back of my neck and knees, that fills the crooks of my arms, the creases of my palms. I stop at a Dunkin' Donuts for a croissant and a Pepsi, and sit at the counter reading someone's discarded newspaper, which, wouldn't you know it, forecasts record-breaking low temperatures for tonight and tomorrow night. In the lifestyles section, I learn that separation from one's spouse or lover can be a wonderful time of personal growth, a time for taking up ballroom dancing or karate or Middle Eastern cooking. *Expand your horizons*, the article urges. *Discover who you really are—a fabulous person capable of just about anything!* I lean my head into my arms and doze briefly at the counter. "Sorry," I murmur as a youngish woman in a pink uniform and frosted hair shakes me lightly. "I was just discovering who I really am."

"Oh yeah?" says the waitress. "Who are you?"

I notice that there is a cast on her right hand, that all of the fingernails peeking out from the cast are ornamented with black polish. "I'm a dentist," I say, though it doesn't feel like the right response. "How did you break your hand?"

"Teaching my kid to ride his two-wheeler. I was running along-side him and tripped over my own stupid feet."

"Is it a new bike?" I say. "What's it look like?"

The waitress narrows her eyes at me. "It's an ordinary bike, okay?" she says. "It cost me $89.95 at Kiddie Kastle and it didn't even come with its own bell. I had to pay extra for that, can you believe it?" Idly (seductively, I think) scratching the side of her face with her long shining pitch-black nails, she says, "Want a refill on that Pepsi?"

I give her a nod somewhere between yes and no and think of my first two-wheeler and its disastrous fate almost thirty years ago. I'd been riding it proficiently for only a week or so when, pedaling it along the perimeter of the Bronx neighborhood where I spent half my childhood, it was stolen out from under me. Incredibly, a family of four—two boys bigger than I was, and their mother and father—approached me with smiles, speaking a language I didn't understand. While the mother of the family lifted me gently but efficiently off the bicycle, the father steadied it on the pavement for one of his sons, who took off with a shriek as the rest of the family raced after him. My own mother and father were furious with me, though I couldn't have been more than six or seven and utterly blameless. Summoning the police, my parents had me ride around in the back of the patrol car, cruising the neighborhood looking for the thieves. This was the worst of it, as I remember—even now I grieve for the small figure sitting desolately in the back seat of a squad car driven by an enormous stranger who joked around with his partner up front, ignoring me except for the moment when he leaned over his shoulder to say, "Tough luck, little guy, huh?" For a long while my parents had refused to buy me another bicycle, and when at last they gave in, they took me to a yard sale and chose some other child's rejected, scuffed-up Schwinn, a bike not even a thief would have given a second look.

"The cast comes off next Thursday," the waitress is saying. "My lucky day."

"That's terrific," I say. I rattle the ice at the bottom of my soda glass, ask if there's a telephone I can use.

Dialing from a pay phone just outside the restrooms, I make a long-distance credit-card call to my parents on Long Island. My mother answers instantly. "What's wrong?" she says.

"It's me," I say. "And nothing's wrong."

"Of course it's you. You think there's a mother on this planet who wouldn't recognize her son's voice, even at this hour?"

"Sorry if I woke you."

"For you I'm always awake." Yawning extravagantly into the phone, my mother says, "Pardon me."

I smile at a baby who emerges from the ladies' room in a stroller, sucking on the tip of a long red-and-green rubber snake. "Remember,"

I ask my mother, "when my bicycle was stolen in the Bronx? You know, I still can't figure out why you were so angry at me."

"Someone stole your bicycle when we were living in the Bronx?"

"It was brand new, a beautiful metallic green. It had this terrific bell, a white button that you pushed like a doorbell; it chimed like a doorbell, actually."

"You never had a bicycle stolen, sweets. Someone once took your best baseball mitt and threw it out the window of the school bus, maybe that's what you're thinking of?"

"You were completely unsympathetic," I remind her. "And then when the police came you told me I had to ride around the neighborhood in the patrol car and find the bicycle. This doesn't sound familiar?"

My mother sighs. "I'm not a young woman, Alex. I can't be expected to remember every little thing that happened to you thirty years ago."

"It wasn't a little thing," I persist. "It was a huge deal, it was a major crisis." Something is digging rudely, sharply, into my back; looking behind me, I see that it's the curved plastic handle of the baby stroller. Realizing the baby's mother is waiting to use the phone, I signal to her that I'm going to be a while.

With a snort of exasperation the woman says, "Thanks for nothing," and yanks the snake from the baby's mouth.

"Who's that crying?" my mother says.

"I'm calling from a pay phone," I say. I watch as the woman glares at me and then takes off with her weeping child, her shoulders bent over the stroller, the rubber snake tucked under her arm, dangling limply, its forked tongue glistening with the baby's saliva. I haven't yet told my mother that I'm no longer living at home, that I've been sleeping in my clothes under a heavy load of blankets, condemned to cold storage by a wife who could not see her way to forgiveness. I decide to skip the announcement of my current troubles and stick to the past, but my mother is already suspicious.

"What do you mean, a pay phone?" she says. "Where *are* you so early in the morning?"

"On my way to work," I say. "I just thought I'd get an early start today."

"You're on your way to work and you stop to make a long-distance call about a bicycle that disappeared thirty years ago?" I hear her repeating this to my father, twice. "Your father's very upset," she reports. "He wants to know if you need anything, maybe a little money?"

"Business is booming," I lie. "You'd be surprised at all the people who aren't flossing like they should. There's still a lot of decay out there, believe me."

"Okay, then," my mother says, though hesitantly. "The family's well?"

"Everyone's fine."

"Are you sure no one's sick? Who's sick?"

"No one," I say. "It's just the bicycle. There were four of them and only one of me. What was I supposed to do?"

I get into my car and ease back onto the busy highway cluttered with rush-hour traffic. When I pull into my parking space outside the low-rise Medical Arts building, I see a little girl hanging around one of the garden apartments next door. There is something old-fashioned about her; her bangs have been clipped comically short and she is wearing a navy blue peacoat, navy leather shoes with a strap, and little white socks. She's about seven or eight, and I smile at her earnest expression as she approaches.

"Have you seen a missing boy?" she asks.

"Excuse me?"

"I'm a member of the Junior Police," the little girl explains, linking her hands behind her back, rocking from side to side, "and we're looking for a missing boy."

"What does he look like?"

"I don't know, but he's been missing for a bunch of years," the girl says impassively. "He might be, you know, dead."

I blink at her in the early-morning sun, dazzled. I wonder if the girl in the clipped bangs and little white socks is real or if I've already begun to lose my grip after so many nights spent in mind-numbing cold.

"You have to go now," I say. "You have to go to school and I have to get to work."

"See you," the little girl says, and salutes me stiffly before running across the parking lot toward home.

My hands are slippery with perspiration; I shake them out in the cold to dry them. "Get your act together, shithead," I tell myself in a whisper. Entering the building, I go first to Josh's ground floor office, where I thump my fists on the locked door until he appears. Josh is a pediatrician; his outer office is decorated with shelves of plastic toys that look manhandled and slightly soiled. There's a VCR running *Stuart Little* in one corner, and a full-sized pinball machine in another. Josh himself is blond and pink-cheeked, a little overweight but immaculately groomed. He's dressed in a heavy cotton sweater patterned with brightly colored diamonds; his expensive tasseled loafers are well polished.

"You look like bad news, buddy boy," he says, as he leads me into one of the three examining rooms he shares with his partners. He asks if I want to come over for a shower tonight, knowing the hot water at the beach house has been only lukewarm lately and that I'm worried the pipes are going to freeze.

Hopping onto an examining table covered with clean white paper, I stretch out on my back, flap my arms dramatically over my chest. "Doctor doctor doctor," I sigh. "I'm a man in need of more than a hot shower."

"Well, you want to crash at my place for a while or do you want to actually freeze to death one of these nights?" Josh slips on his stethoscope and unbuttons my coat skillfully, making his way through a sweater and several layers of thermal underwear. He listens to my heartbeat briefly, then offers a diagnosis. "Self-pity," he announces. "You're clogging up your arteries with the stuff."

I don't know about that, but I'm sure I'm no longer the same self-possessed guy who returned home at the end of each day to a wife and son and the certainty of their love. The thought of warm shelter for the night, for the next couple of nights, exhilarates me, as does the knowledge that it was Josh who did the asking. "What about Marie-Laure?" I say, beginning to worry. "You think your girlfriend's going to be thrilled at the prospect of a clinically depressed houseguest moping around all night?"

"She doesn't want you to freeze to death, either."

"Well, that's good to hear," I say. "Too bad my wife doesn't feel the same way."

•   •   •

Arriving at Josh's expensively renovated brownstone in Back Bay, I present Marie-Laure with a bouquet of cut-rate roses amidst a spray of baby's breath—the best I feel I can afford at the moment. "Very nice," she says, and kisses me on one cheek and then the other. She is even blonder than Josh, and very pale; there's a slight chilliness about her, and also a directness that has always made me wary in her company. I don't like the idea of being indebted to her for anything but cannot see that I have a choice.

"Thanks for having me," I say. "Really."

"It's nothing," says Marie-Laure, who is from Meudon, a suburb of Paris, but speaks nearly perfect English. She's been studying at the B-school at Harvard and has a job in international finance waiting for her when she graduates in the spring. Neither of these facts interests or impresses me much, though maybe if I liked her more, they might. She motions for me to put down the canvas overnight bag stuffed with my belongings, and gives me the once-over; I sense a little sympathy as her gaze travels swiftly up and down the length of me. "You must feel like a displaced person," she says. "You'd think Amy could have waited for warmer weather."

I follow her into the spacious parlor with its fourteen-foot ceiling, and then Josh emerges from the kitchen carrying a scrawny baguette under his arm, and a small teak tray of cheese on his shoulder. "Frankly," he says, "I can't believe Amy's being so hard on you."

"Well, there's no denying I did a remarkably dumb thing," I say. I choose a place for myself on the Persian rug opposite the fireplace. "I did many dumb things, apparently."

"Is she ever going to take you back?" Marie-Laure says. "Or are you permanently in the dog house?"

Am I? This past Saturday, when I went to pick up Matt for our weekly visit, Amy handed him over to me at the door, asked where I was going, told me precisely what time to be back, and then disappeared up the stairs, without even the briefest glance over her shoulder. Perhaps a dozen words passed efficiently between us. "I get the feeling even the sight of me offends her," I say.

"Doesn't sound promising," Marie-Laure observes, and twists off the heel from the end of the bread. Standing at the coffee table considering the brie and *chèvre*, she shakes her head slowly. "I'd say you're screwed, wouldn't you?"

"Knock it off," Josh warns. "Give the guy a little something to live for, for crying out loud."

"Maybe Alex would like to hear how I left my husband once for six months, maybe seven, when I was still living in France. Guillaume called me every single day and then when that didn't work, he sent me notes, sometimes two or three a day. Finally I had to give in."

"But then you divorced him," Josh points out irritably. "No one needs to hear this, believe me."

"It's true that I divorced him, *chéri*, but that was almost a whole year later. So maybe Alex should try sending desperate notes through the mail, it might work, you never know."

"Ever notice this knack she has for passing along just the right story at just the right moment?" Josh says, and I can tell by the way he tilts his head coyly that he's savoring this, every word of it. "What I *really* like is that there's almost never a point to these stupid stories of hers. I can't listen to them, what intelligent person could, but maybe I should start taping them for instant replay, so she can hear how profoundly idiotic she sounds. So what do you think?" he asks me. "Should I get out the tape recorder or what?"

Marie-Laure comes after him now and pokes him in the stomach with the baguette. "You're jealous because my ex was a doctor *and* a lawyer!" she yells. "He was brilliant and he didn't mind listening to my stories at all. He loved them, in fact, he loved everything about me, and I mean everything."

"The poor dumb bastard," says Josh.

"Well, guys," I say, shooting up from the floor, "maybe I'll just go home and count my blessings, whatever those may be." I have the impression I'm talking to myself, that I've become invisible. "Does that make any sense?" I say. "I mean, it does to me."

"Wait," says Josh. "I'm going with you." He smiles broadly, clownishly, as Marie-Laure strikes him over the head now with the baguette, which splits into even halves that fall lightly to the living room floor. And then she gives him a surprisingly powerful shove that nearly causes him to lose his balance. "Are you out of your fucking mind?" he says. "That's assault and battery any way you look at it."

In spite of myself, I laugh, but only for a moment. I would guess, as Marie-Laure throws up her hands and begins to shriek in French, that she is cursing us both. Somehow, I think, I've slipped into the role of troublemaker, bringing my affliction with me and setting off sparks in the middle of my friend's living room. This puzzles me; I have always been a natural at smoothing things over, at restoring peace. Instinctively avoiding conflict myself—in my childhood home, in school yards, in my office, in my marriage—I've always known the right thing to say. And when Matt was an infant and from time to time fell to weeping for no apparent reason, it was me and not Amy who turned out to have the magic touch, who held the baby against my shoulder and endlessly walked the length of our house, murmuring nonsense as I caressed his tiny, velvety back, soothing him into silence. It could not possibly be true, as Amy had told me so accusingly, that I had been a lousy father, that I had lost interest in the pleasures of nestling my son in my lap, of soaping his still-soft back in the bathtub, of listening, while I lay at the foot of his bed at night, to his chatter about kindergarten and his small circle of friends gradually fade as he grew sleepier. Amy had been crazy, I decide now, crazy with resentment and grief, because, in a moment of weakness and also excitement, I'd allowed myself to fall under the spell of a woman offering something irresistible. (In truth, it *had* been thrilling, a hurried, slightly panicky fifteen minutes of exploring an unfamiliar body, a body softer and more voluptuous than Amy's.) Feeling clearheaded now, for the first time since Amy ditched me, it strikes me that I am still a decent guy, a decent father, and probably even a decent husband. I have been walking around for weeks now with my shoulders hunched, my head lowered, as if I could not bear to be recognized. I want to be forgiven, but if that is impossible, the least I can do is forgive myself. Like a prisoner about to be paroled, I've done my time and am more than ready for reentry into the world.

"I'm feeling so great you wouldn't believe it!" I announce, relieved that the words seem heartfelt and absolutely true. Grabbing Josh by the shoulders, I say, "I mean, on a scale of one to ten, I'd put myself pretty high up there."

"Get out of here, both of you!" Marie-Laure howls. "I want you two losers out of here now!" Her pale skin glows crimson with anger; she runs her hands roughly through her pale spiky hair. I stare at the tendons straining in her slender neck as she shrieks at us in French now. "*Vous êtes bêtes comme ses pieds!* What jerks, both of you!"

"Oh, we're going all right," Josh informs her. "But not because you want us to. We wouldn't give you the satisfaction, believe me. We're going because *we* want to."

"Good for us!" I say, seizing my coat and bag in a hurry. I feel myself being yanked from the room and out the door into the bitter cold by my best and wisest friend.

"Keep walking!" Josh orders. "She's standing by the window watching us. Walk *jauntily*, for God's sake."

"Jauntily?" I say. "Like this?" I swing my arms easily, quicken my step. "How'm I doing?" I say over my shoulder. Josh has fallen behind; coming to a halt, I wait for him to catch up.

"Let's go drinking," he says gloomily. "I'm talking about some *serious* drinking, like we used to do in college."

"We were assholes in college," I say. My exhilaration was only temporary, I see, and has already begun to evaporate in the frigid air. Where are we going to sleep tonight? Unexpectedly, I long for the dormitory room I'd shared with Josh almost twenty years ago, a cheerful pigsty ornamented with posters of the Dead, and the Beatles crossing Abbey Road, and littered with balled-up socks and underwear and a carefully constructed pyramid of empty beer cans; in the wastepaper basket under my desk, evidence of the four basic food groups could always be found. My stereo had blasted rudely at odd hours, disturbing the girls who lived directly above us and who periodically pounded on their wooden floor with their heels or a broom handle to show their displeasure. We had lived with a kind of deliberate, adolescent carelessness, Josh and I, sleeping through morning classes, routinely smoking pot on rainy afternoons and weekend nights, always on the prowl for girls who were generous with their bodies and asked for nothing in return. At the start of our junior year, we both decided we were heading nowhere; that was the year we declared ourselves pre-med. Only Josh made it to medical school— I'd shrugged off my disappointment and after a year or so of working as an editorial assistant at a scientific journal, ended up in dental school. Nostalgia overwhelms me now for that two-year fling I'd had with utter self-indulgence, so long ago. How shameless Josh and I had been as we passed one day as idly as the next, hard insistent rock thumping in the background while we earnestly discussed life, about which we knew next to nothing.

"Well, I'm not an asshole anymore," Josh reports now. "I'm just groovy. And also starving."

The dim, nearly deserted bar we've wandered into, just off Comm Ave, has walls made of knotty pine and floors covered with sawdust. There are no menus, but the waitress informs us we can choose between hamburgers or tuna fish on pita.

"That's it?" I ask incredulously, after we've ordered our beers. "You're goofing on us, right?"

The waitress, who is probably not much older than a teenager, bends forward to confide in me. "The cook gets ticked off if you ask for anything else. He's got eggs back there, but I don't think he's doing anything with them tonight."

"I'll have a cheese omelet," says Josh.

"Me too."

"All right," the waitress says uncertainly, "I'll give it a try, but I'm not promising anything." She returns a few minutes later with our Michelobs. "How do you like your tuna?" she asks. "With or without onion mixed in? We've got both kinds."

"How about a hamburger, then, very well done?" Josh says.

The waitress has more bad news. "He shut down the grill for the night. He does that sometimes, when he's really depressed."

"Depressed?" Josh yells. "Tell him I'll write him a prescription for Prozac, Paxil, Wellbutrin, you name it, I can get it for him." More quietly he adds, "I'm a doctor, I can do that, you know."

"The tuna's real good," the waitress says, ignoring him. "It's the specialty of the house."

Taking a sip of beer, I study her T-shirt, which has a drawing of Jesus at the center of her chest, surrounded by numerous little hearts inscribed with the words "He loves me, He loves me not."

"So does he love you?" I ask, unable to resist.

"Stefan?" the waitress says. "When he's depressed like this, he's incapable of loving anyone."

"I meant Jesus."

The waitress smiles sweetly. "Of course He does. And He loves you guys, too."

"All I want," Josh says, "is a simple cheese omelet. I'd go back there and whip it up myself, if Stefan would let me."

"Nothing is ever simple, you know what I mean?" the waitress says, and disappears.

Though I rarely drink at all these days, I finish off my beer in a few indelicate gulps. "She *wants* me to freeze to death, she *doesn't* want me to freeze to death," I say in a singsong as I peel off bits of the label from the beer bottle and toss them over my shoulder. "She wants me to freeze to death, she doesn't—"

"Knock it off," says Josh. "More to the point, will I get my goddamn omelet or won't I? I'm totally starving."

After three beers, our tuna sandwiches arrive on glossy paper plates decorated with the words "Happy Birthday," but I, at least, am too anxious to eat. "I can't stand the suspense," I say. "If she doesn't want me to freeze to death, then it follows that she'll give me a room for the night, maybe not my own room, maybe the room next to it, which wouldn't be too bad, which would be better than sleeping in *your* house, man."

"She'll have to take *me* in, too," Josh says forlornly. "No way am

I going home tonight. Marie-Laure probably changed the locks on me. She was exceptionally harsh, don't you think, tossing us out in the cold like this?"

"Home," I say, sounding bewildered, even to myself. "It seems to me I had a home once. And a family. It was a long time ago, in a little village far away, somewhere between here and there. Every morning I awoke in my big warm feather bed with my princess beside me. And then one day—"

"You're putting me to sleep," Josh complains. "Don't you have any other stories? A techno-thriller, perhaps?"

"Sorry," I say. "Right now it seems to be the one and only story I know."

• • •

During the thirty-five-dollar cab ride back to the suburbs, I can barely sit still; I swivel my wrists and tap my feet to the baroque music playing on the radio up front. Josh rests against me, his eyes closed, his big blond head astonishingly heavy against my arm.

"Wake up!" I command. "Keep me company, will you?"

"Wha?" says Josh. "Wha you talking about?"

"Your speech is slurred," I say, alarmed. "Is my speech slurred?"

"How would I know? I'm only a pediatrician."

Leaning over the top of the seat, I graze the cabby's shoulder. "Excuse me, sir," I say. "Does my speech seemed slurred to you or am I talking like a normal person?"

"As long as you've got thirty-five dollars in your pocket, I don't care how ripped you are," says the driver. "But I'm going to let you in on a secret, okay? You and your friend both could use a little mouthwash. The whole cab stinks, I'm getting dizzy just breathing in the fumes."

"Uh-oh. My wife isn't going to like that."

"Just one more thing to add to her list of complaints," says Josh, murmuring into my sleeve. "Big fucking deal."

"It's necessary to be absolutely punc-til-i-ous," I say with difficulty. "Do you understand what I'm telling you?"

"I can't even hold my head up on my own—how do you expect me to understand foreign languages?"

"Whatever," I say. "I just want things to be right for my homecoming. And if the gentleman behind the wheel says we need a little sprucing up, far be it from me to disagree with him." Taking a comb from my overnight bag, I try to arrange my hair neatly off my forehead. "Notice any improvement?" I ask the cabby, but get no response. As we exit off the highway and drive through the small, darkened town, I feel my confidence waning. I haven't had a shower in two days, and I reek of booze; my hands, as I hold them up to the illumination of a red traffic light, are trembling badly. I'm in no shape to reclaim anything, let alone my wife, my marriage, the home I'm no longer welcome in. "Pull over," I instruct the cabby. "I'm going into that Store 24 over there."

The harshly lit convenience store seems to offer too much of everything, adding to the panic I feel stirring in my stomach. Miraculously, I find my way to the toiletries aisle and a travel-sized bottle of Scope. I ask the cashier for a cup of water, for which I'm charged a quarter.

"You ought to be ashamed of yourself, you cheap bastard," I mumble, and the cashier, a bored-looking kid with a dull silver ring through one eyebrow, gives me the finger as I slam the door. Outside, I stand next to the curb and rinse my mouth vigorously, then spit into the street, a breach of conduct entirely new to me. I feel cheapened by the act, a serious loss of dignity. *This is what you've reduced me to,* I'd like to tell my wife. *This.* Getting back into the cab, I offer the miniature bottle to Josh. "Desperate times, desperate measures," I say.

"Haven't I told you a thousand times not to bother me when I'm sleeping?" he says, and waves the bottle away.

My speech falters slightly as I lead the cabby around a rotary and through a pair of sharp, sudden turns, and then we're home and I'm pulling Josh to his feet. I guide him along the path of slate tiles that follows the curve of the frozen lawn up to the house. "Listen," I say, "try to remain conscious and don't speak unless spoken to."

"Okay, sir," says Josh, "but if Amy viciously attacks you, you can count on me to come to your rescue."

"Don't," I say urgently. "Just stand there like a dummy and pretend you don't understand *nada*." I watch as my finger bravely presses the doorbell, and then I move one step forward.

"Be still, my heart," Josh says, and giggles.

Amy comes to the door in a royal-blue silk robe, my gift to her on one of our anniversaries; underneath, I imagine, is the matching low-cut nightgown that reveals just enough to excite me. I look down at her bare, white, manicured feet, and breathe deeply, noisily.

"What's up?" says Amy, opening the door not much more than a crack. "To what do I owe this honor?"

"You *are* going to let us in, aren't you?" I say.

Without a word, Amy opens the door wider. We slink inside; I contemplate a friendly kiss, then think better of it and stride into my living room, where I plunge into my favorite arm chair. I swing my feet up onto the ottoman, removing them in an instant as I catch Amy's disapproving look, one that tells me not to make myself too much at home. Not in this house, anyway.

"Just trying to get comfortable," I murmur. I wave halfheartedly at Josh, who wanders off in the direction of the first-floor bathroom.

"What for?" Amy remains standing; a warning, I suspect, that she feels no generous impulse, no inclination to settle in for an endless night of impassioned talk.

"You can't imagine how miserable I've been," I tell her. "I'm always cold, always shivering, every single night since I left here." Extravagantly I add, "I think I've got frostbite in my fingertips." I offer my hands, but she will not examine them. "This struggle to stay warm is getting to be too much," I say.

"I *gave* you those two space heaters I found down in the basement. They must help at least a little."

"It's in my bones," I explain. "It's like this sadness I just can't shake. I can't get warm, I'm telling you."

"Maybe you need vitamins," Amy says indifferently, but, to my amazement, there are tears in her eyes. Approaching me, she kneels at my side, lays her head in my lap. "You did this to yourself," she tells me, but nothing more. I stroke her hair, grateful for the familiar silky feel of it under my hand. I remember a shower we'd taken together, a long while ago, the two of us embracing under a steamy spray, our eyes closed, Amy standing on my feet, her privilege. I'd taken our intimacy for granted; shutting off the water, I backed her against the wall of the shower and kissed her from head to toe, knowing I did not have to ask, that she welcomed my touch. And what now, if I were to lead her upstairs and slowly slip her robe from the narrow ledge of her shoulders? I cannot count on anything now, except the certainty that in my own house I am on shaky ground.

"If I did this," I say, "then I can undo it."

Amy lifts her head from my lap, pulls back from me. "I've missed you," she offers. "But where that's going to take us, I just—"

"I'm going to stay the night," I interrupt, emboldened by hope.

She nods. "I want you to understand that I'm not a cold-hearted person, that I'm not that at all. It's just that I can't imagine what it would take to resurrect this marriage. Even thinking about it seems more than I can bear."

"Why do you have to talk like that?" I cry. "What's the point?"

"Fine," Amy says. "I'm going to bed."

"You're not going to stay up all night and let me talk my heart out?" I say, grabbing her by the arm as she picks herself up from the floor. "That was my plan, I think. Or maybe it wasn't." I look at her in confusion. "Do *you* know what my plan was?"

"You're a little drunk," Amy says gently. "But my guess is you were going to give it your best shot and beg me to take you back."

"Something like that." I let go of her reluctantly. "I'm sure I was planning on sleeping in our bed tonight."

"Don't press your luck."

Stung, I will not look at my wife. "Let's go upstairs to my assigned room, then." I head out in front of her, my feet leaden and awkward as I climb the quick flight of stairs. I stand now at the threshold of my son's room, listening to the reassuring sound of his light, steady breathing. Matt's head is at the foot of the bed, his adult-size Red Sox T-shirt drawn up almost to his shoulders; nimbly, I pull the shirt to his delicate little ankles, then turn him around without waking him. I can still do this, at least, I think with satisfaction. Even slightly drunk, I can rearrange a sleeping child with my magic touch.

"Good work," Amy murmurs, and I savor her praise, as though it were something precious. Smoothing back my son's sleep-dampened hair, I bend to drop a kiss next to his ear.

In the hallway, as if I were a guest, I hold out my hands obediently to receive from my wife a small pile of rose-colored towels, a washcloth and my own one-ounce bar of soap, manufactured exclusively for the Marriott Courtyard. I flick on the light switch in the guest bedroom, and the two of us are startled at the sight of Josh asleep on the floor, his arm cast over his eyes, his mouth half-open. Together we cover him with the afghan crocheted by my grandmother, and then I slip a pillow under Josh's heavy blond head.

"Thanks baby," he says in his sleep.

We stand above him, momentarily amused. As I turn to face my wife, it's her wistful smile that breaks my heart. "I wish," I say, raising my arms into the air and then slapping them to my sides, "I could cast a spell over this marriage—"

"What's left of this marriage, you mean."

"I stand corrected," I say.

Amy sighs. "I wish," she recites in a whisper, "I could cast a spell over what's left of this marriage."

And then I'm alone in an unfamiliar bed, hoping for sleep. When it comes, I'm a passenger in an old-model patrol car, my face thrust against its grimy window, searching frantically for a flash of brilliant green metal, listening for the lovely clear chime of a bicycle bell, unable to believe it is lost to me, no longer mine.

Marquise

How hard could it be, you think.

Well, think again.

For starters, the classroom they've given you is perfectly, strikingly ugly; the walls barren, the unpolished linoleum floor littered with candy wrappers, crumpled tissues, crushed paper cups oozing God knows what. Not unlike a movie theatre when the final credits fade and the house lights come up.

"Anyone know where I can find a broom?" you ask.

Two dozen twelve- and thirteen-year-olds stare at you without a flicker of interest.

No broom? Fine. You walk around the room collecting garbage in your small chapped hands. As you're heading for the metal wastepaper basket shoved in a corner near the door, someone beats you to it, a short, delicate-looking African-American kid with a head that's nearly shaved. He spits into the can exuberantly and saunters back to his seat.

"Phlegm," he explains. The class cracks up, giving the kid what he wants. He rises, clasps his palms together high over his head, shaking them left and then right. "Good work, Shane," he congratulates himself.

You understand immediately that this is the one whose mission it is to draw attention from you at every opportunity.

"Very funny," you say.

"*You* don't think so," he says in disappointment.

"You got *that* right," you say.

"Fuck," he says under his breath, and you let it go, pretending you didn't hear.

A white girl in black overalls, her hair woven into dozens of skinny little braids, is peeling a tangerine on top of her desk. She sees you looking at her. "Wassup?" she says.

"Please put that away."

"I'm hungry," she says reasonably. "If you listen real carefully, you can hear my stomach talking."

"Girl, you pathetic!"

"Shut your face, Marquise," the tangerine-eater says, not unpleasantly. "Like I don't see that Cheez Doodle dust on your big fat lips. What am I, blind?"

"Well, here's a news flash for you, Valerie—my lips are the sweetest part of me. And they're thin, too." Taking out a compact from her book bag, Marquise, dark and pretty, inspects her face. "Thin as a white person's," she announces.

"That's enough, girls. I'd like everyone to take out a piece of paper and a pen," you say, sounding so schoolmarmish, you cringe.

"What about the damn tangerine?" Marquise asks. "First you tell her to put it away and then you make like you forgot all about it." She gives you a brilliant smile, revealing splendid white teeth. "You got to take a stand and stick with it, Ms. Whateveryournameis."

Apparently you've forgotten to introduce yourself. "Slater," you say.

"Got a first name, Ms. Slater?"

"Janet."

"Oooh, can we call you Janet, Janet?"

Sure. What the hell. "Call me Janet," you say. "And take out a pen and paper. And hurry up and finish that tangerine, Valerie."

"I don't got no pen," someone calls out.

"I don't got paper," someone else says.

"Borrow some," you say, and almost instantly a blizzard of pens and loose-leaf paper flies through the classroom. "Stop throwing things," you say to no one in particular.

"Can we take a field trip to Burger King?" someone asks.

"Can we watch a video?"

The distinctive odor of freshly made popcorn drifts from across the hall.

"Can I transfer to Consumer Science?" This from a girl wearing a T-shirt with a likeness of the actor John Goodman in a Fred Flintstone sarong.

"What's Consumer Science?" you ask.

"They make popcorn in some kinda scientific way and go on field trips," Marquise offers. "Now why would Dominica here want to transfer into a class like that? Take a guess, Janet."

You close the door, hoping to shut out the popcorn smell. Your stomach rumbles; instead of breakfast this morning, you drank a can of Diet Coke and smoked three cigarettes. You're twenty-nine years old, divorced, the mother of a fifteen-month-old son. You recently left your job as a copywriter at an ad agency because you thought you belonged somewhere else. You thought you belonged here.

Think again.

"No you may not transfer to Consumer Science," you tell Dominica. "You're just going to have to get comfortable here."

"I hate writing," Dominica confesses. "If you ask me to write something, I'll just turn in a blank piece of paper."

"That's because you lazy, girl," Marquise remarks good-naturedly. "You just want to slide right through."

"Yeah, well, they give too damn much homework in this school."

"And the teachers are so damn ugly," the boy who spit into the garbage can says. "They're beasts."

"Shane's right. That bitch Ms. Nolan has a bad hair day every day of the week. I don't know wassup with her," Valerie says.

There's tangerine juice around the neckline of her T-shirt, you notice. And if there's one thing you know for certain it's that Ms. Nolan—Eileen, to you—is no bitch. She does, however, run a very tight ship; classes are orderly, books are actually read, homework is regarded as serious business. There are no guns here, no knives or razor blades concealed in inner pockets or book bags.

So why, when you turn your back and reach for a stick of chalk, is your hand trembling?

"Nobody is to use the word 'bitch' in this classroom," you say as you swivel around and face the class.

"Well, I hate it when that b-i-t-c-h Ms. Nolan blows that damn whistle she wears around her neck in the lunchroom. I hear that whistle everywhere, even in my dreams. Just can't get away from it." Valerie shakes her head vigorously, her braids flying.

"Valerie," you say.

"Wassup?"

"You dis me again and you're out of here."

"Whoa! You hear that?"

"Janet doesn't like bein' disrespected," Marquise says. "Good for her."

"Call me Ms. Slater," you say, having reconsidered.

Predictably, the class groans. You ignore it, having already squandered too much time on garbage collection, tangerines, and inappropriate vocabulary. At the blackboard, you write out a sentence meant to inspire: "I was thirteen years old and still believed that my mother loved me more than anyone ever would."

"What's that shit up there on the board?" you hear someone say.

You clench your teeth, your fists, your toes. You think of your son napping in his playpen, a plastic bottle of milk shaped like a baseball bat protruding from his mouth, and see yourself bending over him to slip the bottle from his juicy wet lips. You unclench your fists.

"The next person who uses language like that in this classroom will receive a failing grade for the year," you announce. "Any questions?"

A hand shoots up.

"Yes?" Your voice sounds squeaky and shrill; it's the voice of a cartoon mouse heading for trouble.

"Can I go to the bathroom?"

You smile with relief. "Absolutely not."

"Please."

Well, maybe.

"Don't make me tell you the reason," the girl pleads. She's a shrimp, like you, with oily hair in a braid long enough to sit on.

You nod. "Make sure you're back in three minutes," you say. "And the rest of you are going to get to work. Write me a story, using the sentence on the board as your starting point."

Another hand is up now, a chubby hand wearing a gold signet ring. "I don't *have* a mother," the boy says. "See, I do, but she moved to Florida."

"That's what she told *you*, Jason, but I seen her right here in the city. In Pathmark," a boy calls out from across the room. "Like yesterday."

"Shut up, Anthony," Marquise says. "You didn't see Jason's mother. Why you sayin' nasty stuff like that?"

Anthony shrugs. "Felt like it," he says.

"Apologize," you say.

"For what?"

"He's an idiot," Jason tells you. "What do I need his apology for?"

Should you pursue this? Before you can decide, Marquise is up out of her seat and rubbing Jason's shoulders maternally.

"Good for you," she says, "you cute little thing, you."

Bless you, Marquise, you say to yourself.

You explain to Jason that the story he is to write should be fiction, the mother in question a fictional character.

Jason looks bemused; he runs a hand through his neat, blow-dried hair. "If my mother loved me so much, why'd she move to Florida with her boyfriend?" he says. "I can't write this story, okay?"

"You dense, Jason," Anthony says. "Don't you know how to write a made-up story?"

"Yeah, but look up there on the board—it says, 'I still believed my mother loved me more than anyone ever would.'"

"The 'I' isn't you," Marquise offers. "You get what I'm sayin'? It's anybody at all, but it's not you."

Jason's soft face searches your own. "It can't be me," he says.

"Get to work, everyone," you say. "And if anyone needs a dictionary, there's one right here on my desk."

There are no takers, but the room is silent for nearly two minutes.

"It's too quiet in here," Valerie complains. "I can't concentrate unless the radio's playing or the TV's on."

"Yeah, me too."

"Yeah."

"Yeah!"

"Now where's she gonna get a radio or a TV from?" Marquise says. "Quit talkin' like such a damn fool," she orders.

"Thanks," you murmur.

"Just doin' my job," Marquise says.

"And what's that?" you ask.

"I'm your lieutenant," says Marquise. "I thought you knew that already."

"As long as you kissin' butt, Marquise, why don't you kiss mine too?" Shane says. He scrambles up onto his desk and shakes his hips seductively. "Come on, baby, pucker up."

You wait for the laughter to die down and then you tell Shane to leave the room.

"You gonna call my mother?" he says, slipping his backpack over one shoulder. "She's just sittin' home waitin' for your call."

"Go out in the hallway and work on your story," you say.

"And write her and me notes apologizing," Marquise adds.

"I don't got no fancy stationery for notes like that," says Shane, and slams the door behind him.

"Get to work," you hear yourself say for what seems like the hundredth time.

Valerie's hand is up, swiveling madly. "Can I go to the bathroom to look for Jaylene? She's been gone way too long. Maybe she fell in or something."

"Stay in your seat," you say. "I'll go." You put Marquise in charge. "Act your age, not your shoe size," you warn, and hurry out.

In the bathroom, Jaylene is perched on the window sill, blowing smoke rings like a pro. The three army-green stalls are empty, you notice. You bum a Marlboro Light from Jaylene; it's clear you're both sworn to secrecy. She lights the cigarette for you, tosses the match out the open window. You inhale deeply exactly twice, then crush the cigarette under your foot. Mutely, Jaylene offers you a Tic Tac.

"Smoking is disgusting," you say, in case she hasn't heard this before. You deposit the Tic Tac daintily in your mouth.

Jaylene shrugs her little shoulders.

"Don't ever ask me to let you out of class to go to the bathroom," you say. "The answer will always be no."

"Okay," she says, and it's a comfort to know you understand each other perfectly.

• • •

You and Teddy, your son, are having an early dinner together. His aluminum-and-plastic Sassy Seat is clipped onto the edge of the dining room table; on the floor underneath him, you've wisely spread a section of yesterday's New York Times. Without warning, he begins throwing bits of American cheese from his plate to the floor. "Bad bad bad," he says.

"What, you don't like cheese anymore?"

He makes a grab for your slice of pizza, leaning rudely into your plate.

"Spicy," you say, then tear off a ragged strip of crust for him.

"Mmmm," he says. He smacks his lips, seizes the piece of crust, sucks on it joyfully.

"So tell me about your day," you urge. "You went to the Y to your Mommy and Me class and hung out with your pals, right?"

"Jess," he says, referring to his baby-sitter.

"Did I say 'Mommy and Me?' Let's call it 'Care-giver and Me.'"

"Yes!"

"As long as you had fun."

Now he's reaching with both hands for an almost-empty two-liter bottle of Coke. Raising it to his lips, he positions the bottle straight up into the air and drains the last mouthful. "No more!" he proclaims, and casts the plastic bottle onto the floor.

"That's naughty," you say. "We don't throw things."

"We do."

"We don't," you insist. "If we do, we go straight to our crib, where we sit and think about where we went wrong."

Glowering, he says, "Dat's bad."

"Dat's true," you say. "And dat's why we make every effort to be on our best behavior at all times."

"I best boy," he says proudly, and flashes a winning smile in your direction.

Unlike his father, who knew just how to break your heart, this boy can do no wrong. You sweep him out of his seat and into your lap. You kiss each of his fingers one by one, and make him promise that, no matter what, he will never leave you.

•   •   •

In several of your classes, there are a handful of endearing little girls who want to please you; the poems they offer you are of snowstorms, sunrises, and family pets. The rest of the girls specialize in personal essays about their best Christmas ever, TV stars they have crushes on, what it's like to share a bedroom with three younger sisters. Most of the boys are obsessed with murder and only slightly less violent acts. Their stories are filled with severed limbs, knife wounds from which thick red blood flows, sadism, and exclamation points strung together till they spill off the page. They dream of matricide and patricide, of blowing away the math teacher who assigned a double load of home-work over the weekend, the assistant principal who booted them from an assembly program for laughing disruptively. Powerless, they're itching to pull the trigger on an endless supply of imaginary guns.

• • •

By the end of your first month, your hands no longer shake in class. By the end of the second month, you think you've seen it all.

Think again.

Marquise, unfailingly cheerful and expansive, self-proclaimed lieutenant, writer of clever haiku about friends and family, turns in a story that makes your jaw drop and your heart sink.

Her handwriting is small and neat, easy to read, her spelling flaw-less. Reading through student papers late at night, you habitually save hers for last; it's the elegant dessert at the end of a long unsatis-fying meal.

You're on your living room couch, ankles crossed on the coffee table, cigarette in hand.

Debbie and I were in love with the same guy. I didn't know this—I thought he was MINE. Well, I was wrong.

I went to her house one night without calling first.

Big mistake.

The door was unlocked and I went in. The house was empty. I called Debbie's name. No answer. I went to her bedroom. She and Shawn were there, lying on the bed, breathing hard.

"Go down on me, baby," Shawn said in a husky voice. "You know what I want, baby."

I just stood there—I couldn't move. It was supposed to be ME giving him that blow job, not Debbie.

My eyes filled up with tears. I wanted to kill them both and myself too. Instead I ran out of the house. I didn't know if they saw me or not. I didn't care.

They were fuck buddies and I was all alone.

I never felt so alone in my whole life.

Your eyes burn with fatigue; you close them briefly. You remind yourself that Marquise is twelve years old. You've never felt so middle-class. So clueless. So fucking dumb.

In the bathroom mirror, your face looks pasty. The light of intelligence is absent from your eyes.

The next day in class you play it cool. Marquise is her usual buoyant self. With her hair pinned neatly in a bun, she looks especially pretty. When you call for volunteers to read a Katherine Mansfield story aloud, her hand shoots up immediately. You intend to stop her after the first page and move on to another student, but she's reading so beautifully and with such conviction, you let her take it all the way home.

"Poor Miss Brill," she says with a sigh when she's finished. "She's gonna be lonely for the rest of her life."

"You think so?"

"Oh yeah. She may even go and kill herself," Marquise says with a half-smile.

At the end of class, as everyone files out, she stops by your desk. She's tall and womanly; you imagine her in a dark business suit and pearls instead of the overalls and low-cut leotard she's wearing. On her feet are big pink basketball sneakers, clown shoes, really. "You read my story?" she asks.

Your face feels scorched, as if you've been humiliated by the memory. You go to the door and shut it hard.

"Wassup?" says Marquise. "You got a problem with my story?"

Pulling out your desk drawer, you find a bag of M&Ms that doesn't belong to you. Unable to open it with your fingers, you resort to using your teeth. You offer Marquise a handful.

She picks out two blues and a chartreuse. "Am I in trouble?"

"The story was inappropriate," you say. Your hands are sweaty, and the M&Ms are beginning to bleed. You can't think what to do.

"You mean the blow job part?" Marquise says with astonishing ease, and helps herself to more candy.

"This is school," you say. "You're twelve years old," you add helplessly.

"Twelve and a half," Marquise says, chewing. "So what? You always say we can write about anythin' we want. And so that's what I did."

"There are certain boundaries . . . common sense," you murmur. *Blah blah blah*, you hear yourself saying.

"Whachu talkin' about? Spit it out, girl."

"Look," you say, and stare past her into a corner of the room. "I don't want to read about the intimate moments of your boyfriend's life. And I shouldn't have to." You wait for her to tell you the story is pure fiction, but all you hear is her throaty laughter.

"You wimpin' out on me, girl! And you know, he's not my boyfriend. Not anymore. You think I'd be with him after somethin' like that?"

You shrug: how would *you* know? "Please don't call me 'girl,'" you say.

Marquise leans forward and ruffles your hair fondly. "You don't like that? It's a whachamacallit, a term of endearment, you know?"

You're flattered, you tell her. "Thank you," you say primly.

"You gonna fail me?"

You count the ways: by not informing the school psychologist of the contents of the story, by not delivering a lecture on safe sex, by not phoning her mother and letting her know just what her twelve-year-old is up to.

"See, if you give me an F on this story I'll be real disappointed in you," Marquise says. "Because *I* know that *you* know it's a nice sad story. It made you cry, right? Because men cheatin' on their ladies is the saddest thing there is. Or maybe it just feels that way."

Silently, you nod. And then, unwisely, you open your big mouth. You tell her what you've never told anyone: that Phil, your ex, left you for someone smarter, prettier, funnier. Or so he claimed. Never having met her, you just had to take his word for it.

"Kill the b-i-t-c-h. Kill them both," Marquise recommends. She casts her long arms around you. You feel her heat; it settles over you like a silken shawl, soft and light.

Outside in the hallway, the next class is waiting, your students jostling each other impatiently, bumping up against the door, letting you know they're ready for you.

"Gotta go," Marquise says, and heads jauntily for the door. "Be cool," she says over her shoulder. "You got that?"

Maybe you got it and maybe you didn't, but at least you got somethin'.

Like Something in This World

Mistake number one, I suppose, was giving up the rent-controlled apartment I'd shared with my wife for almost twenty years. The apartment, which had a terrace that overlooked the Hudson, a pair of generous-sized bedrooms, and a kitchen you could actually eat in, was only three minutes from Lincoln Center. Sunk low and deep in misery after the sudden death of my wife, I'd barely been able to lift my head from my shoulder to stare at the TV set that I kept running continuously, at a weak murmur for days on end, just for the sound of its voice. Gradually, body and soul taking their own sweet time, I'd snapped out of it and back into my old restless self, the one Ellen had complained about in her good-natured way all through the three-and-a-half decades of our marriage. By that time it was too late; I'd already moved into my son's house in the suburbs, just outside of LA, which was mistake number two. I was barely into my sixties; what could I have been thinking? Warren and Nancy, his wife, had arranged everything while I looked on in a teary-eyed daze, allowing my son and daughter-in-law to decide what would go into storage and what I could take with me, what belonged in the trash and what was worth saving. God knows what treasures I'd allowed them to give away to Goodwill or, even worse, toss down the compactor. Doped up on Valium left over from the morning of the funeral, I'd seen it all and missed everything. But, as Ellen had been fond of saying about all the earrings and cuff links and gloves and umbrellas we'd ever lost, there was no sense in crying over anything that couldn't cry over you. *Good advice, Elno,* I whisper in my bedroom next to Warren's vast, cluttered two-car garage. Formerly my grandson's Nintendo room, its walls are still decorated with posters of Shaquille O'Neal in midair, palming the ball, dwarfing it, about to dunk; the Simpson family in their bizarre hairdos; a kitten poised over a chinning bar, with the words "Hang in there, baby!" spelled out in enormous letters above the poor little guy. *Elno Elno Elno.* Sometimes, lying in bed, I think I can still smell the faintly sweet aroma of her honeydew-scented moisturizer on my pillow as I try desperately to fall asleep in this little-boy playroom I've taken over as my own. Predictably, nights are the toughest, the time when I find myself longing for my wife's old-fashioned softness, that generous fleshiness I could sink my fingers into, and occasionally, gently, my teeth. If she had lost the extra thirty pounds and given up her cigarettes she might be lying beside me in our former bedroom high above the Hudson River instead of in a small silver urn plunged into cemetery dirt. Sniffling, I remind myself that, like all those lost umbrellas and gloves, she can't respond to my grief. A perfectly valid reason for the most self-pitying kind of tears, I decide, and let myself go, even though it's the middle of the afternoon and someone is knocking boldly against my door.

"Jake?" Nancy calls. "Anything you want from the supermarket?"

"Hold on a second," I say, and run a wrist across each eye before opening the door. My daughter-in-law, the mother of my two perfect grandchildren, is a pretty, red-haired pip-squeak, barely five feet tall and very self-possessed. I wish I liked her more, wish I felt deeply grateful to her for having taken me into her home, her five-bedroom, four-bath kingdom with an in-ground pool and hot tub out back. Asking me every night to turn off the news and wash up and come to dinner, the tone of her voice seems to suggest that I'm just one more pain in the ass adding to the ordinary confusion of the household's daily life. She knows all about me, too, all about the string of not-very-successful businesses I'd owned—the small jewelry shop in Greenwich Village, the used bookstore, the discount sneaker outlet I'd finally sold at a small profit. In another life, I'd been one of those well-loved teachers in a noisy, over-crowded high school in the city, but after twenty years, I'd had enough. I'd never hungered for money or success, but had simply wanted to earn a living and enjoy whatever leisure time was left over at the end of a day. Ellen had accepted me, without disappointment, as a man of modest ambition; if she'd had dreams of something greater for me, for us, she never let me know it. But it's pretty clear that Warren, and Nancy, too, view me as someone who couldn't quite cut it, someone easy to dismiss. I see it in the way they only half-listen when I'm talking, as if I couldn't possibly be saying anything of real consequence or substance. It's Warren, a slight, boyish-looking guy with a perpetually worried air about him, who's the success in the family. A personnel manager for a Japanese-owned corporation in LA, he earns a surprisingly hefty salary and has a secretary to order his breakfast and cancel his dentist appointments. These facts don't intrigue me much. What does intrigue me is the fact that Warren's stomach goes bad whenever he has to fire anyone. *I feel for people*, my son boasts; on a particularly lousy day, he can only handle soup and dry toast for dinner, or sometimes no dinner at all. This is a crock, I think. *Feel for* me, I want to say. *Make me feel like something in this world.*

If only I had enough for a comfortable place of my own, I'd be out so fast there'd be a heart-stopping squeal of tires and the smell of burning rubber in my wake.

Perhaps I'd even take my grandchildren with me; a five-year-old and an eleven year-old, they're smart enough to recognize that I'm the one with a natural talent for keeping them happy. I take them roller-skating and ice-skating and let Zachary, the older one, soar ahead while I stay behind with Sara, patiently urging her on one hesitant step at a time. At the library, I set up Zachary in the children's wing with a paperback copy of *To Kill a Mockingbird* or *Cheaper by the Dozen* and sit with Sara at a Formica table, listening to her puzzle out the simplest Dr. Seuss books, her sweet little mouth set earnestly in concentration. I've bought them Sixties rock-and-roll CDs (music I learned to love from my students years ago) and a portable CD player, and let them blast it in my room as the three of us dance ourselves into a satisfying sweat. One afternoon, home unexpectedly early from a tennis lesson, Nancy walked in on us just in time to see me spinning Sara out from under my arm in a dizzying circle as Zachary played air guitar and a raucous-sounding Mick Jagger sang *Jumpin' Jack Flash*. "You're all going to go deaf!" she shrieked. "But who cares, right?" She marched out of the room, slamming the door like some pissed-off adolescent. When I ran after her, she looked at me unhappily for what seemed like a long while, as if she just didn't know what to make of me. "You're kind of a weird guy, Jake," she said finally. "And actually, sometimes I sort of like that."

Staring at her in surprise, I said, "I thought I was just your standard pain-in-the-ass father-in-law."

This appeared to bewilder her further, and she began to walk away. "Listen, the truth is I'm premenstrual," she called out over her shoulder. "Everything you say and do today is going to get on my nerves."

"I won't take it personally, then," I said hopefully.

"Right, fine, whatever."

"I'm off to Food Fair," she tells me now. "Watch the kids for me?" Dressed in black Spandex pants and a matching halter top, her hair gathered back in a high pony tail, she looks like a teenager. Her legs are shapely in her skin-tight pants; the sight of her smooth bare midriff moves me in ways I'd rather not contemplate.

"Give me your shopping list and I'll take the kids with me," I propose.

"Really? Thanks," she says, sounding genuinely grateful and startling me with a quick, cool kiss on my cheek, a rare offering. "But promise me you'll go easy on the junk food, okay?"

I promise her nothing and take the list, three twenties, and her car keys, which dangle from a miniature canvas-and-rubber basketball sneaker.

"I wish you were happier here," she murmurs, and flees.

Fifteen minutes later, attempting to maneuver Nancy's two-month-old Mazda into a tight parking spot between a pair of greedy Range Rovers, both of which have taken up too much space and gone slightly over the painted yellow lines, I feel the sweat gathering in the hollows under my arms. "Great," I say, and decide to give up and look elsewhere.

"Who do you like better, Grandpa," Sara says from the back seat, "the Beatles, the Stones, or the Byrds?"

"That's a dumb question, jerk," says Zachary. "He likes all of them."

"Knock it off," I say automatically, and pull into a space miles from the supermarket, which seems to shimmer like a mirage in the distance in the surprisingly steamy summer heat. I settle Sara on my shoulders and keep a hand clamped tight around each of her ankles.

"Why did we come with you?" Zachary complains. "It's so beeping hot out here. I wish I were back home in the pool."

"What are you talking about? You *love* coming to the supermarket with me," I remind him.

"Yeah," says Sara, and pats the springy gray hair at the sides of my head. "Can we buy chips?"

"Your mother says no," I report, just for the record, and all of us laugh, knowing I always let them have their way, that every excursion to the supermarket with me results in an accumulation of junk food that I have to hide in the closet in my bedroom, out of Nancy's sight. Inside the store now, the arctic temperature raises goosebumps along our uncovered arms. We whiz up and down the aisles, with Sara in the back of the shopping cart shrieking joyously. A woman dressed in a low-necked one-piece bathing suit and metallic gold sandals pushes a sleeping infant in a stroller; she shoots Sara a dirty look as the baby begins to stir.

"Lighten up," I urge the woman, as the three of us speed past her toward the dairy counter, where we select enough containers of Nancy's favorite low-fat cottage cheese to last her a lifetime. At the soda aisle I load up on six-packs of Pepsi and then we're off to the snack section, where puffy cellophane bags of chips line the shelves in flashy colors. Leaning out of the cart excitedly, Sara grabs an assortment, reciting, like a litany, "Mesquite, jalapeño, barbecue, vinegar-and-salt, ranch," until at last I sweep her arms from the shelves and away from temptation.

"You're a terrific reader," I say. "You're doing great."

"She memorized them," says Zachary, unimpressed. "Big deal."

"I did not. I *read* them."

"So what, retard."

Patting Zachary's soft cheek edged with white-blond fuzz, I warn, "Put a lid on it, buddy." I watch placidly as they tear open a couple of the bags and dig in right there in the store, something Nancy would never have allowed. I can feel her disapproval long distance, can see her eyes narrowing, hear her saying, *Don't you have any sense at all?* "Big deal," I murmur, echoing the sound of my grandson's indifference. My wife is gone, taking her love with her; in her absence there's only my grandchildren, who adore me openly, and, perhaps, blindly. A fine orangey dust ornaments their mouths and fingertips; unable to resist, I seize a couple of Sara's tiny fingers and suck on them lightly, tasting salt and also something peppery.

"Grandpa!" she says, but does not reclaim her hand.

"Delicious," I pronounce.

The cashier at the check-out counter, a thin, sour-looking teenager whose name badge says "Precious" on it, rings up our groceries without comment. The outer rims of her ears are studded with seven different colored stones; I enumerate them silently. "Having a party?" she says, tossing the bags of chips into a paper sack.

"Something like that."

"Can I get my ears pierced, Grandpa?" Sara says.

"That's your mother's department, you'll have to ask *her*."

"She says when I'm sixteen."

"Ha!" says Precious.

"I love all the colored diamonds in your ears and your pretty red lipstick," Sara offers.

"Uh-huh," says Precious, and makes an effort to smile at her. "Want to come home with me and be my little girl?"

Sara looks frightened; her eyes open wide and she takes a step closer to me. "Do I have to?"

With a noisy sigh of contempt, Zachary says, "Slick, Sara. Real slick."

"This little girl right here is spoken for," I say, scooping her up and into my arms. "You're mine," I say, and slip into my fantasy of moving back to New York with my grandchildren, back into my old apartment overlooking the dark, silent river. I'd have to give up a bedroom to each of them, leaving me with nowhere to sleep but the living room couch, only a small sacrifice, really. I can see myself pleasantly burdened with all sorts of responsibilities I've never undertaken before; cooking decent meals for the kids, shampooing Sara's hair for her and helping her comb through the knots, battling to get Zachary to practice the saxophone every night and then into bed on time. I know I'm a pro at safeguarding their happiness; the rest will come easily enough. (In my fantasy, Warren and Nancy are out of the picture entirely, inhabiting another, distant universe.) I know, too, exactly what I am, just a loony old geezer, wanting what he can't have. A weariness overtakes me now, a weary confusion. I have no idea where I'm going; I can't predict my future with any clarity at all.

The shopping cart I'm propelling into this startling August heat seems unbearably heavy, and I have to ask Zachary for a hand.

"Are you okay?" my grandson asks. "You look kind of sick."

"Oh, I'm a winter person, I guess—I'm never too happy when it gets this hot."

"I'm just like you," says Sara. "My hair gets all sweaty and I feel dee-spicable." Laughing, I buckle her seatbelt and listen carefully to the secret she whispers into my ear. "Zachary said he'll put a knife in my heart in the middle of the night if I tell anyone, but guess what: he's from another planet! And that means he's adopted, you know." She's smiling so broadly, so triumphantly, that I don't have the heart to set her straight.

"Is that right," I say, and go around to help Zachary unload the half-dozen bags into the trunk. "So, I hear you're from Mars," I tell him casually.

Zachary blinks at me. "Uranus," he says. "And that's classified information."

"Try being a little nicer to your sister."

"What for?"

"What for? Because life is short, how's that."

"I don't know what you mean," Zachary says, looking truly perplexed. Hanging just past his collar is a feathery little rat tail left behind by the barber at Zachary's insistence; I can't resist giving it a gentle tug.

"Of course you don't," I say. "Get in the car and let's get going."

I run the air-conditioning a minute or two and then put the car in reverse. I try to remember if there was ever a time when I was young enough to believe that life went on endlessly, a time when the days and years of my life passed so slowly I barely noticed. In an instant, the rear end of Nancy's almost-new car collides with the bumper of the enormous old Cadillac parked to our right, and there's the sickening sound of what I know is a taillight fracturing.

"Shit!" I say, and my grandchildren laugh, delighted. "Shit shit shit." Hurrying out to assess the damage, I see immediately, and with relief, that it's all mine, a broken taillight and nothing more. But for Warren and Nancy, I know, it's evidence to be held up and examined in the harsh bright light of their general disapproval. Stooping to sweep away the bits of shattered red plastic, I feel my face flush with humiliation.

"Are we in big trouble?" Zachary asks eagerly when I'm back behind the steering wheel again.

"Nope."

"We're not?" Zachary persists. "How are we going to get home?"

"Watch and see." Easing the car forward and back and then out of the spot entirely without sustaining any further damage, I congratulate myself silently.

"We could say someone smashed into us," Zachary suggests. "That way we won't get screamed at."

"Not to worry," I say, pretending fearlessness. I switch the radio on to a station that boasts of playing strictly classic rock and roll, and take comfort in the sound of Jim Morrison's urgent voice. "Try to set the night on fi-re," I sing out at a red light, thumping on the steering wheel with both hands.

"Some people," says Zachary, "go crazy when their cars get wrecked. Like, you know, my dad's old MG that he used to have? Actually, maybe I shouldn't tell you this."

"Go ahead," I say. "I'm not afraid of anyone. Especially not your father." I think of Warren and his three pairs of identical shoes, old, worn Top-Siders that he leaves out for himself, one pair each, just inside the front, back, and side doors of the house. "So I'll always have a pair waiting for me," he'd explained to me, "no matter which door I happen to come in." Not a man to be afraid of. I remember him as a three-year-old entrenched in routine, insisting on drinking his apple juice only from his Rocky-and-Bullwinkle plastic mug;

unable to go to sleep at night without counting backward from ten and then twice forward; unable to sit on the toilet unless every bit of his clothing was off. My son, I remind myself, is a man with a wife and two children and three pairs of the same shoes placed precisely where he needs them.

". . . and he kept the MG in the garage all covered over with this special cover he had to send away for from a catalogue," Zachary is saying. "One day he'd just finished polishing the whole car and then the cat jumped up on the hood and scratched it with his claws. And then guess what," says Zachary, pausing for effect. "My dad was so mad he broke a broom in half, just snapped it in two pieces and threw them at the cat. She ran away and we couldn't find her for two whole days."

The thought of the cat sweeping its claws along the MG's shining hood makes me slightly giddy now, and I almost laugh. "Don't worry, nobody's going to throw a broom at me," I promise. "And if they do, I'll just jump out of the way."

Pulling into Warren's smooth blacktopped driveway a few minutes later, I feel an unpleasant pinprick of fear between my ribs, like a stitch from walking too fast. I stretch my legs out onto the blacktop and listen to the furious, sharp buzzing of a hidden colony of cicadas. My son's well-groomed lawn is littered with a couple of bicycles, a pogo stick, and a doll carriage with a pair of pink plastic shoulders and a curly blond head leaning precariously over the side. I hear the sound of water splashing and the high thin shriek of the neighbor's kids in their pool next door.

Indoors, the house is blissfully cool and silent. I see two heads in the swimming pool beyond the kitchen's sliding glass door and a flash of bright yellow towel draped along a plastic beach chair. An arm glistening above the water waves to me as I slide open the door. Behind me, Zachary and Sara are stripping off their clothes and grabbing their bathing suits from the kitchen table.

"The water's perfect," Warren calls out amiably. "Get into your suit and hop in."

"I don't owe you any money, do I?" says Nancy. She side-strokes to one of the ladders and hoists herself onto the top step. "And thanks a lot for going out for me."

"You don't owe me anything," I say, trying not to stare at the sharply defined outline of her breasts as I approach the pool. I roll up my chinos and pull off my shoes and socks. Cupping my hands, I dip them into the water and soak my face and hair. Water trickles down the open neck of my polo shirt; underneath, the staccato pulsing of my heart speeds up frantically. Searching for any inspiration at all for courage or optimism, I remember one of the last days I spent in New York: after tidying up some paperwork at the bank nearly six months ago, still feeling grief-stricken and low, I'd leaned exhaustedly against a pillar in Grand Central, waiting for the train that would take me back to the West Side. Nearby, I noticed a well-dressed middle-aged woman standing alone, fingers flying and thumping in her palm excitedly, a hand occasionally rising to her mouth or tracing shapes in the air. Watching in fascination, I'd suddenly understood that the woman was a deaf-mute, talking to herself in sign language. Mesmerized, I couldn't take my eyes from her, couldn't imagine what it was that had brought her to such a state of agitation. I'd wanted to touch the woman's shoulder, catch the flying hands in my own, offer her *something*. In that moment I saw my old self within reach, saw that I could reclaim at least something of my old life. I watched, relieved, as the woman gradually quieted, her arms coming to rest, at last, at her sides. Hurrying toward a newsstand, she bought a cellophane bag of dyed red pistachios for herself and then disappeared.

"Well, the bad news is I wrecked one of the taillights on the Mazda getting out of a parking space," I address the back of Nancy's head. "But the good news is the other car was fine. And of course I'll pay for a replacement if the insurance doesn't cover it."

Nancy whips her head around at me, her wet ponytail slapping against her neck. "With my kids in the car?" she says. "That kind of stuff can't happen with my kids in the car. Not ever."

"The kids are fine," I tell her. "The truth is, it could have happened to anyone."

"What the hell is your goddamn problem?" yells Warren, who's just within earshot, floating idly on his back. Swimming underwater to the side of the pool now, he surfaces with a lot of noise, flinging his arms above the water dramatically. "For crying out loud!" he says, looking straight through me. With his wet hair slicked back tightly across his skull, his mild features seem sharpened, his face a trifle menacing.

"It's not the end of the world," I point out. "It's a simple piece of plastic we're talking about here." At the far end of the pool, Zachary leaps above the diving board, his skinny arms and legs beautifully arranged in flight. I close my eyes as he vanishes beneath the water.

"You *know* how I hate it when things go wrong, goddamnit," says Warren. He slaps at the pool with his open palm, splashing water in his face. Hauling himself onto dry land, he says, "I'm too freaked to even go look at the car, you know that?"

"Does this mean I'm grounded?" I ask, and laugh at what I see: a teenager who's just reported the bad news to his father. I'm waiting to hear that my allowance has been suspended indefinitely, that I have to come straight home from school every afternoon and help my mother with chores around the house. And worst of all, there'll be no dates with my girlfriend for the next two months. "Two months!" I groan out loud, the groan somehow leading me back to laughter.

"What? You think this is a joke?" says Warren with an exaggerated weariness. "You think I haven't noticed you haven't exactly been on your best behavior lately?"

"I haven't?" I know what's coming, and have an urge to put my hands over my ears or whistle rudely, anything to avoid listening to my uptight buttoned-down disappointment of a son.

"You do as you damn please," he complains. "You hide all that junk food in your closet and hand it out to the kids whenever you feel like it. You stay up listening to Janis Joplin while the rest of us are trying to sleep . . . You don't have a clue what it's like waking up at two in the morning to the sound of *Another Piece of My Heart* blasting all the way from downstairs, do you? And when Sara wakes up in the morning wanting to wear one pink sneaker and one white one, I don't need you telling me, 'If it makes her happy, what's so terrible?' What I need is for you to keep your brilliant advice to yourself, okay?"

Though I could have predicted every word of this, I'm stung nevertheless. "Well, I *am* sorry about the music," I concede. *But how come you're not smart enough to know I'm just doing my best to drown out the sound of my own grief?* I envision asking him.

"I'll buy myself a pair of headphones tomorrow," I promise instead.

"It's not like having you here these past few months has been a *complete* disaster," Warren offers, resentfully, I think. "But you've got to get your act together, get your ass in gear, you see what I'm driving at?"

"Absolutely," I say, nodding politely, and cheered by the imagined sound of my hand broadsiding Warren's flushed cheek, by the yelp of outrage and surprise that follows. But then I can hear Ellen saying, aghast, *Don't even* think *about touching that boy!*

"You just need to have a better understanding of the house rules," Nancy is saying, and I see a flicker of regret pass briefly across her sweet face.

"Perk up," I advise her. "It's not like I'm going to live forever."

• • •

The all-season tent I've pitched for myself in the back yard is officially called an "isolation hut," according to the salesman who sold it to me last week, one afternoon following the accident in the parking lot. I had to laugh when I heard that, bewildering the salesman and causing him to stop in the middle of his spiel and repeat what he'd said a moment earlier, that the four aluminum poles added structural stability and that the single door with its "no-see-um" netting provided excellent ventilation. To me, in fact, the bright turquoise tent looks something like a geodesic dome set beautifully against the lawn; in the five days since I've been living in it, it's served me well.

"What's going on?" Warren had asked, startled at the first sight of it when he happened to come out back for a swim after work. "I mean, what *is* this?"

"What *is* it?" I said. "It's an isolation hut, obviously. It's got forty-five feet of floor area and it sleeps three comfortably. Want to come in for a look around? I haven't got all my things moved in yet, so it's kind of bare, but once I fix it up it'll be nice and homey. And Nancy promised to give me a few decorating tips. She's been very helpful, really."

"So what's it doing in my back yard?" Warren asked, and tugged at his bathing suit, which was fluorescent orange and a little big around the waist.

"Now that's a dopey question," I said cheerfully. "It's obviously my new home."

"You already have a home," said Warren. "One you can actually stand up and walk around in."

I ignored this. "I intend to be very happy here," I said. "I've scheduled a couple of sleep-overs for the kids and they're pretty excited about it."

"You *have* a home," Warren repeated. "And let me remind you it's got central air-conditioning and heat and, more important, running water and electricity. What more could a man ask for?"

"Well, it's just not a place I find particularly cozy." Unzipping the nylon taffeta door, I crawled through, and into the tent. The heat had broken overnight, and it was surprisingly comfortable inside. I stretched out along my brand-new state-of-the-art sleeping bag, arms crossed behind my head. I whistled the theme song from *Ally McBeal* and a couple of ancient Broadway show tunes. In the middle of "I'm Not at All in Love," Warren appeared on his hands and knees.

"You can sit up now," I said. "There's plenty of room, as you can see."

"You're going to be a squatter in my back yard?" said Warren. "Is that the way it's going to be?"

"Do I need official permission?" I sighed. "A permit?"

"People don't do things like this," Warren told me. "This is nuttiness of the highest order."

"What people?"

"Normal, ordinary people," Warren said. "You know the kind I mean." Sitting up finally, with an extravagant groan, he looked at me sharply. "Or maybe you don't."

I decided to let it pass. "I'll be taking my meals in the Big House, if that's any consolation to you," I said. "So it's not as if we won't be seeing each other. We'll just be spending a little less time together, that's all."

Warren looked depressed; his shoulders were slumped and his chin rested on his bare, nearly hairless chest. "You know, I once had a girlfriend in college who kept insisting, despite all the obvious signs, that she wasn't breaking up with me. She kind of eased her way out of the relationship a little bit at a time. First she stopped letting me spend the night in her dorm room, then she wouldn't let me take her to this hangout we always used to go to for pizza, then she began cutting our phone conversations short. And all that time she kept saying we weren't breaking up."

"*We're* not breaking up," I said. "I'm just trying to view this as an opportunity for, shall we say, growth and self-reliance in my golden years." I winked at him. "It's extremely important for old people to feel self-reliant, don't you think?"

"You're not old," said Warren gloomily. "In fact, sometimes I'm convinced your problem is you've never been able to—"

"Sorry, that's all the time we have for now," I interrupted. Bending my legs into a crouch, I made my way to the open doorway and out onto the lawn, then waited for my son to follow. A few minutes passed and he didn't appear, and I poked my head back inside the tent. I saw him lying on the sleeping bag, face-down, his toes kneading the nylon floor.

"I had to fire a guy in the executive trainee program today," Warren confided. "A kid right out of business school, incredibly self-confident, actually. He cried in my office and then after that he got a nose bleed that dripped all the way down his tie. What a mess." Turning slowly over on his side, Warren raised his head in my direction. "Is it all right if I stay here a while? Just a few minutes by myself?"

"You can stay," I said.

·   ·   ·

Arranging Sara's Barbie sleeping bag next to my own, I say, "I hope you'll stay all night, sweetie, but if you wake up and feel homesick, I'll take you right back to your bed inside."

"Can we stay up until four or three o'clock?" Sara asks. She's wearing beach thongs and an ankle-length nightgown that matches her sleeping bag. Sitting beside her, with three flashlights blazing in her lap, Nancy frowns.

"What do you think you and Grandpa are going to do all night? How many ghost stories do you think he knows?"

"None," I say. I choose a flashlight from Nancy's lap, prop it under my chin. Grimacing into a shaving mirror, so that all my teeth are on display and my eyes become slits, I hoot demonically.

Sara grabs Nancy's knees and shivers. "You look so ugly!" she howls. "Could I be ugly like that, too?"

"Be my guest," I say, and hand her the flashlight.

"I just don't know," Nancy says.

"About what?"

"I'm feeling a little nervous," Nancy admits. "There are certain thoughts running through my mind right now, none of them good."

"Like what?"

"Oh, all kinds of natural disasters—fires, flash floods, lightning . . ."

"You don't trust me," I say, and a jolt of anger travels through me, making my hands and feet tingle. "Be honest."

"Well, I'd like to trust you," Nancy says, patting my elbow awkwardly. "But I look at you and never know what you're thinking. Who knows, I could come out here tomorrow morning and find the two of you missing, and then get a phone call from you at the airport telling me you decided to take Sara to see the Statue of Liberty. I could, couldn't I?" she asks me, but I don't answer. Withdrawing her hand, she aims one of the flashlights into a corner where a neatly folded pile of my shirts sits on the floor. Next to it is a plastic bin holding my socks and underwear, and another bin, filled with toiletries. "You're not planning on living in this thing forever, are you?" she says.

"Let's play it by ear," I say, and shrug, enjoying the idea of myself as utterly unpredictable and impulsive, someone who would, without warning, breeze cross-country, all the way to Liberty Island. Who would pitch an all-season tent in his son's back yard just to claim a little peace for himself.

"I want to play gin and also the memory game," Sara announces. She unzips her backpack and empties its contents onto her sleeping bag: a deck of cards, a black-and-white speckled notebook, pencils, a change purse, a roll of Scotch tape, a miniature stapler, a handful of peach-colored tissues. "After we play cards we're going to practice writing all the letters of the alphabet, upper case *and* lower case."

Nodding, I say, "Fine. Just tell your mother to get out of here so we can start enjoying ourselves."

"Get out of here, Mom."

"Not like that," I feel an obligation to say. "*Nicely.*"

"Okay. Get out of here, darling Mother."

"I'm one of those people who likes being treated with a little respect, you know?" says Nancy irritably. She rises onto her knees and heads for the door, flipping it up and out of her way with a single exasperated motion.

I imagine her determined stride across the lawn, the swift swinging of her arms, the tilt of her tanned neck toward the sky. *Your father*, she hisses as Warren looks up from the TV in surprise. *Your father.*

"You have kind of a mean face on," I hear Sara telling me now.

"I do?" Instantly, I make an attempt at rearranging my mouth into a smile. "Better?"

"Not really. Want me to give you a massage?" Without waiting for a response, she comes around behind me, and, in the illumination of three flashlights, sets to work on my shoulders. Under her tiny, eager hands I feel myself begin to relax, feel something like contentment trying to settle in my hard bones and soft heart.

Miss Grace at Her Best

Waiting, one rain-soaked midnight, for her husband to finish up brushing his teeth, Grace found herself doing stretching exercises on a dingy-looking rag rug ornamented with tassels and laid out sloppily alongside his bed. Legs spread wide apart in an imperfect split, she touched her face to her left knee and then to her right, breathing deeply. When Willio finally emerged from the bathroom, a bubble of turquoise toothpaste at the corner of his mouth, he discovered her bending one leg upward to her head.

"Ouch," he said, as if the sight of her in such an unnatural position caused him pain.

"This rug could actually use a quick going-over with a vacuum, sweetie," she said mildly, knowing she was irritating him by saying this, but unable to resist, just as she was unable to resist tidying up his apartment every night when she came over after work. Willio was a jewelry-maker who taught a class at the Y and also at the New School one evening a week; on those nights, he didn't arrive home until after nine-thirty, and Grace had all the time she needed to vacuum and dust and scour the sinks with Ajax and collect all the magazines and newspapers Willio had thrown around during her absence. Three days a week he did word-processing at a Wall Street law firm, and the rest of the time he worked on his jewelry, which he occasionally sold to galleries in Soho—lovely necklaces of hammered silver, and bracelets and earrings made of enameled copper. Unlike Willio, Grace had only one job, working as an assistant at a PR firm where, she felt, no one appreciated anything about her except her typing skills (which happened to be first-rate), and where no one knew she was a poet. Going home to her apartment on the upper East Side after spending half the night with Willio across town, she was, from time to time, greeted with a batch of her poems in the mailbox, along with an unsigned note from a literary magazine saying, "Looks like you've bitten off more than you can chew. Sorry." Or "Sorry, but these just didn't strike a chord here."

"Sorry," she told Willio now. "Did I say 'vacuum'? This rug needs a trip to the cleaners, if you ask *me*."

"I didn't," he said. He came around behind her and blew gently on the back of her neck, sending a pleasing chill down the length of her spine. Lowering her leg to the floor, she smiled at him. "This is my apartment," he reminded her. "So my rug's looking a little grungy, so what. Why do you have to waste your time even thinking about these things?"

His apartment, a studio in a nicely kept limestone townhouse, had excellent light, a tiny kitchen, a bed that was rarely made. He loved living there, he'd told her when they first met. That was a year and a half ago, in Brooklyn Heights, at an uncomfortably over-crowded thirtieth birthday party of a mutual friend. Grace and Willio had left the party together early and gone by subway to a dim sum parlor in Chinatown. She was immediately impressed by his delicate, almost pretty face, and at the way he leaned forward across the Formica table in Chinatown to listen intently to whatever it was she was saying, as if he could not bear the possibility of missing even a single word. When she heard that he was an artist of sorts, the skin across her throat and chest went hot, and she'd had to ease herself out of the blazer she was wearing over her black satin shirt. She had always been a sucker for what her father referred to as "those artsy-craftsy types"—her last lover had been second in command at the Staten Island Children's Museum, and the one before that had been a painter/art teacher at a girls' school in the city. Holding one of Willio's beautifully enameled earrings in her hand that first night, she felt slightly dizzy and weak behind the knees, the way she got after finishing a single Margarita. And after a short while, only a few weeks or so, she could not imagine life without him. They shuttled back and forth between their two apartments that fall (Grace doing most of the shuttling), until finally, when the weather turned icy, she felt compelled to say, "This is ridiculous."

"Move in with me, then," he'd offered.

"My apartment's twice the size of yours."

"The light's terrible," Willio pointed out.

"Maybe the natural light's not great," she said, "but I've got three terrific halogen lamps and I can get a couple more if you want them. I'll have lights blazing for you everywhere."

"Look," he said, "I've been here for seven years. And if you think I'm going to give up a great rent-stabilized apartment like this, you're out of your mind." There were chocolate crumbs left over from lunch caught under his lower lip, and she bent toward him to brush them away.

"You ridiculous stubborn fool," she mumbled. It was the first time she had felt the need to criticize him and the words had an unpleasant taste to them, as if she had just eaten something that had gone bad.

"What?" he said.

"I love you anyway," she told him. "Regardless."

"Irregardless."

"Don't be such a wise guy," said Grace. "And don't try to kiss me when I'm angry at you." She pushed him away halfheartedly, then pulled him back.

"If I moved in with you," he said, "your apartment would be a shambles in no time. Disorder is a way of life for me. I come home, open the door, throw my coat on the floor. My mother used to watch me do that when I was a kid and say, 'Someday some nice girl is going to be tearing her hair out over you.'"

Grace pulled a single hair from the top of her head and presented it to Willio. "Your mother was right," she said.

When they decided, three months later, that they would get married, Willio went downtown to an ancient, shabby store that sold buttons and notions, and bought her a rhinestone that was meant to look like a six- or seven-carat marquise-shaped diamond. He glued it to a silvery band and slipped it over her ring finger while he crouched on one bent knee. She wore it happily; looking at it perched so ludicrously on her slender hand made her laugh. Willio promised he'd have the real thing for her someday if he ever managed to save up enough money, but seemed relieved when Grace insisted she truly didn't care one way or the other. A second promise was offered up hesitantly and after a great many hours of spirited discussion; according to Willio, he was going to seriously consider the idea of moving in with her. He still hadn't come to a decision when they went off to Key West for their honeymoon. Unnerved, Grace tried to enjoy the hot, breezy weather and the sight of so many men like Willio wearing earrings and torn, bleached jeans, walking through the streets in their bare feet. Arriving back in New York after a week, she and Willio took a cab from the airport to her apartment, where they spent the night. In the morning, she watched from her bed as Willio took his clothing from their suitcase and dumped it into two large shopping bags.

"Coming with me?" he said.

"What?"

"I'm going back home."

"We're married," she said stupidly, and burst into tears.

Circling her in his long bare arms, he said, "Stop crying and come home with me."

She looked around at all her things neatly in place, the bright Morris Louis prints in their steel frames on her bedroom wall, her set of shining lacquered chests, a ceramic vase filled with carefully chosen silk flowers—all of it familiar and well cared for—and shook her head. "I've got twice as much room as you," she said. "This is where I live. Why would I ever leave here except for someplace better?"

"For love," said Willio reasonably, but somehow, she thought, it didn't sound reasonable and it didn't seem to be about love. She felt his arms fall away from her, and she began to tremble in her warm bed. She thought of a divorced couple she knew, people who had no love left for each other, but who continued to live together in the same apartment because neither could afford a place of their own. A crazy arrangement, but at least it was one based solely on economics and not the kind of incomprehensible selfishness that she now suspected was at the heart of her husband's unyielding will.

She remembered that she loved him, though no particular reasons came to mind. She remembered her wedding, the look of pure contentment that illuminated Willio's face as they danced together, so slowly they were barely moving, under a canopy of silver and purple balloons, their friends whistling and stamping their heels in approval.

"We'll work it out," Willio said softly, gathering up the shopping bags that swelled with his clothing. "Anything can be worked out."

He wasn't even going to stay for breakfast, she'd realized. "I was planning on making pancakes," she said. "What's the big rush, anyway?"

"I've got a lot of stuff to do. But come over later and spend the night, okay?"

She nodded, saying, "Am I always going to have to wait for an invitation?"

"Are you nuts?" Willio said, and had rolled his eyes at her. "We're married, Gracie."

And here she was nearly a year later, dressed in black leggings and one of Willio's plain white T-shirts, contemplating rising from his rug, getting back into the clothes she'd worn to the office, and going home. It was only a matter of deciding whether to stay a while longer (stay and make love, as she knew Willio wanted), or leave now and get an extra hour of sleep at home. In the ten months of their marriage, neither of them had been able to yield to the other, and they had, only recently, stopped pretending that one of them would concede anytime soon. Grace believed that she had always been a generous, expansive person, that she was still that person, and that she would do anything for Willio except this one thing which was so clearly wrong and therefore impossible. It seemed to her that he was content for now to endure things as they were, that he was simply going about his work, his responsibilities, from one day to the next, all the while waiting patiently for her to give in. And she, too, while not entirely happy, had, against all expectation, grown accustomed to the rhythm of her endless trips back and forth across town, the taxis hailed after midnight as Willio stood alongside her in the hushed darkness, kissing her good-bye urgently and with regret. The odd pattern of their life together had taken on a bittersweet edge that sometimes, on reflection, she actually savored. Although the realization frightened her, she never said a word to Willio, knowing it could not lead them to anything worthwhile.

She suddenly felt too sleepy to move, and allowed Willio to lift her onto his bed, where, miraculously, he managed to arouse her interest in the long slender body he pressed against her. Afterward, she fell asleep for half an hour or so as she usually did, then with great effort sat up and considered the dress she'd worn to work and carefully arranged across a love seat on the other side of the room.

"Stay," Willio murmured, though he knew that leaving had become a point of honor with her, evidence that her persistence still matched his. "Look at it this way—I stay over at your place nearly every weekend."

"You owe that to me for all the time I spend here. And anyway, I don't have any clothes for the morning."

"We'll set the alarm for six or six-thirty, and you can go home and change before work."

Trailing a finger up and down the length of his ribs, she said, "Please don't ask me to do what I can't do."

Out on the street, they waited silently in a fine light rain for a cab to appear. Nearby, a bevy of pigeons shared a slice of pizza that was lying limply in the gutter. Two balding men in yellow slickers sauntered by, holding hands, swinging their joined arms high. Imagining the well-appointed apartment they'd shared for years, the bed from which they rose together every morning, Grace envied them briefly, until they turned the corner and disappeared.

When, at last, a taxi pulled up alongside them, Willio opened the door for her, saying, "Love you," reaching for her face and a lingering kiss. She watched as he hurried away, back into his bed without her.

"I'm exhausted," the cab driver complained as they shot through the Park. "Plus I'm having root canal tomorrow morning, which I'm not exactly looking forward to. You ever go to a periodontist? My gums are so bad they had to be slit open with a knife and then they had to scrape away all the crud that was—"

"Please," said Grace. The hypnotic sweep of the windshield wipers back and forth across the glass soothed her, and she almost succeeded in tuning out the driver's anxious talk.

"It's on my mind, you know? If I could think about something else, I would. And catch this one, I was just telling Tom Hanks the same story a little while ago, three fares before you, and he was real sympathetic. A big star like that, and he still took the time to tell me all about the two wisdom teeth he had pulled. You see *Saving Private Ryan?*"

"No," Grace said, feeling insensitive and inadequate, knowing she clearly couldn't measure up to Tom Hanks and his great reserves of sympathy. "You can leave me off right here, in front of the awning."

The doorman's tiny TV set was tuned to *Night of the Living Dead* and he waved at Grace absently, barely turning his head as she walked through the small lobby. Emerging from the elevator, she went through her bag twice in search of her keys, which finally turned up in her coat pocket, sandwiched between a shredded tissue and a leather glove of Willio's long presumed lost. Eiko, her next-door neighbor, peeked out shyly when she heard Grace at the door.

"Late," Eiko said, and smiled mournfully.

"Yoshiharu's not back yet?" Eiko had come from Japan a few months earlier with her husband, a physician who had a one-year research fellowship at New York Hospital. Unlike Eiko, he spoke excellent English and claimed not to suffer even the slightest pangs of homesickness. He stayed late at his lab many evenings; occasionally, Eiko would be stationed expectantly at the threshold of her doorway an hour or two past midnight, just at the moment Grace happened to be fishing for her keys. Twice they'd had tea together in Eiko's apartment, Grace talking slowly and loudly and excessively, trying to compensate for Eiko's diffidence and the language barrier between them. It was hard to know exactly how much her neighbor understood; she seemed to do better with the written word and sometimes had Grace write a few sentences on paper for her, to which she smiled and nodded in response.

"I'm sorry to have troubled you," Eiko said from behind her partially opened door. "Will you sleep now?"

"I'm very tired," Grace admitted.

"You *are* tired," said Eiko. "And furthermore, I am afraid to trouble you further, Miss Grace."

"Just 'Grace.'" Unable to resist her neighbor's sweet timorous manner, Grace motioned for Eiko to come inside with her.

"Your nice apartment strikes me with wonder," Eiko said as she followed Grace into the living room.

Smiling, Grace said, "Please sit down."

Eiko remained standing, a small figure in a gray warm-up suit and child-sized running shoes. "I will make tea."

"No tea," said Grace, and put her hands on Eiko's shoulders, guiding her to the couch, where they sat side by side. "Let's just hang out for a while."

"It troubles me that I don't understand English enough well. Yoshiharu's friends here think I must be stupid, but at home I am architect."

"An architect?" said Grace, impressed. "Well, you'll be back in Japan soon enough."

"July one. Six months," Eiko said, and sighed.

"Willio was in Japan once. He spent a few weeks there one summer after college."

"And how is your nice boyfriend, who is furthermore very handsome."

"Husband," said Grace.

"Husband?" Eiko said, and drew back in surprise. "He lives here with you? This also strikes me with wonder."

"He lives someplace else."

"Please explain," said Eiko. "If you will. You have paper and pencil?"

"I can't," said Grace, lowering her head. "It's just too much."

Hesitantly, Eiko rose from her seat. "I am afraid that I give you much trouble. Perhaps one day soon, if you wish, I will put beautiful kimono on you in order to see Miss Grace clothe herself in her best."

"Thank you," said Grace. "And thank you for coming over."

"You hope that I go home now?"

"It's late."

"One happy day," Eiko promised, "you will clothe yourself in your best."

• • •

At work a few weeks later, Grace sleeps away most of her lunch hour on an old leather couch in a small lounge of sorts just outside the ladies' room. The lounge, dimly lit and furnished with cast-off arm chairs and a set of end tables, is nearly empty; two secretaries are eating their lunches out of their laps and gossiping quietly. Grace announces that she has a headache and then collapses on the couch, falling asleep to the low murmur of the two secretaries exchanging horror stories about a Xerox machine that collates like a madman. She dreams of a bracelet, a delicate-looking design of thin black rubber and brightly colored aluminum that she helps Willio fashion one night in her living room. She and Willio seem headed for happiness: this bracelet of theirs becomes a big hit downtown as well as in all the department stores. They're able to buy a loft in Soho with plenty of room for them both, but for some reason Willio will not allow her to move in with him. *This isn't what you want*, he insists. *Trust me.* In the dream, Grace is wearing a trio of bracelets on each arm; the purple and green and turquoise-colored aluminum gleams so brilliantly she cannot take her eyes from the shining metal as Willio repeats, *Just trust me on this.* Awakening, she rubs one bare wrist and then the other, surprised that there's no sign of the bracelets she imagined so vividly. The dream has left her bewildered and a little shaky; rising from the couch with a noisy yawn, she has to grab onto an end table for support.

"How's your headache?" one of the secretaries asks. She's the only one left in the room, a skinny woman with a pallor and brittle-looking bleached hair, who is picking listlessly at the remains of a salad in a plastic container. There are rumors that she'd suffered a nervous breakdown a couple of years ago when her fiancé revealed himself to be a cross-dresser and told her he wanted the two of them to be married in matching wedding gowns. Grace has heard the story from so many different sources that by now she almost believes it.

"My headache?" she says. "Just about gone, I think."

"You look kind of under the weather, actually," Patty says.

"Chronic sleep deprivation. Other than that I'm in good shape."

"Try this," Patty says, eager to be of help. "Go to bed ten minutes earlier tonight, ten minutes earlier than that tomorrow night, and so on, for a week. By next Tuesday your bedtime will be a whole hour earlier. You can make a chart if you want, so you'll know exactly what time to aim for every night."

"Great," says Grace, who is utterly depressed by this news. She imagines herself and Willio walking down the aisle in identical wedding gowns, long pure white trains trailing elegantly behind them, the guests in their orderly rows of seats whispering so fiercely it's like the buzzing of insects.

"Want to go for a quick walk?" Patty asks. "I've got to get over to a cash machine."

A homeless person, his bare feet swollen and purple, stands guard at the outdoor machine. "Welcome to the Chase Advantage, sir," he says pleasantly. "May I be of some assistance?" Grace gives him a dollar and watches guiltily as the machine dispenses five twenties to Patty from a metal drawer.

"Ain't no shoes gonna fit on *these* feet," the man says, looking down at the pavement.

Across from the ATM, a small crowd has gathered in front of a vendor selling socks in neon colors arranged on a couple of dark-blue beach towels spread against the pavement. Grace buys two pairs for Willio, who will appreciate the wild colors, she thinks. Passing the homeless man again as she and Patty make their way down the street, she impulsively hands a pair to him without a word and continues walking.

"Thanks for the memories," the man calls after her, making her laugh.

For the first time in a long while, she goes directly home after work. She doesn't know precisely why, doesn't want to know precisely why, but the thought of puttering around in Willio's apartment waiting for him to get home from his class just doesn't appeal to her. Calling him from the phone at her bedside, she thinks she detects the faintest note of relief in his voice.

"Well, I guess it's a good opportunity for you to stay home and catch up on your sleep," he says.

"I took a nap at lunchtime."

"You're exhausted," Willio says. "You think I don't notice how tired you are all the time? You should take better care of yourself."

"Listen to the dream I had about you—I mean us—and our big success," she says, and describes the bracelets for him, along with everything else.

Willio is quiet for a moment, then says, "I love the part about the loft in Soho. It would be perfect for us, wouldn't it."

"Yeah, terrific. Too bad you wouldn't let me move in with you," she says, surprised at how bitter she sounds.

Willio is clearly offended. "What are you angry at *me* for? You're confusing me with someone you saw in a dream. Don't be nutty, Gracie."

"Okay," she says softly. "Okay."

"Want me to call you after I get home from my class? Just to check in and see how you're doing?"

"I'll probably be asleep," Grace says. "Call me at work tomorrow, how's that."

"Love you," says Willio, and hangs up.

Pretending she is a child again, home from school with what her mother used to call a "twenty-four-hour virus," she gets into her bathrobe and heats up a bowl of packaged noodle soup for herself. She arranges it on a wicker tray along with a salad plate full of crackers and the remote control for the TV, then settles into bed, where she watches game shows for an hour, savoring the foolish waste of her time. On one of the shows, an attractive-looking contestant, a woman in her forties, Grace guesses, is asked when middle age officially begins. "Thirty-five?" the woman says, and giggles expectantly. Grace lets out a yelp and snaps off the TV. She is thirty-two years old and married to a man who lives across town for no good reason at all. *You are pathetic*, she whispers, but as soon as the words are uttered she knows this isn't true. She's too angry to be pathetic, she realizes, and sails the remote across the room, watching with satisfaction as it splits open and the batteries leap out over the carpet. She is ready, at last, to play hardball with Willio; she imagines the theme song from *Rocky* booming at full volume somewhere in the distance. And then she has to laugh, because melodrama really isn't her style.

She times her arrival at Willio's to coincide with his return from the Y, but gets stuck in cross-town traffic half-way through the Park.

"How can this be happening in the middle of the week?" she wails to the cab driver, a woman with curlers in her hair and a pink-chiffon scarf pulled tightly over her head. "This is crazy."

The driver takes a swallow from her coffee cup, which is ornamented with an apple and the words "I Love New York." "*Everything* happens in this stupid city," she says. "A guy kills his girlfriend and boils her bones for soup. And then gets off on an insanity plea. And you're upset over a little midweek bumper-to-bumper traffic?"

Trying to compose herself, tossing Willio's brand new electric yellow socks from one hand to the other, over and over again, Grace envisions him behind the wheel of the U-Haul that will transport his things from his apartment to hers on a dazzlingly clear Saturday morning. She sees herself seated beside him in the small truck, an open carton filled with his dusty spider plants balanced against her knees. Just before they pull away from the curb, Willio turns his head toward the windows of his apartment for a final lingering look. She hears his sigh, a mixture of longing and resignation, and then the sound of his foot plunging downward on the clutch, the harsh shifting of gears as the truck takes off.

The keys to Willio's apartment, tied together on a lavender ribbon, are warming in her hand now as the cab deposits her at the curb. She hurries up the half-flight of worn stone steps and through two sets of heavy glass-fronted wooden doors. Outside the apartment, she hears music, Vivaldi's Spring Concerto from *The Four Seasons*. She smiles, enjoying the exhilarating music for a moment or two before letting herself in. What she sees in the clutter of his apartment is Willio bent forward across the small circle of his dining table, one elbow raised upward, chin resting in his palm. His other arm is lying flat against the table, his fingers playing lightly with a hand belonging to a woman whose back is toward Grace.

"Gracie," Willio's voice says, unnaturally high-pitched and a little wobbly. In an instant, both his hands have disappeared under the table. The woman turns around and gives Grace an appraising look. Her waist-length hair is streaked with silver; a single earring of bright feathers hangs low, almost to her shoulder.

"I know you," Grace says in astonishment, and takes a step backward. "I mean, I know who you are." She knows the woman's name is Perri, that she is a widow with two teenaged sons and nothing to lose. According to Willio, she remembers, Perri was the only student in either of his classes with any real talent. He'd spoken of the impressive work she did in silver, and also of the loss of her husband, who was killed in an accident witnessed by Perri as she stood in her skis at the bottom of a steep slope somewhere in Vermont. The story had brought Grace to tears one night not long ago.

"You make me sick," she informs them both, without any inflection at all, simply stating a fact.

"I'm really hoping," says Willio, turning off the music and approaching her slowly, cautiously, arms outstretched in her direction, "that it's going to make you feel better when I tell you that nothing happened."

"You mean I got here too soon," Grace says, shooting the pair of yellow socks over his head and into Perri's lap.

"Listen to him," Perri says, and throws the socks back at her. "He's telling you the truth."

Grace slips out the door and away from Willio, aware that he is struggling to keep up with her, talking too fast in that same foolish-sounding high-pitched voice that's not going to get him anywhere at all. "You listen to *me*," she says. "Talk to my answering machine if you want to talk."

Willio follows her out into the middle of the street, stands at her side as she flags down the first taxi she sees. "What kind of things should I say?" he asks. "What do you want to hear?"

"Only things that are true," says Grace. "So don't try and tell me that this is the first time you've ever brought anyone back to the apartment, because that would be a lie and I only want to hear things that are true." Grabbing hold of the door handle behind the driver, she strains awkwardly to yank the back door open.

Willio gives her a stricken look that betrays him. "I can't believe what I'm hearing," is all he says.

Unrolling his window halfway, the driver says, "Yes or no? What's it going to be?"

• • •

Eiko's living room is small and stark; the only furniture is a television stand holding a tiny TV, and a bridge table and four metal folding chairs. Taped to one wall is a series of postcards depicting scenes of rural Japan in pen-and-ink drawings. The other walls are entirely bare.

"In meeting me tonight, you will have one very good time," Eiko promises. She is in another warm-up suit, this one with Batman's insignia stamped across the front of her sweatshirt in gold. "I will put kimono on you now, if that is what you hope."

"Thank you." Grace doesn't know what to hope for; she no longer knows anything about even the simplest things. Everything is shapeless and hard to read, even her own heart.

"And furthermore, we have HBO."

Grace smiles; tears well in her eyes but she ignores them.

"When you are clothed in your best," says Eiko, "you will feel very good, okay?" She leaves the room and returns with a small pile of silky-looking things and a pair of brocaded thongs, little bells embedded in their rims. Closing the blinds, she says, "Now you must take off clothes. Soon I will dress you."

"Here?"

"I will be in kitchen finding Japanese crackers for you."

Weeping, Grace undresses clumsily, feeling as if she were in a doctor's examining room, half-expecting Eiko to return dressed in a white lab coat, stethoscope drooping from her neck. She dumps her clothes on one of the folding chairs and waits in her underwear with her arms crossed over her chest.

"You will have Japanese crackers now?"

Grace chooses one of the thin rice crackers decorated with a dab of yellowish icing in the center. As she chews, her mouth begins to burn and she coughs uncontrollably.

"Only a little spicy," Eiko says as she offers Grace a glass of water. "You are wimp, yes?" she says with a trace of a smile.

"Absolutely not," Grace answers, when she's able to talk again. "My marriage may be going down the tubes but I'm still more or less in one piece, as you can see."

"Pardon me, please?"

"Skip it," Grace says.

"Please?"

"Never mind."

"Okay," Eiko says, shaking her head. She helps Grace into a pumpkin-colored robe that Grace mistakes for a kimono but which Eiko identifies as underwear. Then comes the kimono itself, a robe of bright orange silk patterned with small white flowers. Tying a yellow sash around Grace's waist, Eiko says, "You will sit, please." She hands Grace a pair of white cotton socks resembling mittens.

"Special for toes," she explains. Grace slips into the silk-covered thongs; there's a light tinkling of bells as she stands up and takes a few tentative steps toward the center of the room.

"Now you are in your best," Eiko announces. "And so you are happy. And furthermore, proud. I must take photograph, which will strike your Willio with wonder."

Hiding her face in the crook of her arm, Grace murmurs, "No." She wants no record, no reminders, years from now, of this moment, when all she is feeling is an icy numbness everywhere. Her hands and feet are leaden; under the soft kimono, her ice-cold heart beats slowly and stupidly on.

"You must look," Eiko says, and leads her down a darkened hallway into the bedroom. Throwing open a closet door, she smiles at Grace in the full-length mirror. "Miss Grace in her best," she says, and applauds briefly, matching the palms of her small hands together in delight.

Grace rubs both eyes with her fingertips and sees with perfect clarity the brilliant feathers that hang boldly from Perri's ear, imagines the look of astonishment that crosses Willio's face as she reaches forward and yanks the earring from Perri's flesh, a single thrilling act of violence in her own utterly unremarkable life.

Solemnly, without a word, Grace takes a bow and then, moments later, blinks at the startling flash of an Instamatic that appears out of nowhere.

"You will strike your husband with much wonder. And so you are happy," Eiko insists.

Marian Thurm's fiction has appeared in the *New Yorker*, the *Atlantic, Mademoiselle, Ms, Redbook,* and many other magazines. She is the author of two previous short story collections and four novels, the most recent of which was *The Clairvoyant* (1997), a *New York Times* Notable Book of the Year. She teaches creative writing at Columbia University.